THE BARD OF BRYN DOON

THE LEGEND OF Q'NTANA
BOOK FOUR

MARK DAVID GERSON

MDG media INTERNATIONAL

THE BARD OF BRYN DOON

First Paperback Edition 2021. Second Edition 2024

Published by MDG Media International
Scottsdale, AZ 85260
www.mdgmediainternational.com

Library of Congress Control Number: 2024945141

ISBN: 978-1-950189-19-9 (paperback)
ISBN: 978-1-950189-28-1 (ebook)

Cover Image: Kathleen Messmer
www.kathleenmessmer.com

Praise for The Legend of Q'ntana

Leaves you turning every single page, hungry for more!
DAVID MICHAEL – AUTHOR OF "THE UNITED SERIES"

Compelling…a magical journey!
KAREN VAUGHAN – AUTHOR OF "DEAD TO WRITES"

An intriguing and exhilarating magical tale.
DAN STONE – AUTHOR OF "ICE ON FIRE"

An evocative and emotionally moving tale.
"MIDWEST BOOK REVIEW"

*I read "The MoonQuest" three times and couldn't wait for
"The StarQuest" to come out. Well, it was worth the wait.
I loved this book, and you will too!*
AMY ROBBINS-WILSON – AUTHOR OF "TRANSFORMATIONAL MOTHERING"

*An enjoyable journey into a wondrous world
that will leave you yearning to return again and again.*
JUDY SMITH ADAMS – SPRINGFIELD, MO

Stunning, magical and inspiring.
PAOLA RIZZATO – GLASGOW, UK

*Magic, music and universal truths
masterfully woven into a gripping tale.*
BETTY DRAVIS – AUTHOR OF "1106 GRAND BOULEVARD"

*Of the hundreds of books I own and hundreds more I've read, this is
the only book I've ever finished and immediately picked pack up and
read a second time. Amazing masterpiece of literature.*
LYNN HUDSON – ALBUQUERQUE, NM

*A fantastical ride to another world…the kind of book
the world should clamor for and read more of.*
MICHAEL HICE – SANTA FE, NM

*Fans of quest-centered fantasy and visionary fiction
as well as New Agers should enjoy this emotionally solid tale.*
"LIBRARY JOURNAL"

More from Mark David Gerson

FICTION

Sara's Year

After Sara's Year

The Emmeline Papers

MEMOIR

Acts of Surrender: A Writer's Memoir

Dialogues with the Divine: Encounters with my Wisest Self

Pilgrimage: A Fool's Journey

SELF-HELP & PERSONAL GROWTH

*The Way of the Fool: How to Stop Worrying About Life
and Start Living It…in 12½ Super-Simple Steps*

*The Way of the Imperfect Fool: How to Bust the Addiction to Perfection
That's Stifling Your Success…in 12½ Super-Simple Steps*

*The Way of the Abundant Fool: How to Bust Free of "Not Enough"
and Break Free into Prosperity…in 12½ Super-Simple Steps*

The Book of Messages: Writings Inspired by Melchizedek

RESOURCES FOR WRITERS & ASPIRING WRITERS

The Voice of the Muse: Answering the Call to Write

The Voice of the Muse Companion: Guided Meditations for Writers

From Memory to Memoir: Writing the Stories of Your Life

Organic Screenwriting: Writing for Film, Naturally

Birthing Your Book...Even If You Don't Know What It's About

The Heartful Art of Revision: An Intuitive Guide to Editing

*Writer's Block Unblocked: Seven Surefire Ways
to Free Up Your Writing and Creative Flow*

Stories never really end, even if the books like to pretend they do.
Stories always go on. They don't end on the last page,
any more than they begin on the first page.
CORNELIA FUNKE

Stories are expressions of our humanity, of our universality.
In our stories, we discover not what separates us but what unites us.
We discover not our differences but our similarities.
Read others' stories, but do more than that.
Tell your stories, whatever form they take.
Share your fears and joys, your failures and triumphs.
Share your humanity. Let us see you...and let us see ourselves in you.
That's how we heal ourselves. That's how we heal the world.
MARK DAVID GERSON

For all who live to tell stories...and all who live to hear them.

As you step from your world into the worlds of Q'ntana, you will experience foreign lands, sample exotic foods and encounter all manner of uncommon individuals and peculiar creatures.

Look for "The Worlds of Bryn Doon" at the back of the book to ease your journey through this unfamiliar territory (and to assist you with some unusual pronunciations).

If you'd prefer to have this guide by your side as you travel these pages, download a free copy of "The Worlds of Bryn Doon" at www.markdavidgerson.com/qntanaworlds.

§ § § § §

With its compelling story, engaging characters and rich, multilayered themes, "The Bard of Bryn Doon" is an ideal selection for any book club.

ONCE UPON A TIME...

I have recounted this story more times than I am able to number, and not merely here in Bryn Doon. I have journeyed with it deeper into Q'ntana and all the way to the Principality of Flor, as well as to far-distant realms beyond the Mir. Yet each time this story has freed itself through me, it has presented me with either a new chapter or a fresh perspective on an old one. For stories are not static. Stories are living, evolving organisms, sentient entities with unique souls, spirits and destinies.

Unlike other living beings, however, stories never end, nor do they die. Other tellers add to them. Other tellers may even adapt them to their experiences and rememberings. These alterations and accretions render a story no less authentic. For as I learned early on in this story, all stories are real and all stories are true.

THE END

Lightning bolts slice through the moonless sky, illuminating shard-like flashes of the cluttered collection of tents, huts and lean-tos clustered around the only structure with any pretense of permanence in this nameless desert village, a domed rotunda. Sporadic at first, the blazing streaks dance silently just beyond the farthest dwellings, striking only sand and dirt.

No one emerges to witness the fiery spectacle. Sheltering indoors accords villagers the illusion of safety, even as there is none. In an instant, the teasing flares can grow deadly, as they have so often in the past.

As they will again this night.

one

Kamela

"Once upon a time…"

Pyrà's eyes sparkled. "A story," he squealed. He sat up, tugging the quilted coverlet to his chin.

"Yes." I forced a smiled. "A story." The lightning had not yet touched the village. It still could. It had rarely spared us in previous storms. Why would it now? If we could neither hide from it nor outrun it, then all that was left for us was to continue as best we could. That, at least, was my view.

I had not draped a heavy blanket over the window to hide from the lightning, as some of my more superstitious neighbors were wont to do. Nor had I masked out the storm to keep Pyrà from panicking. My son would not be alarmed by a storm that had never before distressed him, not even when he was an infant. Rather, I had covered the window to prevent the flashing light from keeping Pyrà from sleep. Because if sleep failed to overtake him, inquisitiveness would. Unlike my neighbors, I was not superstitious. Even so, racing out into the night to chase after lightning did not strike me as the wisest of pastimes. Yet that is what Pyrà did during the first storm after he gained the ability to walk. That my son and these storms should somehow be linked did not surprise me. The first of them battered our village the night he was born.

As entranced as Pyrà was by the storms, stories always cast a more powerful spell, especially the few from ancient times that had survived.

Pyrà dropped his head to the pillow and shut his eyes expectantly. "Which story?" he whispered.

I paused. "Ben," I replied at last, praying that this one would distract him from the storm. "Ben and The SunQuest."

Pyrà grinned, his eyes still squeezed shut. The story of the greatest king and bard of all time was his favorite, not that he had ever been awake for the ending. He was always journeying with the dream-walkers long before I had completed my telling.

Not this night. This night, Pyrà remained spellbound all the way to the end. Even Jeryn, normally the first asleep, listened raptly from her cradle, her eyes opened wide in wonder even as they stared past the candle's reach and up toward the ceiling.

"'The people of Q'ntana are now sovereign and empowered, and stories, visions and dreams live in us all,' Ben declared. 'Now we are all bards,' he said, 'and I am at peace.'" I nudged the cradle with my foot. Jeryn gurgled and tilted her head toward me.

"With that, Ben shut his eyes and fell into the deepest of contented sleeps, the sleep from which no man ever wakes…not in this realm."

I thought Pyrà had followed Ben, into an equally content if less permanent dream state. His breath was even and his eyes twitched under his lids. I had half-risen when he murmured, "Go on, Maminka."

"The end," I whispered. I hovered over my stool, fearing that my slightest movement might push him back into full wakefulness. I needn't have worried.

"No, it is not," he insisted in full voice.

"It isn't what?"

Pyrà opened his right eye a slit. "The end. It isn't the end."

"What do you mean? There is no other." I knew this telling as well as I knew my name. When I was Pyrà's age, Ben and The SunQuest had been my favorite as well. And despite the uncountable generations that had passed since the great king's death, despite the impassable distance between his part of the realm and ours, the story was as alive in my heart as it had been the night I first heard it and as unchanged as when he penned it, at least according to my grandfather. Some stories alter over time or according to the teller's whims. This one was not one of them.

"Say that last bit again."

"The end."

He giggled. "No, silly. Before that."

"With that, King Ben shut his eyes and fell into the deepest of contented sleeps?"

"Before that."

"Now we are all bards?"

"Yeah."

"Now we are all bards," I repeated, "and I am at peace—"

"Don't say it."

"What?

The end, he mouthed. He sat quietly, deep in thought. "If we are all bards in Q'ntana…"

"Yes?"

He lay motionless for so long I thought he must have at last fallen asleep. Jeryn still stared at me, so I pinched out the candle flame, hoping the darkness would coax her as well toward the dreamwalkers.

A few moments later, Pyrà's whispered voice cut through the black stillness.

"If we are all bards in Q'ntana," he repeated, so softly that for a minim I thought I too had drifted off and was dreaming, "then I must be a bard. Is that not so?"

I reached down and stroked his face. "It is, little one."

"You are certain?"

I nodded, then realized he could not see me. "If the story says it, then it must be so. Stories do not lie."

"Then as the bard that I am," he declared, "I say it is not the end. 'There's more to every story. Tell me how it continues.' Isn't that what Eulisha tells Toshar in The MoonQuest?"

How did he know that? In that story as well, he was always asleep before I reached that point in the telling.

"That is a different tale," I replied, doing my best to keep my voice level. "At any rate, I know no more than what I have told you. That is all I have ever known of the Ben story. As far as I am aware, that is all anyone knows. If there is a continuing, I can't tell it to you. I don't know it."

A bolt of lightning streaked across the sky, so near to our hut that it shone through the blanket and illuminated Pyrà's face. He appeared to be deep in thought. Another flash, then another, this last one accompanied by the low rumbling that always presaged the storm's worsening. He jerked up with the next clap of thunder and his eyes shot open. Even in the dark they shone with excitement. "*I do,*" he whispered. "I do."

two

Kamela

I was astounded by Pyrà's claim and, I am not ashamed to admit, skeptical. Yes, he was bright, preternaturally so. In fact, his precociousness revealed itself through a birth so premature that the midwife feared for his survival. So, had he offered a story of his own creation right then, I would not have been surprised, even though such tellings occur only rarely in one so young. Yet to take known history and claim to be ready to add to it previously untold chapters? In any other child of his years, I would have presumed an immature arrogance that ought not to be encouraged.

Pyrà was different, and not merely because of his early birth or because that birth signaled seasons upon seasons of unprecedented dry-lightning storms. Pyrà possessed an uncanny knowingness — a kenning, as they would have said in ancient times — that I would have found extraordinary even had I not been his mother. Not merely extraordinary, but unnerving. When he would stare at me in that certain way he did betimes, it was as though those blue-green eyes that were deeper and more passion-filled than the Mir and sharper than the blade of Orrican could pierce not only through me but back into every moment of every life I had lived…all the way back to the beginnings of time itself. To before that, were that possible.

It was for that reason that no village children would play with him. That reason, coupled with the coincidence of birth and storming, was why no mothers or daughters would mind him and no fathers would show him the traditional games, even as he had no father to teach him those things. My Lucca had disappeared soon after Jeryn was born, and Pyrà carried little memory of him.

Consequently, Pyrà was a solitary child, although I often wondered whether he was solitary as much by choice as by circumstance. Certainly, he never appeared to miss the companionship of his contemporaries, preferring instead the company of the wild stallions that grazed on the slopes of Mòrq'an Mellà a little more than a v'rek's walk from the village. And when he was not with the horses, he would stand across from the Dôma, day or night, staring into the sky, scrutinizing the suns, moon and stars in much the same way he would stare at most villagers — as though he knew their most closely held secrets, including those they themselves had yet to acknowledge. Perhaps that was how he could claim to see beyond the ending of an oft-told and much-beloved story.

What I could not know that night — what neither of us could know — was that he would be unable to recount the continuing until he had lived it…until we all had.

As it was, I placed my hands over his eyes and crooned the lullaby he had never until now been awake to hear.

> *Sleep Pyrà, my child, my own*
> *Sleep through the night*
> *Sleep, though the lightnings come*
> *Your heart will keep you right*
>
> *Sleep Pyrà, my child, my own*
> *Let dreams fuel your sight*
> *Sleep, though the lightnings come*
> *Your heart will keep you right*
>
> *Sleep Pyrà, my child, my own*
> *Sleep through the night*
> *Sleep, though the lightnings come*
> *Your heart will keep you right*

three

Pyrà

I did not fall asleep with my mother's lullaby. I did not fall asleep at all. Instead, I feigned sleep through the interminable drip-drip-drip of time until I heard Jeryn's soft snores and my mother's even breathing and felt certain I would not wake them.

Kamela liked to pretend that the lightning storms were of little concern to her. She acted that way for me and my sister, so we wouldn't be frightened. Yet that is what it was: an act. Many were the nights when I observed her through eyes open a crack as she leaned against the roughhewn doorpost of our one-room hut chewing her thumbnail, her brow furrowed with anxiety — and not merely over whether the lightning would enter the village and, if it did, would spare our home. She was scanning the horizon for my father.

Against all entreaties and common sense, Lucca had set out for lands beyond the Mhor-Jenn three nights after Jeryn was born. Even Fay'dor, who rarely interfered with village life, had urged him to wait. Lucca, however, would not be dissuaded. Since boyhood, he had dreamt of discovering a route out of our barren, isolated province. And despite the legendary impossibility of such an undertaking, he was not only convinced there was a way, he was determined to find it. Once he did, he vowed to return to lead us to more bountiful lands.

Would he return? Although Kamela prayed for it most nights, I knew he would not. Paradox though it was, I also knew we would see him again.

I knew it because he had promised it. More than that, with his parting words, he had echoed the counsel given to Toshar in The MoonQuest story, to Q'nta in The StarQuest story and to Ben in The SunQuest story and had insisted that I heed it.

Kneeling before me so he could look directly into my tear-filled eyes, he said, "We will be together again, my son. All of us. Trust that, Pyrà."

"I-I can't," I sobbed, clinging to him. "I'm afraid to."

"You must." He brushed the tears from my cheeks. "You either trust or you do not, Pyrà. There is no halfway in between. When you doubt, and you will, remember that." Then he kissed my forehead, rose and was gone.

If Lucca's promise set up one paradox, the night's storytelling offered another, equally baffling: How could I know that the story of Ben and The SunQuest continued? There was no explanation. I simply knew that it did. Nor could I have recounted the continuing had I been challenged to do so. I knew that I knew, but I could only trust the knowingness. I could not touch it. Not yet. That would come…sooner than I could have imagined and in ways I would not have wished for.

The lightning flashes more blazingly. The gap between strikes narrows. The gap between each strike and the village narrows. Now, it is but a few paces from the most outlying dwellings.

The next strike slams into the village common, firing clumps of dried mud into the sky and fleetingly illuminating the only living being about: a youth who steals from a simple hut, pauses to ensure that he is unwitnessed, then races past the jumble of shanties to Mòrq'an Mellà, the broad, stumpy knoll east of the village, waving his arms as menacingly as one can at lightning.

As the youth approaches the mound, a low thundering rumbles across the Mhor-Jenn, rolling boomingly toward the village. When it reaches the common, it partners with the lightning and together they roar toward the sole structure of any substance: a domed, circular edifice at the far edge of the common and the only one in all the region constructed of stone. The domed building, older than the village itself, towers over its neighbors, until a single thunderbolt, sharper and brighter than the others, assaults it. The building explodes, flinging jagged rubble in every direction. Incredibly, none falls where it can inflict more damage.

Despite the deafening blast, no curious eyes peer out from behind curtained windows or darkened doorways. No fathers or mothers, sons or daughters, move to assure themselves that friends and family are safe. Not a single villager ventures outside to survey the scene.

Thus, just as no one has noticed the youth, no one now discerns the dark-robed figure who steps beyond the threshold of an unprepossessing lean-to to contemplate the unfolding drama. Bald, clean-shaven and with skin of a translucent scaliness that is neither wrinkled nor smooth, he seems at once aged and ageless, solid and ethereal. After a brief scrutiny, he raises his arms toward the heavens and mutters a few alien phrases, inaudible under the relentless thunder. At his final word, all lightning ceases and all thunder stills.

With yellow eyes that pierce the now darkened, silenced night, he gazes up to Mòrq'an Mellà, where stallions more numerous than there are villagers, munch contentedly on the hillock's scrubby brush, seemingly undisturbed by nature's barely concluded histrionics. A closer look reveals the youth, who weaves among the horses, whispering words he himself does not understand, even as the horses do. In return, the horses nuzzle the youth as though he is one of them. Perhaps he is.

When a sliver of silver translucence creeps above the horizon from the far-distant Mir, the boy makes one final circuit among the horses, then sprints down the hill for home.

four

Hara'q

The pounding intensified, a pulsing throb that rocked the earth. It felt as though a mob of stallions stampeded toward us. Scores upon scores of them. Not our stallions, for ours were placid creatures. Perhaps the passage of time had tamed the fierceness out of them. Or perhaps they had been so battle-weary when the villagers' ancestors rode them here in shameful exile that all they could do was wander lazily among the sparse grasses of Mòrq'an Mellà. That is what they did now, as unconcerned by the earth-shaking roar as my neighbors were alarmed by it.

Nor could it be the explosions of an approaching lightning storm. The sky was a cloudless azure, the two suns beating down on us with their customary relentlessness. Dry thunderstorms such as we had experienced the previous night had rarely been known to strike more than once in a moon, and never during the day. Those tremors that did roll through during waking hours were gentle, soundless swayings. Whatever this was anything but silent, and its unyielding hammer-beat reverberated so deeply that I felt it in my blood.

Two doors from where I stood shaded by the eaves of my hut, Kamela hovered by the entryway to hers, clutching Jeryn tightly to her breast. The fear in her eyes was mirrored on the faces of our neighbors, who had appeared at daybreak with brooms and spades to clear the debris from the shattered Dôma. Now they stood motionless, uncertain what to do or where to go. The rumbling came at us from everywhere at once, so there was nothing for us to run from, nowhere for us to run to, even were escape an option.

Unfortunately, escape was not an option. We lived at the center of the Mhor-Jenn, a remote desert wasteland that began at the Mir and extended countless days' journey east, north and south…not that there was any place to journey to. Our coastline in the west was a formidable headland that jutted into the boulder-strewn cauldron that was the Mir. Even could we have harvested sufficient lumber for a sailing craft from the spare, spindly copses that were all that broke the monotony of the moorland near our village and even could we have managed to transport it as far as the jagged bluffs and lower it to the sea, the Mir would have hacked it to splinters and dispatched its crew to Kea Kana before any course could be laid.

And were one to survive the pitiless heat long enough to make it to the end of the Mhor-Jenn in any other direction, the Do'ana Qi, an unbroken expanse of disappearing sands, would impede further progress. Those deadly, all-devouring bogs, which separated our province from the rest of Q'ntana, sucked in whatever touched them, however feathery the touch. That was why everyone despaired for Lucca — everyone but Pyrà, who could not be dissuaded from the certitude that he would reunite with his father, and Kamela, who never stopped beseeching Prithi for his safe return.

The next jolt that swept through the village was forceful enough that it knocked the half-dozen men nearest to the Dôma to the ground and crumpled three nearby lean-tos. I grabbed onto my doorframe for support, grateful that mine was among the more sturdy dwellings. Solidly built though it was, it would not hold up to much more of this. For all the fearsome pyrotechnics of our nocturnal lightning storms, none had threatened the entire village. If this stormless thundering continued and if Lucca were somehow still alive, would there be a village for him to return to?

If this stormless thundering continued, would it matter?

Then, it mattered little to me, so long in exile that I could barely recall any sensings beyond those few offered by this desolate dust bowl. What did lush forests smell like? What did melodious birdsong sound like? What did crystalline creeks taste like? Even had I possessed the slenderest recollections of these, I would have blocked them from my awareness, so resigned had I become to perpetual incarceration in the bleak prison that was the Mhor-Jenn.

Here, the only trees were shriveled, stunted and twisted, and the only native birds were giant maq'rahs, screechy, coarse-feathered creatures that feasted on flesh — dead or alive, it was equal to them. On a rare occasion, we caught glimpses of a lost ganda, pulled many hundred of v'reks off course by the unceasing gusts howling off the Mir. As for water, we knew of but a single spring; it trickled up in reluctant burblings inside the Dôma. Although other creek beds crisscrossed the land, they were no more than scorched and cracked reminders of a time before the Mhor-Jenn's jungles had withered into this desiccated wilderness.

All that still stood from that ancient time was the Dôma, a structure whose story and purpose were known to no one in the village, except perhaps to Fay'dor. But one did not seek information of Fay'dor. One waited for him to speak, to reveal answers to the questions no one dared to ask.

When it seemed as though the ceaseless booming must have reached its peak and could grow no more violent, a single blast louder and more savage than any of its predecessors convulsed the village. Knees buckled at the intensity of it, and hands flew to ears in a vain attempt to muffle it. I leapt away from my hut, certain that this was the shock that would destroy it. Yet through some miracle that could only have been Prithi's work, it withstood the assault, as did every other dwelling in the village. What did not were the rubbled ruins of the Dôma. As its remaining stones exploded in a rain of fine gray dust, deep fissures sliced through the ground at the edges of the site, drilling farther and farther into the earth until, with one final burst of fury, the land upon which the Dôma had stood since the beginning of time collapsed in on itself, choking off our only source of water and leaving nothing but a cavernous crevasse in its place. Through another of Prithi's miracles, no one was harmed.

For an instant, all was still. Nothing moved but Aygra and B'na, the two suns. As they joined together in the suns-merge moment of midday, a bolt of lightning charged *up* from the crevasse and flung itself at the two-suns-as-one. When it struck, daylight fled. All light fled. And before the villagers could cry out their terror, a new lightning storm had commenced, one unmatched in its brutality.

The day is black. Aygra and B'na have vanished, and it is too early for moon or stars. The only available light flares in abrupt flashes as first one, then two, then a dozen lightning bolts smash into the village. This time, no dwelling is spared. This time, few villagers are left unscathed. This time, there is no sanctuary from the merciless strikes.

"Pyrà. Pyrà!" Kamela shrieks through the panicked cries of her neighbors. "Have you seen him?" she asks each in turn. No one has.

"Pyrà. Pyrà!" She hugs her infant daughter so closely that the young girl kicks in protest, wailing loudly. This only makes Kamela tighten her grip. She must keep her daughter safe. But her son. Where is her son? "Pyrà. Pyrà!"

Fay'dor will know, she thinks. Fay'dor must know. This curious oracle who has come and gone from the village for longer than anyone can remember, says little but sees all. He must know where her son is.

"Fay'dor. Have you seen Fay'dor?" No one has.

Fay'dor is seen only in those moments he chooses to be seen. Those moments have not yet arrived.

"Pyrà. Pyrà!"

Pyrà is again with the stallions on the far side of Mòrq'an Mellà. None but Fay'dor knows this. Fay'dor witnessed him steal away as soon as darkness struck, silently encouraged him to steal away. Now, the boy moves fearlessly from horse to horse, murmuring comforting words to one, stroking another reassuringly. The horses know this is a storm like no other. No storm has ever touched Mòrq'an Mellà, has ever ventured this close to Mòrq'an Mellà. For the first time in their lifetimes of lives in the Mhor-Jenn, they are frightened.

"Pyrà. Pyrà!"

The boy hears his mother's call on the winds that have risen since the great darkness fell. Gentle breezes at first, they eddy and bluster now, whipping the tents and lean-tos so far spared by the lightning from their moorings and *flinging them far into the empty desert. Without understanding why, the boy knows he cannot leave the horses. Without understanding how, the boy knows that only he can protect them. He must stay.*

five

Hara'q

"**N**ot you." Fay'dor set one clawed hand firmly on my shoulder. "You must stay."

Stay? For what? There was nothing left of our village save Fay'dor's lean-to, miraculously untouched by the storms, and the scattered detritus of the only home these villagers had ever known.

I shrugged and stepped aside to let my neighbors pass down the narrow stone staircase that wound deep into the blackness of the crevasse. Had the lightning carved out those steps? Or had it cleared away the structure that had long concealed them? No doubt, Fay'dor could explain it all if he chose to. No doubt, he would not choose to.

All I knew was that when the storm cleared as quickly as it had appeared, the darkness departed with it. Aygra and B'na now blazed down on us as though no thunderbolt had struck them, and this stairway, its steps worn as though by generations of footsteps, had been revealed. The only remnant of the storm was the wind. It squalled around us in sharp bursts, scooping up stray scraps of village life and hurling them out of view, when it wasn't flinging sand into our noses, mouths and eyes. More than once, I was forced to duck out of the way of a flying fragment of debris.

Fay'dor had not indicated where the steps would carry them, only that it would carry them to safety. With their village destroyed and seeing no other options, they filed down and around and out of view — many bandaged and limping and all clutching what few possessions they had managed to salvage from their ravaged homes. A rucksack here, a spare pair of sandals there; a blanket here, a soup ladle there. Kand'q had a book tucked under one arm; his other hugged his mate Valena'a, who wept uncontrollably. Falla carried an empty cage that had once held an injured ganda; her daughter, Mayta, half a doll that had been carved by her father.

The last in the endless procession was Kamela, her long auburn hair whipped by the wind and her eyes rimmed red from crying. Tears coursed down her cheeks, mottling the dirt that caked her face. Jeryn whimpered in her arms. Kamela was last because she kept stepping out of the queue to let others pass. All the while, her eyes darted left to right and back again in search of her son.

"Pyrà?" Kamela's cry had shrunk to a moan. "Pyr'…?"

With a tenderness I had never known him to display, Fay'dor hugged her to him. "He is safe," he whispered, glancing over her shoulder up to Mòrq'an Mellà. "If you and Jeryn are to be too, you must go with the others." Gently, he pushed her from him toward the stairway. She descended a single step then stopped and half-turned back to face him with pleading eyes.

"It is his time," he said before she could speak. "Yours too." She dropped her head and turned away. A moment later, she had disappeared into the crevasse.

"And me?" I asked after the final muffled footfall had silenced.

"It is your time as well."

six

Pyrà

It was impossible to imagine what Fay'dor might want of me. He was a man of few words, most too cryptic to decipher, and a gaze so piercing that most villagers avoided him. No one knew where he had come from or how he got here. If there was no way out of the Mhor-Jenn, how had he found his way in? And why?

In a community as small and isolated as ours, there were innumerable theories, all regularly gossiped about over pots of stem tea or flagons of the bitter ooura ale brewed from the dun-colored flowers of a ubiquitous shrub so hardy that it grew where it wanted and refused all attempts to eliminate it. Some claimed that Fay'dor was a malevolent spirit in human form who had come to worsen our already harsh lives; others argued that he was an agent of Prithi's, come to improve our lot. To date, we had seen evidence of neither. Fay'dor kept to himself for the most part, yet in his own way he was as ubiquitous as the ooura bush. Wherever in the village I found myself, he seemed to be there too, though not standing in full view. Each time, I caught him from the corner of my eye, and he always seemed to be watching me. Kamela insisted I imagined it. I knew I didn't.

Was Fay'dor a man? What man has eyes the color of the suns? And what man's hands resemble more a clawed animal's than a human's? My experience of man and beast was admittedly limited. Of the former, I had only my neighbors to compare him with, and he looked like none of them. Of the latter, we had few here in the Mhor-Jenn. My stallions, of course, the maq'rahs and whatever scrawny livestock we could raise. We were also cursed with nayla, the most deadly and stealthy of creatures, who would scavenge ravenously through the village at night, howling their blood-chilling cry. What else could survive in such an inhospitable land? How we sustained ourselves on the meager, water-starved crops we cultivated and the occasional disoriented flock of gandas or verros was a mystery. Somehow, by Prithi's grace, we did…until the storm snatched it all from us.

I knew nothing of the storm's wave of destruction when Hara'q sprinted down from the Mòrq'an Mellà summit in that bobbing way he had of running, his shoulder-length raven hair flying behind him. He sped up when he saw me.

"Fay'dor," he panted when he stopped. "You. Must. Go. To. Him." He bent over, his hands on his knees, breathing heavily. "Now."

"Why? What—?"

He straightened himself up. "There's no time," he said. "You must go and swiftly…"

Hara'q was nearly as much of an enigma to me as Fay'dor was. Like Fay'dor he said little but saw much and had no more intercourse than necessary with other villagers. And like Fay'dor, he had been in the village longer than anyone could remember. Yet his hair and beard, dark as a moonless night, had never grown a single strand of gray and, apart from a few lines around his eyes, not a wrinkle scarred his dusky face. Other villagers were born, grew old and died. Hara'q never changed.

Other villagers acted as though the stallions did not exist. Not Hara'q. Although he visited Mòrq'an Mellà only rarely, his time with the horses was not unlike mine, moving slowly from animal to animal, although rarely speaking to them as I did. I never witnessed any displays of emotion from Hara'q — he never laughed or cried, smiled or frowned — except on his return from those infrequent visits to Mòrq'an Mellà. On those occasions, both his face and posture betrayed a despair that no mask could conceal. Afterward, he would retreat into his hut for days, and woe betide anyone who knocked on his door.

I would not have left the horses in anyone else's care. Even with the return of daylight, they were still unusually skittish. Although I could not understand Haraq's feelings for them any more than I could understand my own, I knew he would tend to them in my absence.

I embraced T'tammo and Sajàno, my favorites, assuring them that I would return as soon as I could. Then I made my way back toward the village.

Despite the apparent urgency of Fay'dor's request, I was in no hurry to meet him. Hara'q called after me to make haste, but I pretended not to hear. Only when I reached the summit of Mòrq'an Mellà and saw the ruin spread out before me, did I break into a run.

"Ruin" was too generous a description. Where our village had been, as recently as that morning, only a single lean-to now stood. It was as though a giant broom had swept everything else away, for no evidence remained that anyone had ever lived there. Even the half-destroyed Dôma was gone, replaced by a massive black crater.

"Maminka," I shouted into the emptiness. "Jeryn!" But all I saw in the distance was Fay'dor, leaning on a staff at the entrance to his lean-to.

seven

Kamela

We trudged down and around, down around, down and around for what felt like lifetimes. Before long, the sky was nothing more than an asymmetrical blue patch as far above us in this seemingly endless crevasse as the suns had felt up in our village. Too soon after, the patch shrank first to the size of my fist, then to a pinprick. Then it vanished altogether. Yet we did not descend in the dark. Once all daylight had melted away, the steps themselves began to radiate a faint luminescence, bright enough to keep us moving but too dim to disclose our destination.

Fay'dor had instructed us to follow the stairs wherever they carried us. But where did they carry us? How deep into the earth could we descend? How long could we keep going? How would we eat? What would we eat? When would we sleep? Where would we sleep? Didn't Fay'dor realize that there were children and elders among us, and that nearly every villager was injured in some way? How long could *they* keep going?

As if sensing my silent questions, Mayta hugged her doll more closely. "I'm tired, Mama," she whimpered.

"I know, Maytasch," Falla murmured.

"Will we be there soon?"

"A little while longer. You can go a little while longer, can't you, my little bird?"

"Yes, Mama." Mayta swallowed a sob. "A little."

Those were the last words I heard.

The youth races down the hill, not toward Fay'dor but toward the naked land where his home had until recently stood. A half-buried bokka stone is the only evidence that there had once been a dwelling there. He scratches in the dirt to free the smooth, pearlescent stone and presses it to his face, where it catches the tears that fall freely from his eyes.

Sensing a presence standing over him, he looks up.

"You!" He leaps to his feet and hurls himself at Fay'dor, battering him with his fists. "Where are they? What have you done with them? With everyone? You did it. I know you did."

Fay'dor stands in place, not resisting the attack, saying nothing.

A large wet nose inserts itself between Fay'dor and his attacker. It nudges the youth back a step and whinnies, shaking its head. Teal-colored sparks fly off its velvet mane.

The whinnies swirl around and around in the youth's head, deconstructing into a series of staccato sounds, then re-forming as words he understands even as he tries to push them away.

"Trust Fay'dor," they say.

"No," he shouts, pummeling Fay'dor more violently still. "You're in my head. Get out of my head."

But the whispered words will not be silenced.

"Trust Fay'dor," they repeat. And again. And again. And again.

eight
Pyrà

Trust Fay'dor? How could I trust Fay'dor? I couldn't, not if he was responsible for what had happened here. What if it was he who had brought the lightning and the storms? What if it was he who had—? No, Papa *was* alive. But what of Maminka and Jeryn…and the rest of the village? No, I couldn't trust Fay'dor. I wouldn't.

Besides, it hadn't been T'tammo speaking to me. It couldn't have been. Although we had ways of communicating, it had never been through words. No. It must have been a trick of Fay'dor's. I would not trust the words; I would not trust him.

Then I heard it again. "Trust Fay'dor."

This time, it was not some strange translation of T'tammo's whinnies coming from inside my head. This time, it seemed to come directly from the horse.

I spun around and peered into the stallion's eyes, which glowed that otherworldly greenish blue they took on when the suns' light struck them at just the right angle.

"Trust Fay'dor?" I whispered, stroking his muzzle.

T'tammo snorted and nodded. Then he turned his muscular body back toward Mòrq'an Mellà and took off so swiftly that all I saw of him was a black blur.

If our stallions could have been said to have a leader, T'tammo was it. There was a subtle majesty about him, in both stance and gait, that to me distinguished him from his brothers. Perhaps the other horses saw it too, for they treated him with a deference they didn't afford each other. Yet no one else would likely have discerned the distinction. After all, the stallions were solid ebony, with no distinctive markings — all nine score and seven of them. Moreover, who was there to notice? Few villagers gave the horses much thought, let alone climbed Mòrq'an Mellà to visit them.

Still hugging the bokka stone to my chest, I watched T'tammo until he disappeared over the crest of Mòrq'an Mellà. Then I dropped to my knees and sifted through the dirt for any evidence that I had lived here…that anyone had lived here. There was nothing.

All I had was the bokka stone, which my father had pressed into my palm the night before he left.

"Sleep with it under your pillow," he'd said. "It will help your dreams come true."

This was no dream. It was a nightmare worse than any I could have imagined.

"Pyrà." Fay'dor's voice was uncharacteristically soft, dissolving most of my rage, though none of my terror.

I looked up. "What has happened? Where is everyone?"

Fay'dor reached for my arm and pulled me up. I stared into his unblinking eyes, but they remained as inscrutable as ever. "Maminka?" I whispered, fearful of his answer.

"She is safe."

"Jeryn?"

Fay'dor nodded. "As well."

"Take me to them," I insisted as firmly as I dared. "Please?" I entreated when he failed to respond.

He contemplated first one sun then the other, then gazed not at me but into me, as though reading my soul. I felt naked under his scrutiny and yearned for nothing more than to flee or at the least to hide from him. Not that anyone could hide from Fay'dor. Nor was there anywhere to flee to. Not anymore.

"You know I cannot," he said at last.

He was correct. I did know it. I did not know how I knew it, nor was I content to possess that knowingness. Nonetheless, petulant youth that I was, I opened my mouth to argue.

Fay'dor cut me off before I could speak. "You have other work to do, Pyrà. With T'tammo, and his brothers."

What could I have to do with the stallions…especially now? "I don't understand."

"I think you do, young bard."

"You called me 'young bard,' does that mean I *am* a bard?"

"It means what it means," Fay'dor replied, gently propelling me the three dozen steps to his lean-to. He then directed me inside and onto the intricately patterned rug that filled nearly the entire space, a space that seemed impossibly ample. No interior in our village was even one quarter as roomy, nor did any exterior so effectively disguise the scale of what lay beyond its threshold. If that incongruity hadn't kept my feet from proceeding, what occurred next did.

The rug's abstract geometry shifted, fluidly forming and re-forming until I feared I would faint at the mutability of it. Finally, the movement stilled, settling into an outer border of multicolored chevrons and an inner border of entwined roses surrounding a field of dark, star-studded teal. At the rug's center, a silvery moon formed the backdrop for a black chalice that I imagined to be the legendary Nayr. It was flanked by two eagles, their wings outstretched. Each eagle clutched a sun in one of its claws; Aygra, the larger of the two, to the left, B'na to the right.

For all its capaciousness, the space was empty but for a low wooden table that sat slightly off-center immediately above the chalice. Tucked next to the table were two black cushions; one embroidered in gold with the two suns, the other in silver with M'nor, the moon. An earthenware teapot, aromatic steam swirling from its spout, rested at the table's center. It was mud-colored, a double-chevron set in each side — one teal in hue, the other the same shade as Fay'dor's eyes. Two drinking bowls sat alongside the teapot, matching it in all but a single detail: one bore the sign only in teal, the other in yellow.

Fay'dor gestured for me to sit, and as if in a trance I obeyed — on the moon cushion. As I did, the lean-to's opening sealed itself and its canvas roof dissolved. It had been full daylight when I stepped inside; now it was nighttime, and M'nor in all her fullness illuminated the space.

Fay'dor settled onto the other cushion and tented his fingers. He remained like that in silence long enough to render me even more discomfited than I was already feeling. I tried not to fidget, but I couldn't help myself until, finally, I sat on my hands. After a time, he lifted the teapot by its rush handle and poured out two full bowls.

"Choose a cup," he said softly. "Choose a cup and it will be yours for all time…if you let it."

There was something about that sentence…something familiar, even as I knew no one had ever spoken it to me. "Does it matter which?" I asked after a few moments' indecision.

"Only if it does."

I reached for the yellow cup, but before I could touch it, some force pushed my hand to the teal one. I pulled it toward me.

"As I thought," Fay'dor murmured. He tapped the yellow cup three times, and it didn't so much disappear as melt into the table, leaving a faint yellow stain where it had sat. "Now," he said. "Now."

"Now what?"

"Now, drink your tea and tell me what you see."

I cradled the bowl in my hands and felt its heat seep into my fingers, then up my arms and into my shoulders before rushing at the same time up into my head and down through my body. I cried in pain and attempted vainly to release the bowl. It was as though it now held me.

"What do you see?"

"I-I don't understand."

"Understanding is not required. Seeing is. Knowing is."

"I don't kn—"

"You do, my boy, even if you do not always know you do."

I finally wrenched myself free of the bowl, splashing half its contents onto me and the other half all over the table. Yet I felt no hot liquid on me and there was no puddle of tea on the table.

"I don't understand," I cried again. "Not this place, not the tea, not you. Not anything. You always speak in riddles. How can anyone ever know what you mean? I can't. I don't. Not ever. Can you not speak plainly for once? What am I doing here? Where is everyone else?" Frustrated, I burst into tears. "Where is my family?"

Fay'dor rose and paced back and forth in front of the table, his voice rising as he spoke. "You think you are the youth Pyrà who was born in this village in the Mhor-Jenn. You think you are but a boy who mourns the disappearance of his family and neighbors. You think that is all you are. You think—"

I leapt to my feet and around the table to block him. "That is what I am. That is who I am. I don't think it. I know it. Who else would I be? Who else could I be?"

The corners of Fay'dor's lips twitched, forming the closest to a smile I had ever seen cross his face. "Well done, my boy. Well done." He placed his hands on my shoulders and guided me back to my seat.

"More riddles," I muttered.

He took his seat across from me and poured out another bowl of tea. "No ordinary youth would challenge me as you have. Only one as extraordinary as you could possess the courage, and the telling. Now it is time to take those gifts and employ them to meet your destiny…Q'ntana's destiny."

"I-I'm a boy," I whispered.

Fay'dor shook his head. "You may have been a boy when you opened your eyes to this day. You are one no longer."

"He is mad," I thought. "Perhaps the lightning struck the sense out of him."

Fay'dor pushed the bowl toward me. "Look into the bowl," he said. "Look into the steam and tell me what you see."

The steam washed sinuously across the surface. Ordinary steam. Ordinary tea.

"Blow on it. Gently."

As I did, the steam danced to the edges of the bowl, where it continued to flit and flitter. But it was the tea that caught my eye. Instead of rippling on my breath, it stilled and lightened from amber to silver until I saw my face staring back at me from its now-mirrored veneer. Or was it my face? I scratched my chin to see if that other face would follow suit. It did. Yet its chin sported several days' coppery growth, thicker than any boy of my years could manifest. I withdrew my hand. The hand in the tea vanished. I touched my chin again. This time, I felt the same nascent beard I had just seen reflected back at me. My hands fell to my lap and I squeezed my eyes shut.

When I opened them again, I averted them from the tea bowl and, instead, turned them across the table to Fay'dor. His face wavered in and out of focus, as did the canvas walls behind him. I dropped my eyes to the floor, but the rug had recommenced its shape-shifting. Only the tea was fixed. Even the table wobbled unsteadily before my eyes.

"The tea." Fay'dor's voice burbled at me, as though rising from deep in the brew. "Read the tea and tell me what you see."

Doubtful, and shaken by the image of a future me that were Fay'dor to be believed, was now the present me, I returned my attention to the tea.

The vision was unclear at first, as though I viewed it through a thin layer of tulle, and in black-and-white.

"I see you," I began slowly, "standing at the entry to your lean to, watching all the stallions gallop toward us from Mòrq'an Mellà." I paused. "Do I stand next to you?" I shook my head. "No, it is almost as though I see it through your eyes, which makes no sense. Because I'm not there. I don't see myself there. I don't know where I am."

Slowly, the gauzy filter dissolved, bringing color to the scene. And sound.

"All those horses. Scores and scores of them. And I'm somehow in the middle of it. I'm not sure how because I don't sense myself there either.

"It's loud, but not so loud that I can't hear my heart pounding. Why is my heart pounding?"

Why *was* my heart pounding? Not merely in the vision but there, at Fay'dor's table. It was as though I was in the two places at once, and it was making me nauseous. I wanted to shut my eyes again to quell the queasiness. I didn't dare.

"Focus." Fay'dor's voice sounded more distant now, muffled as it was by the pounding of all those horses' hooves. "Stay with the vision."

The vision…the horses…

"T'tammo is at the lead…kicking up so much dust it's hard to see anything but his head and his eyes, glowing more brightly than I have ever seen them…

"He is almost here…although I don't know what 'here' is. All I know is that the dust is thicker now…"

I tasted the dust in my throat and started to cough. Fay'dor thrust a black goblet at me and I took big, long gulps of the sweetest water I had ever tasted. Whether it happened in my vision or at the table, I could not be certain. At least I could breathe easily again.

"Wait. The dust is clearing, and— No, that can't be. Someone is astride T'tammo."

No one rode our stallions. Not ever. Anyone foolish enough to try was immediately thrown, although never seriously injured…merely bruised enough never to attempt it a second time. Who would dare?

My breath stopped. Not because of the dust and not within the vision, which was forced to continue without me for in my disbelief I knocked over my tea bowl a second time.

"Th-that was me," I stammered.

"Indeed."

nine

Pyrà

That was all Fay'dor would say for a time, responding to none of my questions. Instead, he righted my tea bowl, refilled it and bade me focus again on its contents. My first inclination was to refuse, to insist on answers and explanations, and not simply regarding what I had visioned in the tea. My second was to leave. The first, I knew, would achieve nothing. As for the second, even were I able to leave this place, where would I go? As far as I knew, everyone other than Fay'dor and Hara'q had vanished. By now, for all I knew, Hara'q might also have disappeared. Perhaps the horses had gone as well. Maybe the maq'rahs too, although that would be viewed as a blessing by everyone, if everyone numbered more than two.

Me, Fay'dor and an empty Mhor-Jenn. Was that to be my world? Would I ever see Maminka and Jeryn again? I dropped my head into my hands, overcome with despair.

"You have all the answers you seek," Fay'dor said gently but firmly. "You *are* all the answers you seek. Continue, and you will know them."

"But—"

"Continue, and you will know them and more." He nudged the bowl closer, until it touched my elbow. I raised my eyes. "The knowingness is already there." He reached across the table and touched my chest. "And there." With his other hand, he touched my brow. "It is but for you to acknowledge that knowingness and own it."

"I can't," I whispered.

"You must."

My head felt heavier than the heaviest of boulders when I finally lifted it. My breath felt ragged as I blew away the steam. And my eyelids struggled to remain open as I stared into the bowl.

The boy astride T'tammo *was* me. Yet he was no boy. He was the copper-bearded youth I had seen in the tea. Nor was this a vision of some future me. Not only did I have the whiskers to prove it, my voice now seemed deeper than it had when Fay'dor sent Hara'q for me.

You may have been a boy when you opened your eyes to this day. You are one no longer.

It made no sense. None of what I was seeing and experiencing made sense. Was this all a dream? Would I wake on my own sleeping pallet in a short while? Would I then slip out of bed, sneak out the door and view our village exactly as I had seen it the night before? How could this not be a dream?

Understanding is not required. Seeing is. Knowing is.

I knew what I had seen to be true, even if I didn't understand it. Even if I never understood it. Did I dare continue?

You must.

I refocused my eyes on the tea, again calmed to mirror-like stillness.

"I still see you standing there," I began haltingly, "but now I also see where I am. I am riding toward you on T'tammo. The other stallions follow behind. All of them. You make a sign as we gallop past. Like this." I formed a circle with my left thumb and forefinger and crossed it with my right forefinger.

Fay'dor nodded.

"Now, the site of village is far behind and all I see in every direction is empty Mhor-Jenn. I don't know where we are or where we are going, but T'tammo seems to, so I hang on." The vision faded and I waited for more. None came.

"Close your eyes, count to eleven, slowly, and look again."

One more thing that made no sense, but I did as Fay'dor asked. Again, I felt as though I had no choice. *Eight...nine...t—* My eyes were still shut, but suddenly there was more. I didn't see it so much as sense it.

"It's nighttime and M'nor has yet to rise, so all I see is whatever light is cast by our flickering campfire. Someone sits with me, across the fire pit, but their face is in shadow. I can't see who it is. Is it you?"

Fay'dor said nothing. I continued.

"The only sound is the fire's crackling and the burble of running water. There must be a stream nearby. I'm aware of lapping and snuffling sounds, so some horses must be with us, if hidden in the shadows."

I opened my eyes, hoping the tea would somehow reveal more of the scene. It did. "Yes, the horses are with us. All of them, it seems. I see more of where we are: camped on a mountain plateau and backed against a wall of sheer rock that rises to the summit.

"I cannot see into the valley, but I sense our elevation to be very high. If it is, we must be far from home, for no mountains are visible from our village. There's a storm on the horizon. It is too far to hear any thunder, but the lightning…there is so much of it that it's bright as daylight… It moves toward us. More swiftly than any ordinary storm. And— It's here… Oh…*NO!*"

I pushed the tea bowl away.

"It needn't end that way," Fay'dor said softly.

"What way?"

"Tell me what happened."

I shook my head. If I didn't speak it, maybe it wouldn't be real.

"If you do not speak it, you cannot prevent it from being real." Fay'dor flung the contents of the tea bowl over his shoulder, where the droplets transformed into sparks. Once they had extinguished, he poured me a fresh cup. "Drink it. It will give you courage, and the necessary words."

As doubtful as I was, I held the bowl to my face. I closed my eyes as the steam washed over me. This brew was different. Where the other had been odorless, this one smelled fruity, spicy…and sweet.

"I have brewed it with extra honey, the way you like it," a voice spoke, not Fay'dor's. My eyes shot open and for the briefest of instants, an old woman sat across from me. She smiled at me as I imagined a grandmother might. The moment I blinked, she was gone.

"Eulisha?" I whispered.

"Who?"

"Eulisha. I saw her. I know I did." I sipped on the tea to steady myself. "Like in the story of Toshar and The MoonQuest."

"Who is Toshar and what is a MoonQuest?"

"A story. Toshar is in it. He's a bard. It's one of Maminka's stories." My voice caught. Would I ever see her again? "It's one of my favorites, after Ben and the SunQuest." Tears longed to come. I swallowed them and took a deep breath, then another. "It's just a story."

"There is no 'just a story,'" Fay'dor said. "All stories are real. And all stories are true. As a bard you must know that."

"Then I am a bard."

"What I say is precisely what I mean. No more, no less."

Fay'dor folded his hands on the table, his clawed left over his right.

I stared at them, aware of their significance in a way I never had been before. It couldn't be. How could I never have noticed?

"You're O'ric," I said at last. "You must be. He has hands like yours." I studied his face. "And eyes."

Fay'dor raised an eyebrow, saying nothing.

"He is in both those stories. He is a mysterious sort of wise man, and he…and you— You must be O'ric."

"I must be Fay'dor, for that is who I am," Fay'dor said in a voice that brooked neither contradiction nor argument. Yet there was a laughing glint in his eyes. *Was* he the O'ric of those stories that weren't 'just stories'? If he was, was this also a story? If it was, who was I? My mind refused to grasp any of what was happening.

You have all the answers you seek. You are all the answers you seek. Continue, and you will know them.

"Drink your tea," he said aloud. "You will need it in order to continue. For continue you must. Your destiny demands it."

I gulped down the rest of the hot, sweet liquid, set the bowl onto the table and pushed it away. "I died," I said without emotion. "So did whoever was with me. And the horses. All of them."

"What happened?"

"Must I?"

"Yes, if you wish to avert that outcome." He filled my tea bowl again. "Drink," he said.

I shook my head. "When lightning struck the summit — three thunderbolts at once — the mountaintop collapsed on top of us. We were buried alive." I gasped for breath as though still in the vision, as though my lungs were filling with dirt and dust.

Fay'dor pushed the tea bowl at me. "Now," he said.

I nodded and tried to swallow, even as I choked. Somehow, I managed to down a mouthful. The choking stopped and I could breathe again.

"Another," Fay'dor said, this time with an urgency I had never known him to express.

As soon as the liquid hit my throat, I knew — what I was to do and why I was to do it. What I did not know was how to avoid the fate of my vision.

"You will," Fay'dor replied to my silent question.

"Why me?" I asked.

"You are the Bard of Bryn Doon," he said. "It is your destiny."

ten

Hara'q

The Bard of Bryn Doon. Was it possible? If it was, then perhaps I wasn't doomed. No, it couldn't be. How could I have lived in the Mhor-Jenn for so long and not known that the Bard would return, here? Could return here? Was already among us?

Perhaps I should have suspected something of Pyrà. What boy had ever been so devoted to any horse as Pyrà was to my brother stallions? Almost from the moment he could walk, he spent as many waking hours among them as he could…as Kamela and Lucca would allow. It was as though the horses satisfied a need in his young life that nothing else could. Somehow, his parents had known; somehow, his parents had permitted what no other parents would. There were times he even slept among them. They belonged to him and he to them in a way that could only have been true of the Bard of Bryn Doon.

For all that, I did not see it.

Perhaps had I still been in my natural body, I would have. But the magic that had cursed me with humanity yet failed to remove my immortality must have left me blind to such things. That same magic cursed my brothers to forget me and themselves, but not I them nor our shared history. I spent little time on Mòrq'an Mellà, even as I longed to spend more, for my brothers did not trust me. They trusted no humans, and rightly so. They would have trusted the Bard of Bryn Doon. Was that why they trusted Pyrà?

The boy had seemed different when he returned for me. In fact, he did not resemble a boy at all. Not only did he look and act less child-like, he came across as more resolute, not in the headstrong way of a stubborn young lad but in the earnest single-mindedness of a young man of purpose.

Being human in body alone, I was never certain what about humanity I ought to regard as peculiar, given how peculiar humanity had always appeared to me to be. Still, other than my own, this degree of transformation was nothing I had previously encountered.

It was an extraordinary feat, even for Fay'dor, whose actions were inevitably out-of-the-ordinary, and rarely in ways that I would view as desirable.

Thus, I had been no more keen to heed Fay'dor's summons than Pyrà had been. But I obeyed. What was the alternative?

"You know why I have called you to me," Fay'dor declared once I had seated myself at his table.

I shook my head.

"I say you do." He poured out a bowl of tea and pushed it toward me. I shook my head. In my experience, Fay'dor's teas offered more trouble than they did refreshment.

"You give me too much credit," I retorted. I would say nothing until I knew what he sought from me.

"Perhaps," Fay'dor said. He stared past me, through the flap of the lean-to and out into the empty desert. "We have known each other a long time," he began.

"Long enough that I once knew who Fay'dor truly is," I said, "but so long that I cannot remember, although I remember much else. For example, I remember that taking tea with you is to be avoided. No good ever comes of it."

Fay'dor refused to dignify my insolence with a response. Instead, he asked, "What else do you remember?"

"I remember that I was forced to take on this body and this life, while retaining full memory of my previous body and life."

"Do you remember why?"

"I do."

He poured himself a cup of his own and sipped on it slowly while scrutinizing me with those piercing yellow eyes that always seemed to see more than I chose to reveal.

"To retain the memory my brothers could not," I said at last when I realized he could outwait me by more years than I cared to sit there. And would.

"For…?

"For the day when I could restore it to them." After so many generations in this village that Prithi had so clearly forgotten, any faith that such a day would ever arrive had long ago been dashed. So Fay'dor's next words stunned me.

"That day is nearly upon us."

Were my spirit still housed in my true body, I would have reared up on my hind legs, shaken my head until sparks flew off my mane and galloped off toward the horizon, if only for the exhilaration of the run. As it was, I did not know what to say or do. It had been so long since I had experienced joy, and never in this awkward, two-legged body, that I sat paralyzed in my seat until Fay'dor spoke again.

"It cannot be done here in the Mhor-Jenn, Hara'q. It can only be done once you have left this place with your feet pointed toward Bryn Doon."

I frowned, any spark of hope extinguished. Had we possessed the ability to leave the Mhor-Jenn and return to Bryn Doon, wouldn't we already have done so? I had lived long enough in this body in this place to know that there was no way out of the Mhor-Jenn. Unless Fay'dor… No, as powerful as he was — and I knew him to be powerful even if I could no longer recall how — he would not flout Prithi's will.

"There is one way," he said. "Only one."

What could he mean? I scoured the dusty cobwebs of my memory for "the way." I even emptied my bowl of tea in the hope that it might help. Perhaps it did, for after scratching my beard until my chin was raw, I remembered. It still seemed impossible.

"He is here," Fay'dor said when he saw that I knew.

"But— But no one is here. They are all gone."

"Not all."

This time, I knew what he was looking at when he gazed past me and into the desert…out toward Mòrq'an Mellà.

Pyrà, the Bard of Bryn Doon? Impossible. Or was it?

In the highest chamber of the highest tower in the land, in the darkest moments of the darkest night, a lone sorcerer, nearly as old as the land itself, stands by an open window, arms outstretched. Thunderbolts flare off his spear-like fingernails and into the northern sky, one after the other after the other in rapid-fire succession. In the far distance, beyond this land and the next, the lightning smashes into homes, barns and shops, igniting wooden structures and straw roofs and razing entire villages. Those unable to escape their shelters cry out as they are burned alive. Those who attempt to flee are struck dead as individual lightning flashes single them out.

Although the land is hundreds of v'reks away, the sorcerer sees and hears it all with the assistance of his scrying stone. His face, furrowed with centuries of wizardry, is impassive. Yet his eyes, motionless and unblinking, glow as fiery as the lightning.

When nothing more is to be seen or heard, the thunderbolts retreat into the sorcerer's fingernails, illuminating his body and radiating through his coarse, cotton robe to light up not only the chamber but the entire tower all the way into the earth surrounding its foundation.

Only when the tower is plunged back into the blackness of the moonless night does the sorcerer pick up his staff, twined of the contrasting woods of the red and white sha'maya trees, and descend the winding staircase, a grim smile barely visible among the sea of wrinkles and creases. As he steps onto the cool, loamy earth, the tower vanishes behind him. Moments later, he too is gone, swallowed by woods in a grove so dense that no one else in the land dares enter it.

THE BEGINNING

Golden sparks swirled up into the indigo sky from the flames dancing in the fire pit. I could almost imagine them to be the first stars twinkling overhead as the day's final vestiges of light faded into black. Unfortunately, this scene too closely resembled my nightmare vision at Fay'dor's for me to surrender to its visual poetry. As in the vision, the soft trickle of a nearby stream played in counterpoint to the crackling of the fire, which illuminated enough of our surroundings to reveal the sheer cliff face that rose from our high mountain plateau to a craggy summit. Here, even if his face was veiled in shadow, I knew my companion to be Hara'q, as wordless as he had been in the vision. From where I sat, I could make out the silhouette of T'tammo, who stood statue-like between our tiny campsite and the rest of the horses, grazing just out of sight. There was no lightning on the horizon, but that didn't mean a storm was not imminent.

We had been on the road for five days, not that there was any road to follow. The Mhor-Jenn had no roads. Roads served no purpose when none could find their way here, not that any would choose to. As for those of us who lived here, there was nowhere to go, as Hara'q had been reminding us for as long as I could remember.

Events had now proven Hara'q wrong. My mother and sister and all our neighbors were gone, although the means of their departure and their destination remained a mystery. Hara'q and I were also gone, from our village if not yet from the Mhor-Jenn, on a mission to guide nearly two hundred horses back to their homeland.

Had Fay'dor revealed all we were to experience, this journey would have seemed even more impossible than I knew it must be. Instead, he had offered little more than that with Hara'q's assistance, I was to return all the stallions to Bryn Doon, not that he disclosed where that was. It might as well have been on the far side of M'nor. For I could see no way that one hundred eighty-seven horses, however intelligent, could survive long enough in this unforgiving land to reach either the Mir or the Do'ana Qi, let alone cross them. If through some miracle we did, what then? Perhaps the Bard of Bryn Doon was meant to know. I did not. I did not even know what a "Bard of Bryn Doon" was supposed to do or be, other than that, apparently, I was one.

I suspected that Hara'q knew more than I did. But he would only grunt in answer to my questions as we led the stallions off the slopes of Mòrq'an Mellà and deeper into the Mhor-Jenn, me astride T'tammo, and Hara'q, who refused to mount any horse, on foot.

Hara'q and I had met Fay'dor on one final occasion, this time together, before setting off. Through this meeting, Hara'q had sat in sullen silence, an attitude he maintained for the next several days. For my part, I pressed Fay'dor for practical answers to real questions. In which direction were we to travel? How were we to sustain ourselves through what was certain to be a lengthy and treacherous journey? If we somehow managed to find our way to Bryn Doon, what we were to do once there?

"How would the Bard of Bryn Doon answer those questions," Fay'dor asked in return, "were he so untrusting as to feel the need to ask them?"

Hara'q rolled his eyes.

"It is the journey itself that will ask the questions and supply the answers," he continued, "your journey not only to Bryn Doon but into the full expression of your bardship. Remember," he repeated for an umpteenth time as Hara'q mouthed the words along with him, "you have all the answers you seek. You *are* all the answers you seek." He touched my heart. "When you feel doubt or fear, turn to your heart. It will guide you always." He paused, perhaps to provide the space for me to accuse him of more riddle-making. I chose to say nothing.

I had no more enthusiasm for this odyssey than Hara'q did. But what was the alternative? With Fay'dor refusing to reunite me with my mother, there was none. It would have been suicidal to stay. The journey might also prove suicidal, but at least it offered the possibility, however marginal, of a hospitable destination. I would do what Fay'dor asked not because I wanted to or felt called to, but because there was nothing else to be done.

As Hara'q and I stood outside the lean-to, little wiser than when we had arrived, Fay'dor reached into his pocket and pulled out a long, slender feather, the largest, most brilliantly hued I had ever seen. Maq'rah feathers were black and brittle. Ganda feathers were white with deep wine tips. This silver-spined feather was iridescent, every color known to man and several I had never encountered shimmering when he held it to the light. And when he angled it so the suns struck it a certain way, the colors formed a pattern that suggested a simple crown.

When he offered it to me, I refused. I didn't feel unworthy, as Toshar had felt in The MoonQuest when O'ric presented him with the fabled dagger, Orrican. A dagger might have proved practical on a journey such as ours. But a quill? And one so elegant that I would be in constant fear of damaging it or, worse, losing it? Fay'dor would claim to have never heard of The SunQuest, but this feather looked identical to the one Kumba, the Great Dragon of Creation, had plucked from its wing to give to Ben, the same one Ben had used to carve his story into the Scriving Rock. Could it be that feather? Of course not. That was a story.

All stories are real. All stories are true.

I shook my head. Even if all stories were real and true, which I doubted, how could it be that feather? Or was it a fresh feather from the dragon's wing? No, that was more fantastic still.

"You must take it," he insisted. "It is yours. It has been waiting for you, for this moment. For your moment."

"I don't underst—" There was no point in continuing. Fay'dor would only repeat that understanding was not required. "Why?"

He studied me as he weighed my question and for the briefest of breaths, I saw myself through his eyes. It shocked me. I did not see the youthful Pyrà of the Mhor-Jenn. I did not see the Mhor-Jenn at all. I was in another land — an emerald realm of undulating hills dotted with groves of ancient trees, all of it sliced sinuously through by a broad, sea-green river. And I was not a youth. I was mature enough that tendrils of white wove through my beard and hair. As the vision faded, I caught a glimpse of fields upon fields of mixed hues in the far distance. I thought them to be flowered meadows, but only when the vision had evaporated did I realize that what I had seen were horses, hundreds upon hundreds of them, not a black beast among them.

"What did you say to your mother two nights ago?" Fay'dor asked.

I gaped at him as though he had spoken in a foreign tongue. My mind was still trying to decipher what my eyes could not believe they had seen.

"Two nights ago," he repeated, "what did you say to your mother?"

Two nights ago? He could as easily be asking me about something that happened two years ago…or two hundred. What did happen two nights ago? Oh, The SunQuest story. The continuing.

Fay'dor nodded as though he had read my thoughts. "This is the Bryn'qà, the quill of Bryn Doon, and you are the Bard of Bryn Doon, the *Bard* of Bryn Doon. The Bryn'qà will reveal to you that continuing. With the Bryn'qà's help, you will scrive the stories that dwell within you, that have dwelt within you since the beginning of story…since the beginning of time. It is their time, stories' time, as much as it is yours. And you are their story as much as they are yours."

He pressed the quill into my hand. "With the Bryn'qà," he continued, "you will scrive your destiny."

*　　*　　*

My destiny. I pulled the Bryn'qà from the belt of my tunic and held it up to the firelight. The crown flared through the iridescence and for the first time, I noticed that the crown was pierced by a quill identical to the Bryn'qà. What was my destiny? I glanced across at Hara'q.

"It is time," he said, breaking his long silence.

"For what?"

He pointed to the quill in my hand. "To scrive your first story."

It must have been pleasing to the eye, this castle…once upon a time when the stone was scrubbed and shiny, the windows sparkled in the suns-light, the wooden gates and drawbridge were polished and smooth, and the waters of the moat glinted silver in the moonlight. That was the picture Gran Mattilde painted for me when I was still a young girl. That was how her Gran Mattilde had described it to her and her Gran Mattilde before her, all the way back to the long ago days when Castle Flor rose stately and tall from the sylvan meadows at the heart of farm-rich Flor.

Today's Castle Flor was none of that. There were few hints of the stone's original pearly hue, which the burning of many of the meadows had long ago stained a sooty black. The same smoke and ash had coated the glass with a gray, greasy film that blocked not only the views but most light, casting all halls and chambers in grim shadow. The scarlet qanaria wood, once the pride not only of our castle but of the principality, was scratched, scored and begrimed. And the qanaria trees themselves? Gran believed that only one remained in the entire realm, spared not by any official decree but by an enchantment so powerful than anyone who came within a dozen steps of it was hurled back by a mighty wind. Not that approaching that close was possible anymore. Thick krysh bushes, their spiny thorns ejecting a paralyzing poison without even being touched, had already grown up around it in Gran's time. Most meadowland surrounding the castle was now blackened stubble, and nearly all the nearby farmland was so overgrown with massive weeds that the skeletons of once prosperous farmhouses were barely visible.

Gran Mattilde was no more. A sudden fever took her a few days after we celebrated the thirteenth anniversary of my birth. It was then, four years past, that I replaced her as majordoma in the castle. Normally, the position passed from mother to daughter, all named Mattilde, as had occurred in an unbroken line in my family for as long as anyone could remember. My mother, however, was so thoughtless and irresponsible as to die in childbirth; that was how Beneficia put it to me, frequently.

Beneficia was doyenne of the castle and ruler of Flor. She fashioned herself as "Beneficia, Queen of Flor," and insisted on being addressed as "her most beneficent and royal highness and majesty," although her mean, covetous nature was the antithesis of beneficent, and by tradition Flor had a First Lady, not a monarch. She had long pestered Ardoxx to preside over a formal ceremony crowning her as queen. He had always refused, and it was dangerous to argue too strenuously with a sorcerer who could, if he chose, turn one into a slavering mandopleth.

Graceless and overly large with a lumbering gait and mottled skin, she half-resembled one already. Worse, she drooled unremittingly, although it was more disgusting at mealtime, when bits of food lodged in her spittle and dribbled from the corners of her mouth to her chin, only to drop onto her bodice. To keep her presentable, her ladies pried her out of one too-tight-fitting dress into another after every meal; often again before the next. Beneficia took five meals most days, six or seven when she entertained.

Her physical appearance and table manners would have counted for naught had her heart been as generous as her name suggested. Yet she possessed not a single redeeming quality. Were there any, I would have been the one to know. I was in and out Beneficia's chambers throughout the day and night, summoned for the most trivial of tasks and errands. Not once had I heard her utter a gentle word or perform a kind-hearted deed. Rather, her tone was imperious and all her actions revolved around her personal comfort.

Servants lived in terror of her temper, which showed itself most forcefully when her barked orders were not strictly and immediately obeyed. Arbitrary punishments ranged from holding back meals and wages to dismissal. In an impoverished land where malnourishment was common, a temporary loss of wages often brought severe hardship to a servant's family. Permanent loss through dismissal could lead to death by starvation.

As majordoma, I was spared some of Beneficia's worst excesses, thanks to the terms of my indenture, which explicitly laid out both my responsibilities and hers and which would be enforced by Ardoxx were they to be breached. For example, I could be neither dismissed nor ill-treated, but nor could I resign. Unfortunately, ill-treatment, left undefined in the contract, was for Ardoxx to adjudicate. And as much distaste as he had for Beneficia, I was of no more consequence to him than a slimy g'goma bug.

That was the life of Castle Flor's majordoma. It was not the life I had chosen. It was the life I had been born into, as my foremothers had, and it was the life I was expected to die out of, having borne one child to replace me — a daughter. That child would not be of my husband; majordomas were not permitted to wed. Beneficia and Ardoxx would select my bedmate — several, if the first failed to seed a girl child. Were I to birth a boy, he would be given to a peasant couple to raise.

That, too, was explicitly laid out, not only in the terms of indenture that bound my family to Castle Flor, but in the laws of Flor itself... laws I felt increasingly ready to defy.

I was sulking. I had been sulking since Fay'dor dispatched me on this so-called journey with this so-called bard. To be honest, I had been sulking since the time of the first King Fvorag, all those generations ago, when everything I loved had been brutally destroyed. For all Toshar's deeds, Kyri's heroism and Ben's alleged greatness in vanquishing the instigators of our humiliation, the only reward my brothers ever received for our sacrifices was exile to this hellish outback. Now, to be offered the possibility of restitution, but only by babysitting a counterfeit bard on an impossible quest? It was a cruel joke. Of course, I sulked. Who wouldn't?

Pyrà tried often to engage me in conversation through our first days on the road. The most he was able to elicit from me was the occasional grunt. I felt bad, but not bad enough to respond otherwise. Fay'dor had insisted that the youth was the Bard of Bryn Doon, but how could he be? Surely, I, who was of Bryn Doon, would recognize the legendary bard when I encountered him. I refused to believe that I had encountered him in this unseasoned youth, even if Fay'dor's wizardry had added to his years.

I came close to believing when Fay'dor gave him the Bryn'qà. Yet the true Bard of Bryn Doon would have known this quill on sight, not as some artifact from some long ago story but as a symbol of his eloquence and bardly power. He would have known it as the welcome restoration of something familiar, not as something alien and inconvenient. After all, the Bryn'qà was to the Bard of Bryn Doon what a scepter was to a sovereign. If he could not see that, he was no bard of mine.

Pyrà said nothing to me through our fifth day. I was pleased.

Maybe he had finally sensed that I was an unwilling participant in this journey and had agreed only because I would not be separated from my brothers. At the end of the day, after we had set up camp near the mountain summit and taken our meal, in silence, Pyrà retrieved the Bryn'qà from his belt. As soon as he held it to the light, I saw it reflected in his eyes. Or perhaps his eyes had merged with the Bryn'qà in some way, for they grew as iridescent as the quill. And where his pupils would normally have been was the crown. This was not the crown of kingship, but the crown of bardship, representing the singular vision that was the Bard of Bryn Doon's alone. As improbable as it still seemed, could Fay'dor have been right? Was this youth truly the Bard of Bryn Doon? Seeing him now with the Bryn'qà, I was forced to ask a different question. How could he not be?

I pulled back my hood. "It is time," I said.

As startled as he was to hear my voice after my long silence, he didn't take his eyes off the Bryn'qà. Instead, he lowered the quill and peered at me through it. "For what?"

"To scrive your first story."

He said nothing, still mesmerized by the Bryn'qà. Finally, he set it on his lap and looked directly at me. "My first story?"

"Your first of this journey," I replied. "As the Bard of Bryn, you will have scrived many."

He uncorked his water skin and drank deeply from it. "Then you agree with Fay'dor that I am this bard?"

Did I? In manner and appearance, he still seemed an unlikely candidate. Even with the years Fay'dor had added to his age, Pyrà was young, too young for such responsibility. Or was he? After all, he was not much younger than Toshar had been when he set out on his MoonQuest, and he had accomplished much…although not nearly enough for me and my brothers. Was he the Bard of Bryn Doon? It made no sense, but… "I know you are," I replied at last.

He stood and stepped away from the fire. His back to me, he stared into the blackness of the night. "Did Fay'dor tell you about my vision?" he asked softly.

"He did."

"Nonetheless, you came," he said after a few moments.

"Like you, I did not have much choice."

"Yes." He scanned the horizon then turned back to the fire. His eyes glowed and I could again see the Bryn'qà's reflection in them, although the quill was now tucked into his belt. How could I have doubted, even for an instant, that he was the Bard of Bryn Doon? "This is where it happened," he said, "in the vision...where we all perished." He dropped to the ground and crossed his legs.

"Fay'dor is many things, many of which I dislike. One thing he is not is a murderer. We did not come here to die."

Pyrà nodded. "The lightning will come. I know it will. As for the rest..."

"The rest," I said with as much confidence as I could muster, "lives in the story...in your story."

He sighed. "It is the story that will bring the lightning, you know."

I did not. Yet it did not surprise me. I knew that forces existed that were determined to prevent us from reaching Bryn Doon. What surprised me was how much Pyrà knew without knowing he knew it.

"Once upon a time," he began, staring into the flames, "in the early days of the Golden Age of Q'ntana—" A low rumble of thunder rolled toward us from the distant desert. Pyrà stopped, his mouth still open.

I gazed out into the dark. No lightning. Not yet.

T'tammo whickered and moved closer, stationing himself behind Pyrà. A chorus of whinnies and neighs answered back as the remaining horses jostled to form a tight circle around us. T'tammo whickered again, nuzzled Pyrà's neck and stamped his foot.

"I know," he whispered. He gulped several more mouthfuls from his water skin, took a deep breath and started again, as a second wave of thunder rumbled toward us.

The sorcerer strides into the castle's throne room, sweeping through the gaggle of fawning courtiers gathered before the dais. His eyes are dark, his brow is creased with furrows of rage, and he grips his staff with knuckles whiter than the terror that has bleached all color from the courtiers' faces. As he reaches the dais, he points a spindly finger at the ceiling and mutters a terse incantation: "Ankiàna ka'eyna tookà jooq." With that final syllable, every flame in every taper in each of the chamber's two dozen chandeliers is snuffed out and the light from all the throne room's ten floor-to-ceiling windows is extinguished.

Outside it is mid-afternoon. Within, it is as black as the sorcerer's temper.

"You dare—" Beneficia bellows, only to be silenced by a thunderbolt that flies from the sorcerer's staff and lands at her feet, igniting a small fire where it pierces the scarlet carpet. The fire, now the only light in the chamber, burns green, throwing eerie shadows into the mirrored walls and casting her face in a sickly viridescence.

The courtiers have fled, although only as far as the throne room's giant gilt doors, for the sorcerer's magic has bolted them shut. There, the courtiers moan and wail in fear.

"Silence," the sorcerer speaks in a whisper so powerful and clear that it is audible throughout Castle Flor and beyond, to the farthest reaches of the land. All Flor obeys, and not one sound — human or animal — is heard from one frontier to the next.

Only Beneficia attempts to defy the sorcerer. However, when she opens her mouth to speak, no words emerge.

"Know this, Beneficia," the sorcerer says, now so softly that only she can hear. "I cannot unseat you, but I will not serve you. I serve my will, not yours. Never yours." He steps onto the dais and climbs the three steps to the throne, a capital crime were it to be committed by any other person or creature in the realm. He stands over her, the shadow of his towering frame blocking all light from her face.

"Know this too: All I do, I do to enhance my power not yours, as I have done since long before you played at being sovereign, since long before you played in your nursery, and as I will do long after your ill-bred bones have disintegrated into dust and dissipated on the wind. Order me about again, as you have done today, and you will yearn for death to take you. I promise you that."

He turns his back on her, descends from the dais and thrice strikes his staff on the marble floor. Every mirror in the chamber shatters. He strikes it thrice more, and the chandeliers' crystal pendants implode, splintering into knife-like shards that rain onto Beneficia and the courtiers. On the third of the third series of strikes, he is gone.

A third crash of thunder shattered the desert silence, closer and louder than its predecessors. I clenched my fists so tightly that my fingernails drove into my palms. Although I knew lightning flashed behind me, I didn't dare turn. I didn't know whether the story ready to move through me would save us…could save us. Yet this was the continuing I had sensed to a story that was not meant to have one. I had to let it urge itself through me, whatever the outcome. So I began again, praying that I could somehow block out enough of the storm rolling toward us to keep listening and scriving.

"Once upon a time, in the early days of the Golden Age of Q'ntana, the great Ben faced the first challenge of his reign as king and elder-bard: what to do with the Black Riders and their mounts who had ter-rorized the land for so many seasons, first under the command of King Gravel and then, once Gravel was deposed, as rogue highwaymen who ransacked the countryside unchecked. All had surrendered with Ben's ascension to the throne. Could they be trusted to reform their marauding ways? And could a Q'ntana so long tormented by these men and their horses accept them as neighbors?"

A piercing thunderclap shook the ground beneath me, and the sky strobed white from what must have been a series of lightning bursts. I flinched and clenched my fists more tightly. I didn't dare look. Instead, I raised my voice so I could be heard over the rumbling…so I could hear myself over the rumbling.

"Ben's advisors urged imprisonment. The new king, however, refused to inaugurate his reign with mass incarcerations.

"'What of their families?' Ben asked. 'Are we to imprison them as well?' His advisors had no reply. 'What of the stallions?' To this question, too, his advisors had no reply."

The next crash dislodged a dozen boulders from the cliff face. They smashed to the ground steps beyond the circle of horses. The stallions ignored them, but I eyed the summit anxiously. Would the next strike be the last, the one that would bury us alive? I swallowed hard and went on.

"'Yet,' Ben said to himself from his aerie atop the Eagle Tower of Castle Rose, 'they cannot live among us. The animus toward them is too strong, and justifiably so.' He raised his eyes to the heavens and prayed to Prithi for a fair and merciful solution. Then he waited.

"Voices rose in waves from the corridors and courtyard below, accompanied by the arrhythmic beat of hammers, buzz of saws and gratings of wood across stone — all in preparation for the coming evening's coronation feast, a gala that was to extend beyond the castle to surrounding fields and meadows, for all in Q'ntana had been invited.

"Then it ceased — all sound and movement, not only in and around Castle Rose but across the land. It was as though the world held its breath. Perhaps it did. For Aygra and B'na, moments before their sacred suns-merge, halted their journeys across the sky. And Ben, whose kinship with the suns was more intimate than that shared by any living being before or since, felt one ray from each bathe him in the golden glow of celestial light, a light which, for that brief breath, reminded him of all he had ever known or would know."

I stopped. As in the story, everything around us had stilled. Thunder had broken off mid-roar, lightning bolts hung suspended in the sky and a shooting star hovered above us, its light trail a motionless streak of platinum.

Hara'q looked as though he was about to say something, but no words emerged. His eyes stared past me unblinkingly. The horses, too, were rooted in place, like statues.

Was I also a statue? If I was thinking and breathing, I couldn't be. Or could I? Could I wiggle my fingers? I could. My toes? Those too. Could I move my head? I did. What did it mean? Of all the peculiar things I had experienced in recent days, this had to be the most peculiar.

Up in the sky, the stars were bright pinpoints of light. Strangely, they did not twinkle. But the moon… Unlike the suns in my story, the moon had moved. More accurately put, it had let itself be seen. The night had been moonless as I began the story, and M'nor had barely peeked over the summit when time stopped. Now it was fully visible, shimmering as nothing else in this stationary world did.

"M'nor?"

The breath of the slightest of breezes washed across my face in reply. The moon did not sing to me as she had to Toshar in The MoonQuest. But I was certain I detected words in that gentle current. "Trust," it seemed to be whispering. "Trust the story. Trust *your* story. Trust it enough to let it continue."

To let it continue…

I took a deep breath in, then let it go as I freed the story to move through me once more. As I did and as I spoke the telling's next words, time, and the storm, returned to life.

"When the world exhaled and both time and the suns resumed their journeys, Ben summoned one representative each of the Black Riders and of the stallions. They convened in the Castle Rose courtyard and—" I gaped at Hara'q. "You!"

Hara'q moved his head in the hint of a nod.

This truly made no sense. "But—"

Before Hara'q could respond, the earth beneath us heaved and four massive thunderbolts struck the mountaintop. Shallow fissures careered through the ground in all directions, and the summit exploded in a hail of rocks and dirt.

We're going to die. Like in my vision. I should never have gone on with the story.

"The story," Hara'q shouted over the cacophony. "You must finish."

More lightning strikes. More rocks. More dirt.

The story. I can't…

The air was black with dirt. The fire vanished in a hail of dirt. The sky was veiled by dirt. Even the lightning flashes were masked by dirt. Yet one thing was not. Through all the filth and darkness, I still caught glimpses of M'nor. And through all the deafening din, I still heard her, more clearly now than when all had been still.

Trust the story. Trust your *story. Trust it enough to let it continue.*

"To the Black Rider and the stallion," I spoke, not trying to be heard over the chaos, "Ben said, 'I welcome you and thank you for sparing the land more grief.' The Rider, whose name was Azùl, and the stallion, who was called Abray, bowed their heads and awaited their fate."

It didn't seem possible for the thunder to cannon more blaringly and for the lightning to stab the summit more single-mindedly, yet it did. And the summit reacted by erupting more explosively. Now, though, the rocky shards it flung heavenward froze in midair, as though waiting for my story's outcome before deciding whether to crush us.

"'Here is my decree,' Ben declared. 'All Black Riders and their stallions will be exiled to the Mhor-Jenn, a remote desert province on Q'ntana's southwestern frontier. You will be transported there through Kumba's magic and will be provided with all you need to start a new life and to sustain yourselves in that new life.'

"Neither Azùl nor Abray dared look up as Ben proceeded. 'And this *will* be a new life, for Kumba's magic will, in addition, exchange all memories of this lifetime with freshly created memories of an ancestral history in the Mhor-Jenn.' He paused. Azùl and Abray kept their eyes to the ground and made no sound.

"'Only one of you will be cursed with a memory of these times,' he continued, 'a curse that will transform itself into a blessing when, once upon a future time, you will return home and reclaim your heritage, a heritage that long precedes these present times.' He paused again."

All thunder ceased. The lightning receded toward the horizon. Yet the rocks suspended over the summit had not moved, jagged blotches of black against the glimmering moon. I went on. "Their heads still bowed but their eyes raised, Azùl and Abray nodded. 'Have you any questions?' Ben asked.

"'One, sire,' Azùl replied.

"'Speak.'

"'Who is it who will remember all?'

"Ben stared first into Azùl's eyes, then into Abray's. Then he scanned the sky. The suns had crossed. Aygra traveled westward, B'na to the east. And halfway between them, hovering directly overhead, far overhead, a giant, green-scaled dragon, four claws on its right foot, six on its left, breathed fire earthward. It was nearly time."

Something within me prompted me to follow Ben's gaze. M'nor had risen higher, past the rocks that still hung in the sky. And silhouetted against her silver light I could make out a fire-breathing dragon. I gasped.

"What is it?" Hara'q asked.

I pointed a trembling finger at the moon, but Hara'q shook his head. He saw nothing.

Trust the story. Trust your story. Trust it enough to let it continue.

I would trust the story.

"The new king touched Abray's forehead with his middle finger. 'When you arrive in the Mhor-Jenn,' he said, 'you will no longer be in this body. You will be a man, retaining not only all memory of what has come before and of this decree but your immortality, which is your birthright as a stallion of Q'ntana, as one of the original stallions of Bryn Doon. And you will no longer be known as Abray. From this moment forward, you will be known as Hara'q, He Who Holds the Memory of His Race.'

"Abray, now Hara'q, blinked back tears. To lose the freedom…the grace…the elegance. To be forced to exchange them for clumsiness… awkwardness…ungainliness. To be cursed with humanity…and memory. Hara'q longed to beg the king to make a different choice. He dared not.

"Ben saw the grief in the stallion's eyes and his heart broke, for he knew from his journey the limitations of a man's body and mind. He also knew their gifts."

The Hara'q before me wept openly, and my heart broke along with Ben's. "Go on," he sobbed.

"'This is not a punishment,' Ben told the horse. 'The memory must be held, and of all the stallions your wisdom and maturity render you best-suited to the task. You do me great service by taking on the burden of this knowledge.' He stroked the horse's muzzle and wiped away the tears rolling down his face. 'Do you understand?' Hara'q shook his mane one last time and stamped his foot.

"'Then the moment has arrived.'"

As I spoke those five words, it was as though not only M'nor whispered them with me, but as though all creation did. The words continued to echo, growing louder and louder with each reverberation.

"Before Azùl and Hara'q could draw another breath, Kumba swooped down from the heavens, fire shooting from its mouth and nostrils. When the flames touched the Black Rider and the horse, they vanished from the courtyard as though they had never been. In that same instant, every stallion and every Black Rider and all their family members vanished with them, wherever in that instant they had been."

I had barely finished speaking when the dragon I could still see outlined against the moon exhaled a giant gust of fire. As the flames enveloped us, I witnessed, as if through its eyes, myself, Hara'q and all the horses vanish from the plateau as one final quaking of the earth smashed the mountain into dust.

fifteen
Mattilde

I loved Gran Mattilde's stories, and bedtime could never arrive swiftly enough on those evenings when her duties didn't keep her from our quarters. In another land at another time, she could have been a bard, possibly an elderbard. But we had no bards in Flor and certainly no elderbard. Stories and storytelling weren't forbidden, as they were in one of Gran's favorite tales. Beneficia, however, viewed them as frivolous time-wasters and did her best to discourage them, at least in court. I was only rarely permitted to venture beyond the castle walls, so I couldn't know whether Beneficia's subjects paid her any heed in that regard.

In a strange way, though, she hungered for stories as I much as I did. Certain stories. If I happened to be in her bedchamber when Ardoxx was present and if she and Ardoxx weren't battling as they so often did, she would press him to speak of the King's Men and the Black Riders. She had an almost addictive fixation on stories involving those marauders and their stallions.

At the time, I believed Ardoxx to be sharing different versions of two of Gran's tales. And I believed them to be just that: tales… legends…fictions. I would soon discover them to be far more than entertaining make-believe. I would soon discover them to be true histories. And I would soon discover my place in those histories.

*　　*　　*

"I must have those horses," Beneficia declared to Maroona, her cousin and closest confidante. They perched on the edges of over-upholstered armchairs, the bustles on their gowns too puffed up to allow them to lean back in comfort, waiting for me to carve a pair of roast gandas, a rare delicacy in landlocked Flor.

As I touched the knife to the golden skin of the first of the two birds, light from the tapers flickering in the centerpiece candelabra sparked off the blade's polished silver. How easy it would be, I thought, to slice through Beneficia's throat instead. Stuffed into that ridiculous outfit, she could never outrun me, even were she able to pry herself out of that chair. I might spare Maroona. Maybe. My eyes darted to the doors of the dining hall, one of the many chambers in the castle dedicated to that purpose. This one, on the top floor, was the most intimate. I would never make it past the two sentinels who stood, lances crossed, outside the door. Could I get out through a window? I tried to imagine how I could shinny down the wall and—

"Mattilde," Beneficia barked.

I curtsied, mumbled an apology and pressed the knife into the crisp skin and through the soft flesh of the first bird.

"The stallions," she said to Maroona. I had already been forgotten, consigned to the invisibility shared by all efficient servants. As demeaning as it was, my invisibility made me privy to much that I ought not know. Although there was little I could do with whatever information I gleaned, being in possession of such forbidden knowledge gratified me nonetheless.

"Storybook horses?" Maroona asked, her mouth as jammed with ganda as the bird was with stuffing. "What in the Great Flor's name can you do with storybook horses?" She chugged her cup of wine and pushed it at me to refill.

"Were you not listening?" Beneficia slammed her fist onto the table. The crystal jangled, the china rattled, and I caught one of the candelabra before it upended onto her lap.

Beneficia ignored me. She must have been referencing an earlier part of the conversation, one I would have missed while I was heading the parade of footmen who bore the evening's feast up from the kitchens.

"Listening to what? Ardoxx told us a story." Maroona ripped a wing off the ganda and shoved it into her mouth, bones and all. She wiped her hands on her dress.

Beneficia rolled her eyes, and I tried not giggle. When Prithi was apportioning heart, Maroona was given the family's full quota. The same could not be said for wits...or refinement. She was far kinder and more gracious, even to servants, than her cousin ever was. Yet although she lacked intelligence, she was shrewd enough to not act on her tenderness in Beneficia's presence.

"Ardoxx does not tell stories," Beneficia said with what patience she could muster, which wasn't much.

"But—"

"Ardoxx does not tell stories. He tells histories."

Maroona nodded, although it was clear that she couldn't trouble herself to discern the difference.

I withdrew from the table and did my best to melt into the shadows. Beneficia rarely thought about me unless she had a task for me to perform. However, I did not want this to be one of those exceptional moments when, tired of my presence, she shooed me from the room. I wanted to hear about these horses. For reasons I did not understand, I needed to hear about them.

"Kamela. Can you hear me, Kamela?"

I tried to open my eyes to see who was speaking. My eyelids refused to cooperate. My mouth did no better. And my ears felt as though they were wrapped in an infant's swaddling, for the voice sounded muffled and indistinct.

Jeryn. Where is Jeryn?

I could not tell whether my arms were empty or full...whether I had arms at all...whether I had a body at all. I felt nothing. And no body part, assuming I still had any, obeyed my command to move.

"Here," I heard, "drink this." Something cool pressed against my lips.

I have lips. They parted of their own volition and accepted the liquid, which tasted at the same time alien and familiar as it passed through my mouth and down my throat. *If I have lips, a mouth and a throat, I must have a body. Why cannot I feel it?*

"Is that better?" The voice sounded clearer now, though not clear enough to perceive anything about its speaker. Was it a man? A woman? A child? Old? Young?

Jeryn. A stifled cry escaped my lips. *I have a voice.* I tried to speak, but all that emerged was something between a cough and a grunt.

"Your child."

I tried to nod my head but couldn't tell whether I succeeded.

"She is safe. Asleep. By your side." A woman. Grown but young, by the timbre of her voice.

I commanded my lips to form a grateful smile. Did they comply? Only this mysterious caretaker could know. She pressed the cup into my hands — *I have hands* — and guided it to my face. This time, I drank thirstily, draining the cup not once but four times.

My eyes opened, yet refused to focus. Either that or the world of this place was naturally hazy and indistinct. I groped next to me to assure myself that Jeryn was nearby and breathing. She was. I blinked a dozen times, trying to force some clarity of vision on eyes that remained clouded. When I finally succeeded, I stared in disbelief at the woman who knelt before me.

She had milky skin and long silver hair and was dressed in a diaphanous robe as ethereal as she was…as this place was. We could have been perched upon a cloud, for all I could see was a luminous, gently swirling mist. Through it, I caught glimpses of my fellow villagers, all deeply tranced.

"Na'an?"

"You know me," she said. "Good. That will save us time, although there is no lack of it here." Her speech was at the same time dreamy and assertive, and when she laughed it sounded light as a wind chime yet solid as the bell in the Dôma.

"How would I not know you, from my dreams?" I managed to ask, though the words still felt forced and my voice, hoarse.

"All dream, yet not all recall their dreams," she said. "Of those who do, not all see the Tikkan dreamwalkers who bear them. This, too, is good."

"Is this a dream? It must be. How could it not be?"

"Dream and waking are one, Kamela. There is no difference. They merely inhabit different forms of the same reality."

I knew those words. In The StarQuest story, the star Àna speaks them. I had spoken those same words to Pyrà in my storytelling.

"I-I don't understand. Where am I? Where are we? Where is Pyrà?" In my mind's eye, I saw him as I had seen him last, shortly before terror rained onto our village. "Where is he? Is he safe?"

Na'an reached for my arm. Her touch was soft and delicate as a rose petal and strangely reassuring. "Look," she said, as with her other hand she drew an elaborate symbol into the air. The mist immediately before us cleared and there was my son, with Hara'q and the horse T'tammo, in a forest glen, dawn's pale light filtering through the leafy canopy. Pyrà slept, curled into a ball under a tan-colored cloak decorated with what must have been scores of black stallions. I couldn't see his face, but I knew it to be him. Hara'q stared directly at me, nodding his head almost imperceptibly, as though acknowledging me. That was impossible…or was it? T'tammo nibbled at the luxuriant ground cover, the moistest, greenest grass I had ever seen.

Na'an dropped her arm and the mists returned. Barely a breath later, those same mists again veiled my senses as I reentered the trance state my neighbors had never left.

Horses dream, so I knew Na'an well. I knew her brother, Rev'Àn, too, including the more unsavory periods in his history when he fashioned himself as Bo'Ra K'n, the brutal architect of Q'ntana's submission to foreign kings and an accessory to the Great Enchantment that enslaved me and my kin. I had lived that long. Longer.

I was not the only horse to have been blessed with longevity. All horses of Bryn Doon were immortal, in the sense that we could die of neither disease nor old age, nor any other "natural" cause. We could, however, be slaughtered in battle, as had occurred too often in the days of the kings Fvorag and Gravel. We could also be massacred, as most of our sisters had been at the time of the Enchantment.

By the grace of Prithi, I had survived all that, which is how I now found myself with the Bard of Bryn Doon in a strange forest glen. How we had arrived here, neither of us could fathom.

One moment, we were engulfed in Kumba's fire, which felt not at all fire-like; more like a snug, comfortably warm, silky blanket. In the next, it was dawn and I stood bewildered and disoriented by a limpid creek in a land too verdant to be the Mhor-Jenn. Only T'tammo and Sajàno had traveled with us. There was no sign of the other stallions. This alarmed me. Had Kumba left the others behind to perish? Why were only three of us to make the journey back to Bryn Doon? Nor was I pleased to see T'tammo and Sajàno treated as common packhorses, kitted out as they were with heavy saddlebags. If Kumba's magic could convey some of us here, why could it not convey all of us here? And, surely, it could find a less demeaning way to transport our supplies and foodstuffs. During our five days' travel through the Mhor-Jenn, we had carried little with us; whatever provisions we required had always awaited us wherever we stopped to rest or for the night.

Kumba's magic had done more than move and supply us. We now wore new traveling gear — sandals, sand-colored tunics, sky-blue trousers and hooded cloaks. Many men clothed in myriad fabrics had ridden on my back through my centuries in my natural body, yet I had never encountered materials such as these. Unlike the scratchy, ill-fitting fabrics forced upon us in the Mhor-Jenn, these felt satiny against the skin. And they were anything but flimsy, possessing an astonishing tensile strength. My cloak fell below my waist and was the deep green of the forest. Pyrà's, a few shades darker than his tunic and constructed of a heavier, coarser weave than mine, hung to his calves, more cape than coat. Most striking of all was its pattern. Woven into it were scores of black horses, all eerily life-like.

Had Kumba's magic also woven my dream-vision of Na'an, Kamela and the villagers? Or had it been more than a dream? Or perhaps what I now experienced was the dream and we had never left the Mhor-Jenn.

As for Pyrà, he stood transfixed. His eyes were blank, barely blinking, and his face was expressionless. Was he experiencing a dream of his own? If so, I hoped it was the same one as mine and that he was finding it reassuring.

I didn't dare rouse him. Instead, I surveyed our surroundings. If we were still in Q'ntana, it was a part of the land I knew not, for the birds and flora were alien to me. The trees in this glen— I would later discover them to be jaq'òras — were exceptionally tall and bore no limbs other than those that formed a leafy pyramid at their apex. The translucent lemony yellow of their dense foliage cast the glen in the golden glow of dusk, even when the suns passed behind a bank of clouds. Nesting at the peak of several of the nearby canopies with their massive, purple-streaked wings outstretched were ruby-beaked, coal-black birds the likes of which I had never seen. They seemed displeased that we had disturbed their haunting, minor-key melodies, for they now screamed angrily at us in sharp, staccato shrieks.

Even these failed to wake Pyrà. It was only when one of the verros, as these birds were called, swooped down and wildly thrashed its wings in his face that he opened his eyes. "There you are," he said and held his arm out. The verro circled him three times before setting onto his wrist.

"This is Baq'shì," he said to me in a tone that suggested that he and I had been engaged in an ongoing conversation and that being in this place, wherever it was, was the height of normalcy.

"Hara'q," he said to the bird, touching my shoulder with his free hand before introducing T'tammo and Sajàno to her.

"Baq'shì is to guide us into Flor," he added, as though those seven words explained everything about our extraordinary situation.

I was too baffled to speak.

The bird nodded, winking first its gold eye then its silver eye. Then it hopped down from Pyrà's wrist and clawed the earth, carving out a double chevron that pointed south, deeper into the woods. She then stretched her wings to their full span, flapped them twice and took off.

"We need to go," Pyrà said, tugging on my arm.

"No." I shook my head. "Not without the other horses. Does this Baq'shì bird know what happened to them?"

With an ear-splitting screech, Baq'shì charged down from the sky and onto Sajàno's back. The horse ignored her as she bobbed from one clawed foot to the other in a manic jig. She bounced from Sajàno to T'tammo and back, continuing her strange dance until, with a second screech more piercing than the first, she pointed her beak at B'na and, with her wings tucked tightly against her sides, spiraled heavenward.

Pyrà watched her ascent. "We have to follow her before she disappears," he said.

I would not leave without my brothers. "The horses. Where are they?"

"If I tell you they are safe, will you believe me?" Pyrà eyes were still on Baq'shì.

"You know this for a fact?"

Pyrà nodded.

"Tell me where they are."

"It's complicated."

"Go on."

Reluctantly, he tore his gaze from the sky. "Can I tell you while we follow Baq'shì? Please?"

I grunted a grudging assent.

"Thank you." He mounted T'tammo and looked up. Baq'shì was a black speck against B'na.

"Wait," I said. "Before we go—"

"I promised, didn't I?" he growled. "We need to get going." He tugged at the reins. "Now."

"It's about your mother and sister."

All agitation about Baq'shì forgotten, Pyrà leapt from T'tammo. "What? What about them?"

"I saw them, in a way."

"What do you mean, 'in a way?'"

"It was like in a dream, before I opened my eyes to this place, so it's not entirely clear in my mind—"

Pyrà grabbed my arm, squeezing it so tightly I was certain it bruised. "And? And?" he cried. "Where are they? Are they nearby? Are they safe?"

I wrested my arm free and rubbed where he had gripped it, wishing he could see that my concern for my brothers was as real as was his for his mother and sister. "All I know is that I saw them, with Na'an. I don't know any more than that." I did, but that was all I was ready to say. The sooner we got going, the sooner I would hear about the horses.

"Thank you," Pyrà said, wiping his eyes. "I hope that means they're safe."

Baq'shì streaked around us, shrieking shrilly. Then, still screaming, she shot back up into the sky.

"We had better see where she wants us to go." He climbed back onto T'tammo. Without any prompting, the horse stepped forward, ushering us deeper into the forest.

The sorcerer examines his scrying stone, a smooth slab of polished slate set into an irregularly shaped table of rare qanaria wood. He sees the horse man and young bard accompanied by two stallions setting off through the Forest of Baranna, guided by a noisy verro. He cannot hear the verro, but its beak opens and shuts nonstop and its green tongue darts in and out as its throat vibrates. Nor can he hear the conversation between the horse man and the bard. However, he reads lips well enough to capture its essence, and it does not please him. It will please Beneficia even less. That does please him.

If the horse man and the bard have arrived in Flor, the stallions have not. Where are the stallions? It is they that matter, not the bard. The bard is surplus to his plans.

Something is broken, and as powerful as his sorcery is, he cannot identify it. If he cannot identify it, he cannot repair it. And if he cannot repair it, then the Great Enchantment is at risk and Q'ntana and the stallions cannot be his.

Beneficia believes that the only plan is to acquire Q'ntana and the horses, for herself. She is misguided. For the present, that is best. She, too, is surplus to his plans. Although the sorcerer cannot harm her directly, he can employ his sorcery in ways that will place her in the path of harm. This he will do when the time is right. However, the time cannot be right without the stallions.

Where are the stallions?

The image in the scrying stone sputters and fades. Its reach does not extend into the heart of the Forest of Baranna. The sorcerer will have to find another way.

My eyes jerked open. Yes, I still lay in my bedchamber. And, yes, everything was as it had been before I shut them too few hours earlier. Not that I would not have welcomed change. A proper mattress, for a start, instead of this flimsy straw pallet whose stalks poked at me through the night. Maybe a window that overlooked something other than a stone wall slick with slime. A sizable window that I could fling open to feel the evening breeze wash across my face, rather than a narrow slot into a lightless ventilation shaft that I could not shut against its damp, dank, foul-smelling currents.

Oughtn't a majordoma merit something less dismal? Less noxious? Compared to the other servant quarters, two airless dormitories tucked into Castle Flor's windowless, low-ceilinged attics, this was sumptuous and salubrious. At least I had this cell of a space to myself.

In the dream, the one from which I had just opened my eyes, the same one I had been having for more nights than I could count, I was traveling — on horseback, something I had never experienced while awake. I was dressed differently in these dreams, in supple fabrics that moved with me instead of stiff ones that struggled against me. I did not recognize the landscape, not that I would know much beyond the immediate grounds of Castle Flor. Nor could I determine our destination or our reason for journeying there. "Our" destination, for I did not journey alone. Yet even as I knew that, I could not see my companions' faces.

The dreams always ended abruptly and in a similar manner, as I was trapped in some way and about to die. In one, I was tangled in heavy ropes underwater, and I was drowning. In another, Castle Flor had collapsed on top of me and I was pinned under the rubble. In a third, I had been thrown into a pit and left to die. In each dream, the threat originated with Ardoxx. And in each, I was saved by the same shadowy figure.

I lit a candle. What did it mean? I knew from Gran Mattilde that no dream was without significance, that all dreams bore some message from the dreamwalkers. I knew, too, also from Gran Mattilde, that while Tikkan speak only what we know in our hearts to be true, they also communicate in a form that is rarely literal or clear. What would Gran have said about these dreams? She had a way of finding meaning in the most cryptic of visions, a gift she promised to pass on to me. She never got around to it. Consequently, I rarely understood the dreamwalkers' intentions. As for this series of persistent nightmares, I could make no sense of it.

I was accustomed to rising before dawn, apart from those mornings when Beneficia's bell roused me earlier. Years of waking with Gran had trained my body to know when I needed to get started on the day's tasks. When I woke from this latest nightmare, I knew it was not yet time. I could return to sleep if I chose…if I could erase the dream from my memory. Or I could attempt the escape I had long fantasized about. At this hour, it would be easy to steal from the castle without notice. But where would I go? I knew no one beyond the castle walls and nothing of the countryside, and none of my skills was suited to journeying.

Reluctantly, I snuffed out my candle, lay back and shut my eyes. Within a few breaths, I was asleep. Or was I? If I was, how to explain the stranger who suddenly appeared to me swathed in silvery light? He was tall and slim, with shoulder-length blond hair framing a youthful face. Youthful, not young, for his azure eyes shone with an ageless wisdom that belied his looks. Under a luminous navy cloak, he wore a cream-colored, open-necked linen shirt and gold-flecked trousers of a similar color and cut.

My eyes were open, so how could I have been dreaming? But if it wasn't a dream, where had he come from?

"Mattilde," he said.

"Y-yes." I shrank back.

"Do you know me?" His voice was soft and dreamy, and although his lips moved, he didn't appear to be speaking through his mouth.

The words seemed to float off him. I could almost see them form in the air around him.

I shook my head.

"You do," he countered. "You simply do not remember."

I tried to think where I might have seen him. In the castle? In a dream? Again, I shook my head. One such as he would have been impossible to forget.

"Those dreams that so puzzle you—"

"How do you know about them?" Could one dream know about another? If this was not a dream… My head started to ache.

"I sent them." He pulled my one chair, a rickety wreck of a hand-me-down, to the edge of my pallet and sat, spreading his cloak behind him. "I am Rev'Àn."

"Na'an's brother?"

The briefest flash of a frown crossed his face, then vanished. "Na'an is my sister, yes."

"Then I *am* dreaming." I felt better knowing, and I felt reassured realizing that my nightmares had been sent by Rev'Àn. Now, finally, I would learn what they meant.

"Yes, and no. You are dreaming or I could not be sitting here before you. You are also awake."

The pounding in my head intensified. I touched my eyelids. They were open.

"The mechanics of it are of no import. You are awake to ensure that you retain all I say. You are asleep because—"

"You could not be here otherwise. So you said." I sat up. "I don't wish to be rude, but please tell me what more you have to say, then go." Were this visitation to continue much longer, I would be late for Beneficia's morning attentions. Although I could ignore her tongue-lashing, she had lately taken to expressing her displeasure with me through the same beatings she meted out to other servants.

"Beneficia's needs are no longer your concern," he said. It should not have surprised me that Rev'Àn could read my thoughts, yet it did. "You have spent your final night under her roof," he continued. "You will not be required to attend to her whims on this morning or on any other."

I tried to shake my head free of its throbbing. This dream made less sense than the others. Would I wake from it and be forced to face Beneficia's wrath? Or would I never wake from it? Or I had lost my mind only to be sealed in the special dungeon that Ardoxx had conjured up to house Flor's madmen and madwomen?

"Your faculties are entirely intact," Rev'Àn said, once again knowing my mind before I could speak it. "That is fortunate, for you will need them to be sharp if you are to embark on the journey you have dreamed of."

Journey? Then I would be leaving here. I leapt from bed. I had to dress. I had to pack. Much of the little I owned meant nothing to me, but I would need a change of clothes and a hairbrush. And I would have to take the silver-framed pocket mirror and pearlescent bokka stone Gran had left me, passed down to her from her mother and her mother before her. Concluding that modesty was pointless in the presence of a dreamwalker, I pulled my nightgown over my head and rummaged through my chest before realizing that I possessed no suitable travel garments. Why would I? I had never traveled. Not anywhere.

Then I remembered, and I slumped back onto my pallet in tears. "You are delivering me to my death," I whispered between sobs. "In every one of those dreams you sent me, I nearly died."

Rev'Àn observed me in silence, his eyes never leaving mine. "Yet," he said at last, "you did not."

nineteen

Pyrà

Following Baq'shì through the nearly impenetrable woods proved challenging. For all her screeching in the glen, she was largely silent now. And largely invisible. It was only by catching the occasional glimpse of her ruby beak through the treetops that we were able to make our circuitous way — single file and on foot, for the forest was almost immediately too thick for me to ride T'tammo (Hara'q continued to refuse to ride Sajàno) or for us to walk side-by-side.

And it was circuitous. More than once I was so convinced that we traveled in circles that I scored a series of tree trunks with a large X. I wanted to see whether we would pass those same trees a second or third time. We never did. Still, it was difficult to trust that Baq'shì knew where she was going.

Yet Rev'Àn had been unequivocal on that point. "You must trust her unconditionally," he had said. "She knows where you need to go and she will guide you there by the safest route, and in the right time."

Unfortunately, it proved impossible to share with Hara'q what I knew about the other stallions as we made our way through the forest. To ensure that we didn't lose them, we'd had T'tammo and Sajàno file between us as we walked, rendering conversation nearly impossible. Now, we were parked where Baq'shì had left us: on the meadowland side of the shallow stream that marked the end of the greenwood. The dense growth may have scratched our arms and faces mercilessly and snagged our hair into knotted tangles, but it did offer one compensation. From the armloads of dried branches and twigs we gathered, we built a massive fire — less for heat, though the night was chilly, than for comfort and a feeling of safety.

Hara'q had wanted to know about the stallions as soon as we stopped but, assuring him again that they were safe, I convinced him that it would be wiser to first set up camp. Even once we were more or less settled, I insisted on telling the story my way, from the beginning.

If Hara'q's "journey" from the Mhor-Jenn had seemed to him to be instantaneous, mine was more challenging to explain. How could I describe an encounter that originated in a dream that, soon after, dissolved into reality? And how could it not have been a dream if Rev'Àn had not only delivered it but appeared in it?

"I thought for sure I had died," I spoke into the fire, "like in the vision I had with Fay'dor."

Hara'q sat next to me, the hood of his cloak veiling his face. He muttered a curse at the mention of Fay'dor's name.

"Everything was black and stayed black for what seemed like forever. I remember thinking that if this was Kea Kana, it was nothing like the Kea Kana of my mother's stories, and I wondered whether everyone's experience of Kea Kana might be different." Kea Kana, often called Prithi's Garden, was where the souls of the newly dead came to rest before being assigned a new life and body.

"After a long while, tiny pinpricks of light sparked into the blackness. First one, then a dozen, then more than I could count. They danced around in front of me until, finally, they took the hazy, somewhat solid form of a man.

"'You know me,' he said. It was not a question.

"I didn't, not at first, so all I could do was to ask whether I was dead and in Kea Kana.

"The figure responded with gales of laughter. The more he laughed, the more light he radiated until the blackness melted away.

"At first, I thought he was standing on a cloud. If he was, it was no ordinary cloud. Instead of vapory strands of white, it was a weave of silver that seemed neither solid nor wispy. A castle shimmered far behind him, emitting a kaleidoscope of ever-changing colors.

"Only when he reached out for me to join him, did I realize who he was." I paused, uncertain whether Hara'q would believe me. It had felt more real back in the glen. Now, it seemed too incredible to be true.

Hara'q turned to me. "Who was it?" His face was still in shadow, yet for the briefest of instants, I thought I saw the profile of a horse not a man silhouetted against the fire. I couldn't tell him. Whether I had seen it or imagined it, it would only distress him. "Rev'Àn," I said.

Hara'q said nothing. Had he believed me? It couldn't matter. I had to continue. "It was only when I took a tentative step toward him that I realized I still had a body. 'Will it support me?' I asked before lowering my foot.

"'If your heart is light,' he replied.

"How would I know? Did I dare risk it? Did I dare not risk it? I would have to trust.

"The moment I stood next to him on the silver cloud, all doubt dissolved. 'You *are* Rev'Àn,' I exclaimed.

"'And you are the Bard of Bryn Doon.' He placed a hand on my shoulder and his touch immediately erased all memories of his past as Bo'Ra K'n, a name that had always filled me with dread when my mother mentioned it in her storytelling. 'No one is so evil as to be beyond redemption,' he added softly, as if to himself. 'Redemption, however, is a choice,' he continued, more loudly. 'You will be wise to remember that as you journey.'

"'Then this truly is not Kea Kana? I am not dead?'

"He laughed, more loudly than before. 'Far from it, young bard. You have only begun to live.' He whistled a brisk high-pitched tune and a ruby beak took shape above his head. The beak opened wide, a green tongue curled out of it and a short, sharp screech answered back, piercing the stillness that until now had surrounded us. As Rev'Àn repeated the melody, the body that belonged to the beak took shape, dropped to what passed for ground in this cloud-like place and bobbed her head."

"Baq'shì," Hara'q said.

"Baq'shì."

"The horses," I pressed, not attempting to hide my frustration. I had done my best to listen patiently to Pyrà's account, but these were my brothers who had vanished. Despite his insistence that they were safe, I needed to know more. What had happened to them? Where were they now? When would they rejoin us?

"They're here." Pyrà grinned.

Even had they gathered beyond the firelight's glow, I would have heard them or sensed their presence. After all, there were nearly two hundred of them.

"Where?" What kind of game was he playing?

"Here." Pyrà stroked the sleeve of his cloak. Had the horses he'd touched moved? No, they couldn't have. I must have imagined it. I had lived longer than any human and seen much that would confound the most imaginative of souls, but this?

I scrutinized the cloak more intently. If to human eyes our stallions were largely indistinguishable one from the other, equine eyes could easily tell them apart. My vision was no longer fully equine, but nor was it fully human. The same was true of my sense of smell. I leaned into the sleeve, inspected the horses woven into it and sniffed them.

Those *were* my brothers. I recognized Matté, Yùq'a and Fyràm'i, and when I caressed Vee'qo's back with my finger, he winked at me.

"They are all here," Pyrà said, before I could ask. "All hundred eighty-five of them. I didn't believe Rev'Àn when he told me, so I made him wait while I counted."

I was dumbfounded. "But why?"

"Imagine all these horses trying to make it through that forest."

"True." It had been challenging enough with only two.

"Rev'Àn also said it would be safer for them, and for us, this way."

I was gratified by Rev'Àn's concern for our safety, though I didn't fully trust it. "How do we get them out again?"

"He wouldn't say."

"What?" I leapt to my feet and paced around and around the fire in an attempt to dampen my rage. Those Tikkan; they were as maddening as Fay'dor. "Did he say *anything* about it?"

"Only that the horses would be able to leave the cloak when necessary, and that they would return to it the same way."

"Typical dreamwalker," I muttered, dropping to the ground across from Pyrà. I stared into the fire in silence, letting my temper cool. When it had, I glanced up at Pyrà. He was watching me.

"What is it? You look upset. Don't you think the horses are safer this way?"

Something was weighing on me, although it wasn't the horses. If Rev'Àn's vagueness still annoyed me, I knew the dreamwalker to be right, even as I hated to admit it. No, what upset me now was my cowardice.

I had not spoken to anyone with concern or compassion in more years than I could remember, and I was not certain I was brave enough to do so now...or whether I remembered how. In my horse's body, before the Great Enchantment turned me and my brothers into killing machines, I'd had neither cause nor desire to be callous. While centuries of exile had melted other stallion hearts hardened by service to Bo'Ra K'n's surrogates, it had only embittered mine, which had suffered a double exile — once from my native land and once from the body into which I had been born. This journey — no, Pyrà himself — had begun to chip away at the resentful shell I had been wearing for so long.

It would be difficult, but I would have to find the courage to speak. "In that dream I had between the Mhor-Jenn and here," I began. Could I let myself be this vulnerable?

"What about it?"

"I...I asked Na'an to tell me more about your mother and sister, about when you might see them again."

"Why didn't you tell me before now?" There was an edge to Pyrà's voice. He had every right to be annoyed.

"Because she was no more forthcoming with me than Rev'Àn was with you. All she would do was reassure me that they were safe." I lowered my eyes. "And because I did not want you to know that I had asked…that I had asked for you."

Pyrà fidgeted with the strap on his water skin, and for an instant I caught a glimpse of the boy he had been only days earlier. Yes, the boy Pyrà had been precocious, though his maturity always seemed to mask an underlying sadness. It was his sadness I sensed in that moment; that, and a hint of fear. What human would not be frightened by this senseless journey? Admittedly, its aim was far from senseless: to get my brothers home again and to return me to my right land and body. But the means of getting us there? That made the kind of sense that only Fay'dor and a Tikkan could conjure up: The kind that took longer than necessary and was unreasonably convoluted. The kind that could get all of us killed. Too easily.

I wanted to be angry with Fay'dor, Na'an and Rev'Àn, for what they had put us through and for what was to come. Yet I must truly have been softening, for no anger would come. Instead, I forced myself to remember that, for all the many centuries I had lived, Fay'dor had lived longer — since the beginning of time, as had Na'an, Rev'Àn and their fellow Tikkan. I would have to find a way to believe in their greater wisdom and trust it.

It would not be easy.

Lightning stabs the sky. Thunder convulses the earth. Torrents of rain burst from the heavens. From one end of Flor to the other and beyond into neighboring realms, the tempest storms through the land, slashing through farms, fields and villages. Even the driest of deserts is not spared its merciless battering.

In Q'ambra, as in most towns and villages, frothing eddies of mud flood the roads and walkways, scooping up clothing, crockery, furniture and any structure too flimsy to resist. What the waters fail to swallow or smash, they fling onto the sludgy verge. The devastation is cataclysmic, yet not a single living being is harmed.

On a farm fifteen v'reks from Q'ambra, one of the storm's refugees huddles, soaked and sobbing, in an empty barn that has miraculously withstood the squall's savagery. With every clap of thunder, she burrows more deeply into the giant stack of hay that sits just inside the broad double doors and worries that her worst nightmares are about to be realized. Eyes closed, she murmurs half-silent prayers and clutches a pearlescent stone to her breast.

The refugee cannot know that she is not alone. An identical barn painted an identical ocher stands on the other side of a low knoll on this same farm. In it are more refugees: the bard, the horse man and two stallions. Unlike their neighbor, they are fortunate to be dry, having sought shelter as the first rains fell. They are equally fortunate to be comfortable. The horses have hay to eat, and the bard and horse man have hauled a table and two chairs down from the loft. The sole currency in short supply in this barn is patience, for the storm's fury shows no signs of abating. Worse, it grows more violent.

Hailstones as large as bela nuts pound against the roof, and tree limbs ripped from their trunks lash against the walls. The barns quake but refuse to yield. Other structures, in Q'ambra and elsewhere, are not as steadfast. Still, no living creatures are harmed. Yet.

For once, this assault is not the sorcerer's doing. As potent as his magic is, it has its limits. The sorcerer is wise enough to know that. The sorcerer is also wise enough to be awed by the storm's terrible scale and unparalleled scope. His nominal mistress, the self-styled doyenne of Castle Flor, is not so wise.

When the waters of the deluge overflow Castle Flor's moat, driving its sewage infested waters into the dungeons, she does nothing. "Should the prisoners drown or die of disease, there will be fewer of them and fewer mouths to feed," she says.

When the waters of the deluge sluice through the long-neglected cracks in Castle Flor's masonry, she is indifferent. "My apartments face eastward," she responds when informed that rains drilling in from the west have engulfed all west-facing apartments. "Let those on that side of the castle mop up their own messes."

When the waters of the deluge pierce the castle's rotting roof-work, she is unmoved, for only servants' quarters lie beneath the decaying tiles. Her apartments and throne room are unaffected.

Only when the stench of the moat wafts into her bedchamber does she attempt to summon her majordoma to seal her windows and doors against the miasma. By then it is too late. As one, the weakened roof and east-facing walls crumble. An instant later, all interior walls collapse. Unsupported, the ceilings cave in. Then, with the next roar of thunder, what remains of the castle implodes.

When she regains consciousness, naked and floating in the moat, the doyenne no longer knows who she is or where she is. She wades out of the muck, climbs through the debris and weaves limpingly away from what remains of the castle, singing her favorite childhood rhyme in a high-pitched off-key voice: "Oik and Ork pursue an Awk / The Awk will not be caught / The Awk turns 'round, scoops up a rock / Now Oik and Ork are not."

twenty-one

Mattilde

I had barely passed beyond the castle grounds when the heavens erupted. I was soaked instantly. Worse, the rains were so fierce that it was impossible for me to see where I was going.

My first instinct was to race back to the castle, but the moon had vanished behind storm clouds and I couldn't get my bearings. It was all I could do to stumble on, in any direction. I lost count of the number of times I tripped over a tree root and fell face-first into the muck. More than once, I was tempted not to get back up. It felt easier to let myself die. Each time, however, I recalled Rev'Àn's words in the moments before he suspended time for everyone in Castle Flor but me, holding it at bay long enough for me to escape unnoticed.

"You believe yourself to be unimportant," he had said. "You believe you do not matter beyond these castle walls because you do not matter within them."

He was right. Those were my beliefs. More than that, they were my certainties.

"You are wrong. There cannot be a life for you within these walls." He stared at me with a purposeful intensity that I would understand only much later. I had yet to understand it when, soon after, as an earthquaking explosion ripped through the countryside, I collapsed into the barn. I was still ignorant of its import when, early the following morning, I spied a naked madwoman weaving drunkenly past the barn baying nursery songs.

"Your life lies elsewhere," Rev'Àn continued. He pointed to the blank wall, and a window appeared through which I could see M'nor in her fullness, as well as constellations that were not of this place. It was not an illusion, for I could feel the embrace of the moonlight. He then snapped his fingers and all sound and activity within the castle ceased. "Your destiny lies elsewhere."

I was relieved to hear it, for I had felt it as far back as when Gran told me her stories. Now, I felt it each night when I peered wistfully through Beneficia's window before drawing her curtains and returning to my windowless cell.

"It is time for you to go to it," he said. "It is time for you to claim it, for you to claim your destiny."

I forced myself to repeat Rev'Àn's words as I bolted the barn's massive double doors against the weather. I continued to repeat them, mantra-like, as the barn heaved and creaked with the relentless pounding.

I must have fallen asleep because my next awareness was of absolute stillness, so alien after the clangor of the storm. Then came the first light of a new day and the sound then sight of the madwoman.

She ignored me when I called out to her from the window. Only then did I realize who she was. "She has no more awareness of me without her faculties than she had with them," I mumbled. Under other circumstances, I might have thought it not only just to see my former mistress like this, but funny. In this moment, I could find nothing about either Beneficia or my situation to laugh at.

I waited until she had disappeared from view then stepped outside. The earth was wet and the air felt charged, as though it met each of my breaths with a volley of sparks. Not only did I feel reborn into a new life, the world itself felt renewed. I did not know where I would go from here, but it no longer mattered. Whatever this destiny was that Rev'Àn had spoken of, I *would* find it and claim it. I would.

twenty -two

Hara'q

As suddenly as the storm had begun, it stopped. Rain, hail and, for a time, snow had been pelting the barn without letup for what seemed like days, and the thunder and lightning had been equally unyielding. Then, it was over. With one final shriek of wind, the roiling clouds dispersed, taking with them the merciless precipitation and revealing the blush of dawn.

After the unceasing tumult, it was impossible to trust the silence. Had heaven's hostilities truly ended, or was this but a lull before they resumed more ruthlessly than before? Even the birds held their breath, uncertain whether to resume their singing. Not T'tammo and Sajàno. They shook their heads, stamped their hooves and neighed loudly. They were ready to feel fresh breezes riffle their manes and to nibble on damp, rain-cleansed grasses, even should their emancipation prove fleeting.

I unlatched the doors and flung them open, startled to discover that despite its battering, the storm had spared both the barn and the narrow corridor of meadow upon which it stood. Not so the world beyond our extraordinary oasis. There, everything had been flattened. Those trees that hadn't been felled had been stripped of leaves and limbs, and the land was a mucky morass. A single tree, a jaq'òra, stood intact at the perimeter, a lone witness to the devastation.

I had barely stepped outside before T'tammo and Sajàno flew past me along the undamaged gravel path that wound through the meadow toward a nearby hill. I raced after them, having retained sufficient equine blood to bridle at enclosed spaces. My appetite, however, was entirely human. I would not be joining them for their grassy snack.

When I looked back, Pyrà was watching us from inside the doorway. From the expression on his face, it was clear something troubled him.

"Come out," I called. "Enjoy the weather. Enjoy the freedom."

He stepped outside and knelt to pluck a few blades of grass. He clenched them in his fist for a few breaths then opened his hand, letting them flutter to the ground. "Where are we?" he asked, still staring at the scattered grasses.

I was never good with human emotion, especially the sad, confused variety that Pyrà seemed to be exhibiting. Horse emotions were more straightforward, less layered. That I was both horse and human and at the same time neither had rendered me alien to both. That was why I preferred solitude. Companionship bewildered me. Pyrà was proving to be particularly bewildering.

I left the horses to their gamboling and ran back to Pyrà. "You know where we are. We're in Flor. You said as much yourself."

"Only because Rev'Àn said as much. What is Flor? Where is Flor? Why are we here? Why have we left Q'ntana? How do we get this… them—" he fingered the cloak "—back to Bryn Doon? What do we do when we get there?"

Perhaps humans were not so complicated after all. One had only to dig for the single question that lay beneath all the others. "This is about Kamela and Jeryn, isn't it?"

He nodded and turned away so I wouldn't see the tears collecting in his eyes. It was then I realized that he was as much a hybrid as I was. Even as he inhabited a young man's body, the boy he had so recently been had not fully grown into it. Just as he was guiding me and my brothers home and back to our true natures, I was to help him grow into his. It was not a calling I felt equipped to carry out. But, then, I was certain he felt equally ill-equipped for his. Somehow, we would both have to find a way.

The sorcerer surveys the world from atop his tower and frowns. The slightest hint of a frown is the fullest display of emotion he will permit himself. Revealing this much emotion is rare for him, although less rare now than once it was, and it suggests the churning inside him. The story is not unfolding as it should…as many scores of years of assiduous planning would have it unfold. If it is not unraveling, the danger of it doing so has multiplied one hundredfold with recent events.

"I will not allow it to unravel further," he mutters, gazing into his scrying stone, now clouded over. He commands the fog to clear yet knows it will not. Scrying stones do not offer limitless viewing, and no amount of magic can extend their visionary capabilities. However rock-like their appearance, they possess a sentience that can express itself in willful stubbornness and a magnetic aura that prevents more than one at a time in a given space from scrying accurately and effectively. They are also unable to perform unceasingly without pausing for periods of regeneration. As extensive as his powers are and despite his best efforts over countless decades, the sorcerer has not discovered a way to override these constraints. He swears softly at the stone, which grows murkier in response, and stares out the window. All he sees are trees, their leaves still dripping from the storm, and mists rising from the forest floor.

"I forbid it to unravel further," he speaks in full voice. He turns to the west-facing window and draws a clockwise circle in the air with his right middle finger. A wavery parchment scroll takes shape in front of him, unfurling to reveal not words but animated symbols that leap about in jarring, jagged dance on the page until they form a bucolic scene of suns-dappled woodlands and rolling meadows, their emerald grasses bespecked with horses of every imaginable hue. With an uncharacteristic cry of rage, he punches his fist into the center of the scene, which fractures back into symbols that clatter to the stone floor and dissolve. Then, with his index finger, he stabs the scroll. It rots at his touch.

The sorcerer's fingers are long and knobbly, with nails pointy enough to not only puncture skin but draw blood. Should he will it, the tips of his nails *can coat themselves in a deadly poison, one that inflicts searing pain while at the same time merging with a victim's blood to paralyze his heart and lungs. Or hers. He affords no mercy to the so-called fairer sex.*

This manner of death is slow, torturous…and inevitable. He employed it often in his long-ago younger years, when he engaged more directly in his cruelties. Now, in his maturity, he views such methods as unnecessarily vulgar. Why sully his hands with another's blood when a simple incantation or gesture can accomplish a similar end with considerably less effort? And in those instances when direct action is required, why not summon a willing surrogate and savor the inevitable outcome in his scrying stone, preferably accompanied by a leg of roasted mandopleth and a flagon of ale?

Because he knows his first circle cannot on its own produce the desired outcome, he draws a second, counterclockwise this time. His fingernail makes a screeching sound as it passes through the air. As the circle completes, it erupts into flame as dark as coal. He feels none of its heat when, with both hands, he pulls the fiery edges together as though they are curtains. With a piercing shriek, a giant bird that could be Baq'shì materializes out of the fire, wildly beating broad, purple-tipped inky wings that set off sparks in the tower chamber.

The bird could be Baq'shì, but it is not. It is her twin brother, Bàq'sha. If Baq'shì has pledged her allegiance to Tikkana and the dreamwalkers, Bàq'sha has only contempt for both. He owes his life and power to the sorcerer and serves only him, although never, in his mind, with the obsequious servility of his twin.

The sorcerer plucks a wriggling bylta'a from one of the sparks and offers it to Bàq'sha, who devours it live in a single gulp. He belches loudly, flies out the western window, circumnavigates the tower five times, squawking noisily, then returns through the northern window and lights on the stone ledge.

"What Baq'shì does," the sorcerer commands, "you must undo. Where Baq'shì brings together, you must keep apart. Where Baq'shì guides, you must lead astray. Whatever Baq'shì attempts, you must see that she fails."

Bàq'sha flaps his wings and half-bows.

"Mock me, Bàq'sha, and you will wish you did not live to regret it. All I have given you I can as easily take away." He touches a fingernail to the top of the bird's head and it croaks in pain. "Like that." He removes his fingernail and the pain vanishes.

"Kill who you must, but not the horses. I will have the horses. I will have Bryn Doon. And I will have Q'ntana." He waves his arm and Bàq'sha returns to flame. He waves it again, and he and the tower melt into the forest as though they were never there.

twenty -three

Pyrà

The bird Baq'shì had disappeared once she guided us to the safety of the barn, and now we were on our own with neither maps nor directions. How were we to find our way to Bryn Doon from here when we weren't even clear where "here" was?

Back in our village, when there was a village and I was a youngster, neighbors were always saying how fearless and precocious I was. I took childish pride in that. Now that I was suddenly older, I felt neither. Only confusion and dread. My stomach, always so strong that Kamela joked that were I able to chew them I could comfortably digest rocks, was today knotted and tight.

I ran my fingers through the grass. It was soft and pliant, unlike any part of me in that moment. It was also unlike anything I had experienced at home, where everything that grew, in a land where so little could, was sharp or brittle or both.

"What's Bryn Doon like?" I asked Hara'q. "Is it green like this? Or is it more like h—?" I started to say "home," but I couldn't because it wasn't. Not anymore. "Is it like where we came from, dry and empty?"

Hara'q didn't answer right away. He was panting heavily from having raced around the barn with T'tammo and Sajàno. I had never seen him run before, and just as his walking gait hinted at his origins — he walked not with heel and toes on the ground but on the balls of his feet — his running gait was a cross between a prance and a gallop. How could I have not seen him for what he was? Then again, why would I have?

"Not like either," Hara'q said once he caught his breath. "Not like anything you can imagine." He gazed past me, beyond the farmland and toward the darkly forested hills in the middle distance. Yet it was not the forest he was seeing. And his eyes, for the first time in my experience, were wet with tears.

"Sweet," he continued after a time, "as honey. The grasses are sweet. The waters are sweet. The air is sweet. We also have woodlands not unlike those you see up in the hills, but they carry not the slightest hint of threat or malice. Even from this distance, those seem to carry both." He shivered.

"Is it mostly forest, then?"

Hara'q laughed a neighing kind of laugh. I had never heard him laugh before, either. "We also have meadows that ripple to the horizon and lakes that sparkle in both suns-light and moonlight. And we have the River Alanda, that pellucid ribbon that winds through Bryn Doon and much of Q'ntana."

"It never makes it into the Mhor-Jenn."

"No."

I closed my eyes, but Hara'q was right. I could not imagine it. He knelt next to me and placed a hand on my knee. "I cannot wait to show it to you." He paused for so long that I opened my eyes and saw his, limpid and limitless, staring into mine. "Again."

"Again?"

"You are the Bard of Bryn Doon. That means you have been there before, perhaps in another lifetime. That means you are returning home...to your true home. Like me." He stroked the side of my cloak. "Like all of us."

"But—"

"I know it makes no sense, but it is no less true for that."

Hara'q was right. It made no sense. Yet I had to trust it or we were lost. I had to do more than trust it. I had to know it.

From a clearing deep in the forest, a large jet-colored bird ascends past the trees and into the sky, its wings barely moving. It continues to ascend, wings outstretched, far above the tree line until it is but a tiny smudge in the sky, barely noticeable from either end of the winding gravel path that links the two ocher-colored barns. The bird hovers at the edge of a cloud and focuses on first one barn then the other. Distance is no barrier to this bird. Its vision is so acute that if it chose, it could count the pebbles in the path and the stalks of grass that line it. Yet, neither pebbles nor grasses interest the bird, although a fist-sized bylta'a scampering out from one of the farm buildings does. The bird considers diving for it. It is already nearing suns-merge, and the bird would like nothing more than a crunchy snack. But no. Far greater rewards than a spindly bylta'a await it when its commission is complete.

The bird observes the horse man and his two horse companions cavort around the barn and indifferently counts the tears rolling down the youth's cheeks. Its eyes — one gold, the other silver — follow the young woman as she steps tentatively along the path from the barn in which she has been sheltering.

"What would Baq'shì do?" he asks himself. "Something ingratiatingly unctuous," he concludes, rolling his eyes disdainfully. "She would first make herself known to the young woman, a more pliable victim…er, target. Then, she would guide her to the others, introduce them in some sickeningly obliging way and lead them in whatever direction ordered by that Tikkan toady."

The bird snaps his ruby-hued beak at a passing marella bug and swallows it whole. "Makes me want to puke," he mutters. Instead, he belches loudly.

The bird is relieved when the young woman and horse man meet without him. He cannot hear what words are exchanged, for his hearing is nowhere near as keen as his vision. Each is unsettled, and neither is glad to have encountered the other. That is clear from the mistrust in their eyes.

What he wouldn't give to see them claw each other to death. What a feast that would be. That would save him much trouble, yet it would never satisfy the sorcerer. In his experience, there is no satisfying the sorcerer. Not for the first time, he wonders why he let himself become involved with him. Then, he remembers the promised reward.

He hoots excitedly, unheard by those on the ground, watches and waits.

twenty-four

Pyrà

Mattilde struggled against Hara'q's grip as he marched her toward me, her dun-colored tunic and leggings streaked with mud, as were her sandals and feet and the torn bindle she clutched under her left arm. T'tammo and Sajàno followed close behind.

She was the tallest girl I had ever seen. If Hara'q stood a head taller than I did, and I was not short, Mattilde stood a head taller still. And when the suns lit on her wild, waist-length amber hair, she resembled a living torch. Her eyes, a lighter amber, were equally fiery, her cheeks were flaming, and her mouth, set grimly in a straight line, signaled a stubbornness I would soon come to know more intimately.

"She was spying on us," Hara'q snarled, his angry face a match for hers.

I waited for Mattilde to refute the charge, but she remained silent.

"Let her go," I said.

Hara'q opened his mouth to argue, then shut it. As he released her wrist and moved away, he signaled to T'tammo and Sajàno. The horses stepped forward to flank her.

I valued Hara'q's vigilance, yet I knew her to be no threat. I knew more than that. I knew her name. I also knew her to be integral to our journey. Once again, I didn't know how I knew. I just did, even if I still found it difficult to fully trust that knowingness.

"You have nothing to fear from us, Mat—" I tried to catch myself before speaking her name. It was too late. "Mattilde."

The fire in her eyes turned to alarm. "You know my name?" She tried to back away, but the horses blocked her. "Who sent you?" Alarm turned to resolve as the fire in her eyes returned. "Whoever it was, I will not go back," she declared. "Not now. Not ever."

I offered my hand. "We are not here to force you into anything."

She refused the gesture, clasping her hands behind her back. "How do you know my name?" she asked cautiously. Then her voice hardened. "Did Ardoxx send you? Are you also a sorcerer?"

"We— That is, I— I mean…" I struggled for words. How could I explain our presence in Flor without sounding like an imbecile and causing her further distress?

"We are strangers in Flor," Hara'q said in a hurried monotone, not to reassure her but to rescue me from speechlessness. "We know no one here. Not Ardoxx. Not sorcerers. Not anyone. We arrived in your land shortly before the storm and took shelter in this barn. We know nothing more."

Mattilde glared at Hara'q then spun around to me. "I don't believe you. I don't believe either of you. You know no one in Flor, yet you know my name. And I know enough of Flor's geography to know that we are many days' travel from any frontier. Even were these the swiftest of stallions, they could not so shorten the journey." She stepped free of the horses. "You are liars, the two of you, and if you are through spinning your fanciful tales, I will be on my way."

She surveyed the area in every direction, but it was clear from her frown that she had no more idea where she was than we did — because she had wandered into an unfamiliar part of Flor or because storm damage had rendered the area unrecognizable.

"You have nowhere to go," I said softly.

"I will find somewhere to go," she countered, attempting a defiance she clearly did not feel. Yet she didn't budge.

"I know your name," I said, "but you don't know ours. I am Pyrà, and this is Hara'q. You have met him, though not by name."

"No," she said, glowering at Hara'q, "not by name."

No one said anything.

"This barn," she asked at last, "whose is it?"

"We're strangers here, remember?" Hara'q snapped. "If any of us would know, it would be you."

I touched his arm and he turned away.

"It was here when we needed it," I said.

"Mine too," she said.

Hara'q whirled back around. "Yours?"

Mattilde ignored him. "Like this one, it was not damaged in the storm. Not a single window was blown out. If that is not sorcery—" She paused. "Unless…"

"Unless what?" I asked.

She shrugged. Whatever she knew or suspected, she was not ready to share it. I shook my head subtly at Hara'q before he could press her.

"Your barn," I asked, "where is it?"

"Not far over that hill. It's identical to this one; from the outside, at any rate." She strode to our barn's open doors and peered inside. "Inside, too, apart from all the food laid upon that table." Her stomach gurgled loudly and she grimaced, no doubt embarrassed by the involuntary display of vulnerability. She tore her eyes from the food, likely to avoid the temptation it presented. "If all this isn't your sorcery," she demanded, "whose is it?"

"Why ask if you already know?"

She pressed her lips together and said nothing.

"It is the same sorcery that brought you here," I said.

Still, she said nothing.

"Rev'Àn," I said at last. It had to have been Rev'Àn's work. Perhaps not the storm, but certainly the sanctuary of these barns and, more than likely, this meeting, which felt not at all random.

Mattilde stared at me as if seeing me for the first time. Her eyes widened, either in terror or in awe. "Who are you?" she whispered.

How to respond? Rev'Àn's was not the only magic in a story that could make no sense to her. It barely made sense to me.

"Pyrà is the Bard of Bryn Doon," Hara'q said before I could come up with a reasonable answer. He stated it matter-of-factly, as though it would explain everything.

Strangely, it did, although not in a way I would have preferred.

"You?" Mattilde burst out laughing, all apprehension gone. "Now, I know you *are* mad, the pair of you. I may not know where I am, but I know who I am and I know better than to hang about with someone who claims to be a storybook character, and not a particularly convincing one."

I interrupted Hara'q before he could defend me. "Perhaps you're right, Mattilde." Again, she started at her name. "Perhaps I am mad. I know there have been moments in recent days when I have also thought it. So, go to wherever your destiny calls you. But before you do, you must be hungry. Thirsty too. And madmen though we may be, we are well-provisioned." Whatever magic had brought us here had also ensured that we had an abundance of bread, cheese, fruit, salted meat, water and wine. More than enough for two. Certainly enough for three.

"I'm not hungry," she said without conviction. "Or thirsty." Later, we would learn that not only had she not eaten in a full day, but that Beneficia half-starved all her servants, believing they would lack enough strength at the end of a workday to contemplate leaving her service.

I moved toward her and again offered my hand. She considered it before, this time, accepting, if warily. Her fingers were rough and callused, although her fingernails were clean and manicured. Close up, her tunic was well-tailored but worn. Her sandals were of equal quality and wear.

"Why do you speak of my destiny?" she asked, her voice trembling. "What do you know of my destiny?"

I would need to choose my words carefully. Whatever I said and however I said it could determine whether Mattilde stayed or left. "All I know for certain," I said slowly, "is that you being here, right now, with us, however mad we may be, is part of it. Can you trust that, at least long enough to break bread with us?"

She didn't answer right away. Instead, she scanned the sky. A verro — Baq'shì? — circled high overhead, but that was not what she looked at. She was staring at the only cloud in the otherwise clear sky.

"Before she died," she said in a distant voice, "my Gran promised to always watch over me. She said that if I was ever troubled, I was to look for her in the sky and ask for her help." The feathery cloud drifted westward. "I know it's silly, but whenever there's a single cloud in the sky, I like to think it's her."

"I don't think it's silly at all," I said and thought of my grandparents. Kamela's mother and father had died before I was born; Lucca's, before I was old enough to remember much about them other than their kindly faces. It would have been reassuring to think that they were watching over me, especially now.

"It was Gran who told me about the Bard of Bryn Doon," she said wistfully as she let me lead her into the barn. "I loved her stories." She stopped and regarded me sternly. "But they *were* only stories."

"All stories are real," Hara'q mumbled under his breath. "All stories are true."

"What?" Mattilde asked.

Hara'q grunted.

"Never mind that for now," I said. "Eat whatever you want, as much as you want, and I'll tell you what I can of our story."

Mattilde picked at her food at first, either not trusting a madman's offerings or assuming them to be enchanted in some malevolent way. Finally, her empty stomach won out. That, or my telling of our scarcely plausible story convinced her that no one crazed enough to weave such a tale could be clever enough to do her harm.

Despite Hara'q's obvious disapproval, I shared most everything we had experienced, all the way back to the storm that had destroyed our village. However, I held back Haraq's true nature and the significance of my cloak. I viewed the former as his to tell and the cloak as the most precious of our cargo. I had to be more certain of both my sight and Mattilde's character before revealing its significance. Nor did I disclose how Fay'dor had "aged" me. No one could be expected to believe that.

Mattilde uttered not a word while she ate, and her appetite was ferocious. "You were right," she said, when she finally stopped. "About Rev'Àn. I could never have escaped without his magic, and I had to escape. Had I been forced to spend one more night in that castle and one more day at that witch's beck and call, I would surely have killed her, or died in the attempt."

A piercing screech interrupted her as a large verro streaked into the barn, snatched the last slab of jeeka meat from the table and whipped out again. We raced outside, but it was already gone.

"If that was your Baq'shì," Mattilde said sourly, "I would not want her as *my* guide. Thankfully, she won't be."

"What do you mean?" I asked.

"You claim to be a storybook character who is returning horses no one can see to a storybook land that is not real." She scooped up her bindle and tucked it under her arm. "I had enough of mad people in Castle Flor. I will find my destiny, whatever Rev'Àn means for it to be, on my own."

"Let her go," Hara'q urged when I tried to stop her. "We do not need her. Her destiny is not ours."

"Wait," I called after her.

She slowed her pace but didn't stop. "Why?" she asked. "Your friend is right. My destiny is not yours."

I caught up with her and touched her shoulder. This time she stopped but didn't turn around.

"Are you so certain?" I asked.

twenty-five
Mattilde

I was not at all certain. Little about their story was credible, and what was still made no sense. And yet… And yet was their situation any less believable than mine would be to a stranger? Dreamwalkers did not show themselves as Rev'Àn had done. Entire forests were not felled in a storm that a wooden barn could withstand. Not one wooden barn. Two. And Prithi alone knew what had transformed Beneficia from cold-hearted ruler to guileless simpleton.

Even so, I had no reason to trust them. I knew my experiences to be true; I could not say the same for theirs. Best to shrug Pyrà's hand from my shoulder and keep walking, as far from these lunatics and their lunacy as I could.

Yet something stopped me. Maybe it was my Gran, because when I reached into my pocket for her bokka stone, it was hot, nearly too hot to touch. It had only ever done that twice before, once when Gran gave it to me on her deathbed and again when Rev'Àn offered me my freedom.

Who is this Pyrà and why should I credit any of what he says? Like the tales Gran told me, his story is too fantastic to be real. I know he appears to be within a few seasons of my years, but I would swear this Pyrà is little more than a boy. Is that why he pretends to be the Bard of Bryn Doon? There is no Bard of Bryn Doon outside of an ancient fable. How could there be?

Then there's Hara'q… Can he honestly believe all that Pyrà professes to be true? If he does, he must be as mad as Pyrà; if he doesn't, he's a charlatan. Either way, I dislike and distrust him as much as he dislikes and distrusts me. More.

If I am certain of one thing, it is that Hara'q is not who he seems to be and that Pyrà is not who he claims to be. Whoever they are, let them herd their invisible horses to their make-believe Bryn Doon. That is not destiny, it's insanity. I want no part of it.

Pyrà's hand on my shoulder was now as hot as the bokka stone. And as much as I longed to pull away, I couldn't…any more than I could let go the stone, which I still gripped in my pocket. Without releasing my shoulder, he stepped around to face me, and for the first time I noticed his eyes. How could I not have noticed them before? I had never seen the Mir, but his eyes were what I imagined it would be like, in color, depth and clarity. They bore into me as though they could read my essence, as though they knew more about me than I did. My face reddened, and I again longed to be gone from him and from this place. Prithi knows I tried, but it was as though my feet were staked into the ground. I could not move.

"You know something about our horses," he said softly. It was not a question.

"I-I…ah…" I shook my head.

"You know something about our horses," he repeated, more firmly but no less gently. "What is it you know?" His hand still on my shoulder, he guided me back toward the barn. I didn't resist. I couldn't. Hara'q followed a few paces behind.

I felt neither threatened nor forced. Yet I felt I had no choice. If this was what destiny was like, I didn't care for it.

Once inside, Pyrà passed me a water skin. I uncorked it and took a sip. It was wine not water, and it seemed to settle me…to return me to myself, if it was to myself I was returning, for I no longer felt eager to be gone. I wasn't certain whether to be alarmed by that or relieved.

"Horses?" Pyrà asked again.

"Very little," I replied. "Bits and pieces, really. Things I overheard Beneficia say. Or Ardoxx. I never connected them with the stories Gran told me." Why would I? Beneficia's horses may have been magical, but they were real. Gran's were stories.

I shut my eyes and felt myself a child again, Gran's face hovering over mine in the flickering candlelight as our nighttime ritual of weak tea and a story came to an end with a bedtime kiss on my forehead. I missed nothing about my time at Castle Flor apart from those moments. And I missed her. Not merely her stories, but her wisdom. She would know what I was to do. I reached into my pocket for the bokka stone. It pulsed reassuringly.

"I used to think they were only stories, but…"

"But what?"

"Something she said to me once. I'd forgotten it until this minute. She said, 'All stories are real, Matushka.' That's what she called me. 'All stores are real and all stories are true.'" She turned to Hara'q. "Isn't that what you said before? I only half-heard."

Hara'q said nothing, his face a blank.

Pyrà's eyes, however, widened. "That's what Fay'dor said to me!" He poked Hara'q. "Didn't I tell you?"

Hara'q's mouth twitched. Still, he said nothing.

"Now, I'm certain," Pyrà continued. "Our destinies *are* linked."

Can they be? I walked to the door and scanned the sky for another cloud, but the only one was far in the distance. Moments later, though, a cloud-like flock of gandas sailed by. As high as they were, I clearly heard their *ee-ya-EE* cry as they sailed past. *Gran?*

No. It wasn't possible. It couldn't be. Could it?

twenty-six
Hara'q

I was ready to dismiss the significance of Mattilde's Gran having made the identical declaration about stories that Fay'dor had. After all, proverbs and maxims could as easily be timeworn clichés as timeless wisdom. Then, a bokka stone tumbled from her pocket. It flashed brilliantly as its iridescence caught the afternoon suns-light streaming in through the barn door. Pyrà dove for it, but Mattilde was quicker. She slapped his hand away, scooped it up and returned it to her pocket.

"How did you come by that?" Pyrà gasped.

"That is my affair," Mattilde snapped. She turned to leave.

"Wait," Pyrà said. "Please."

"Why?"

"Because of this." He retrieved a bokka stone of his own from his pocket and set it on the table.

Mattilde dropped back into her seat and laid her stone next to his. While they gaped at each other, equally astonished, I studied the stones. Irregularly shaped though they were, I could see that were one to be pushed against the other, they would nestle together like two puzzle pieces. I stared from Pyrà to Mattilde. *How is it I never knew of Pyrà's bokka stone? Now, Mattilde has one too? That one should be carrying a bokka stone is singular enough. But both of them? And linking stones? This can only be Prithi's work.*

Clearly, despite my initial reservations, Mattilde *was* part of this journey. As holder of a bokka stone, and one that linked with Pyrà's, there could be no doubt. When I said as much, and included what I considered to be a generous apology for my treatment of her, she scowled.

"Your explanation means nothing to me," she retorted. "That Pyrà and I should be carrying similar stones *is* curious, but that is all it is. As for your apology, if that's what you call it, could it be any more grudging?" She grabbed her bokka stone from the table, stood and turned her back on me. "Thank you for your kindness," she said to Pyrà. "I wish you good fortune on your journey, but I will be seeking my destiny elsewhere."

"It saddens me to hear that," Pyrà said, "but before you go will you tell us how you came by your stone?" He picked up his and held it in his palm. "My father gave this to me the night before he disappeared." His voice cracked. "It is all I have left of him."

How would Lucca have come by this? Could he have known of its significance? Only Fay'dor could answer that, not that he would, unless it served his purposes.

"Does Fay'dor know you have it?" I asked.

Pyrà nodded and wiped his eyes.

"He never told you anything about it?"

"Ought he to have?"

"That, and so much more," I grumbled. "Where did you get your stone?" I asked Mattilde.

"I will tell *you*," she said to Pyrà, ignoring me. She pulled it from her pocket and held out it for him to see. "From my Gran. She got it from her mother. Like yours, it is special only as a keepsake, because it reminds me of someone…of someone I have lost." She closed her fist over it and a shiver shuddered through her.

She can feel its power, even if she cannot know what she feels. I must regain enough of her trust that she will reconsider. This is her journey as much as it is ours. I am certain of it now.

"It may be a keepsake," I said, "but it is special for more reasons than that. Both stones are. You might say they are sacred."

Mattilde turned the stone over and over in her hand. "What do you mean, sacred? It's a pretty stone and I cherish it because it was my Gran's. But it's only a stone."

"Bryn Doon is a real place," I said.

"What does Bryn Doon have to do with anything?"

"That is where these stones come from." Did I dare? The real question was, did I dare not? "That is also where I come from."

"But—"

"Bryn Doon *is* a real place," I repeated. "All stories *are* real, especially those most difficult to believe. You may find this to be one of those." That all stories were real did not make me any more eager to share mine. For as long as I had been cursed with a human body, I had been forbidden to speak of my history. That proscription had suited me. Even when Pyrà learned of my origins, it was the Bryn'qà that had done the telling. If only the Bryn'qà could do it again. I swallowed hard.

"If, after I tell you this story, you still choose to leave us, I will not try to stop you. Will you stay long enough to listen…if not for me, then for Pyrà?"

Mattilde nodded without enthusiasm and sat.

"May I hold your stone?" I asked her. "For a minute?"

"You may not." She pressed it against her breast.

"Take mine," Pyrà said.

"Thank you." As I examined the stone, I tried to imagine Bryn Doon's golden cliffs, frothing rivers and emerald valleys in its glinting ridges and whorls. But I had been gone from Bryn Doon for so long that it was almost easier to believe I was inventing it, that Mattilde was right to dismiss it as one of her Gran's stories.

"Bryn Doon is a *real* place," I forced myself to say again and to believe it, "the only place in Prithi's creation where bokka stones can be found. The *only* place." I tried again to imagine myself there.

"Go on." Mattilde interrupted my reverie.

I returned Pyrà's stone to him and continued. "In Bryn Doon itself, bokka stones are rare, for they can be found only deep within the crater at the summit of Bokka Baka'à, the crystal mountain island that rises from the salt waters of Lago Bana'à. How the lake can be salty when the river that feeds it is not is but one of the many mysteries of my homeland.

"Another mystery is how bokka stones found their way to your families, when access to Lago Bana'à and Bokka Baka'à are forbidden to humans. It is said that only the Bard of Bryn Doon is permitted to cross the lake and set foot on the island. It is also said that the Bard of Bryn Doon is no ordinary human."

"What do you mean, 'no ordinary human?'" Pyrà asked. "What am I, then?'"

"You are the Bard of Bryn Doon. What that means will be for you to discover. Even if I knew, and I don't, it would not be for me to say. What I can say to both of you is that however your bokka stones found you, you must have an extraordinary connection not only to Bryn Doon and not only to Bokka Baka'à but to Benq'a Baka'à." I bowed my head. If Bryn Doon was my homeland, Benq'a Baka'à was my birthplace.

"Benq'a Baka'à," I continued, "is the sacred creation portal that lies deep within the crater...*was* the sacred creation portal, for it has been sealed."

"I know the name, and not from Gran's story," Mattilde whispered. "How do I know the name?"

"Me too," Pyrà said. "It's as though...as though..."

"As though it's a part of you?" Mattilde asked.

Pyrà nodded. "But how—?"

"Perhaps the stones themselves told you," I said. "Or perhaps the stones came to you because Benq'a Baka'à already lived within you." I paused. "It lives within me too. That is where I was born, where all Q'ntana's horses have been born, since the beginning of time...where none but horses are born." I waited for Mattilde to grasp the import of that. When she did, her jaw dropped.

"But—but—you're—"

"I was and in many ways still am, even as I am forced to wear a human body."

"That can't be. I mean—I mean, how—?"

"All stories *are* real, especially those most difficult to believe. If you choose to journey with us, and I pray you do, I will let Pyrà tell you the 'how,' for as difficult as this story is for me to recount, I doubt I would have the strength for that one."

"The portal," Pyrà asked, "what happened to it?"

"It was buried in a massive avalanche, caused by the most powerful earthquake ever to strike Bryn Doon. Since then...since then...since..." Overcome with grief, I looked pleadingly at Pyrà and Mattilde, hoping they knew what I could not bring myself to speak.

"No new Bryn Doon horses have been born since then?" Mattilde asked.

"So the stallions we are carrying back to Bryn Doon..."

"They are the only surviving stallions," I said. "The only ones. Unless Benq'a Baka'à can be reopened, there will never be any more."

"Where are they, these stallions?" Mattilde asked. "You have made it sound as though there are many. I see only two."

Pyrà caught my eye. I nodded.

"In here," he said, stroking his cloak. "We were told it was safer for them to travel this way."

"You are jesting," Mattilde said. "You must be." She touched my sleeve and moved her fingers from one horse to the next. "It isn't possible. They are the same fabric as the rest of your cloak. Someone has taken you for a fool."

"Nine score and five horses are woven into this cloak," Pyrà said, "and I knew them all as living, breathing stallions before the magic that laced them into this fabric brought us to Flor. Rev'Àn's magic. The same magic that allowed you to escape your mistress. Would you like me to name them all for you?"

Mattilde shook her head. "All stories *are* real, especially those most difficult to believe?"

"Yes," I said. "Especially those."

"Nine score and five, plus T'tammo and Sajàno. That still isn't so many. Why are there so few left? What happened to the rest? What happened to the mares?"

"Did your Gran ever speak to you of the Great Enchantment?"

Mattilde shook her head.

"I myself do not know the full extent of its evil, other than that it cursed me and my kind. It was the Great Enchantment that destroyed all but two of Bryn Doon's mares, enslaved too many of its stallions and stripped the remainder of their immortality. Because of the Great Enchantment, the only horses that remain are those we have been tasked with returning home, to Bryn Doon. There may be more to the Great Enchantment, but that is all I know of it."

"I know something else," Mattilde said. "From what I overheard in the castle, I know that Ardoxx is after the horses. Beneficia too, although I doubt she is any threat." She explained having seen her former mistress transformed into a madwoman. "But Ardoxx is exceptionally powerful. I have known him all my life, and I have never not seen him get what he wants."

"Then he is as dangerous as he is powerful," I said.

Pyrà pulled his cloak tightly around him. "All the more reason to get the horses back to Bryn Doon, and as quickly as possible."

Yes, but how? Mattilde had returned her bokka stone to the table, and it sat close to Pyrà's. At least part of the answer had to lie with those stones, even if I could not see how. Still, although there was much about this journey that remained hidden, some of its puzzle pieces were beginning to fit together. Flor, at first a seemingly purposeless destination, now made the glimmerings of sense. Ardoxx was here, determined to get his hands on the horses. Also here were Mattilde and her bokka stone; not any stone, but one linked to Pyrà's. There had to be more to it, but my gifts did not lean toward the visionary. I would have to trust Pyrà for that. More to the point, I would have to find a way for that trust to be less grudging than it had been.

As I gazed at the two bokka stones, I felt for mine. Yes, I had one too, and I couldn't help but wonder whether it was linked to those. Mine had not been inherited from an ancestor. How could it have been, when I had none. Nor had it been in my possession when I was a horse. Horses have no possessions. Rather, I found it under my pillow, tucked inside a smooth-hide pouch, soon after we arrived in the Mhor-Jenn. Though I recognized what it was, the how and why of its appearance plagued me for days until, finally, as much as it pained me to do so, I approached Fay'dor. Not surprisingly, his characteristically vague explanation left me wondering why I had bothered.

"The day will come," he said, "when you will know why the stone has come to you and what to do with it. Until that day, hold it close to your person and keep its existence to yourself. Share it with no one. *No one.*"

Now that two other bokka stones had revealed themselves, had that day come?

No. The voice was Fay'dor's, and it came not from my stone but from the two on the table. Pyrà and Mattilde heard nothing, but the voice was as clear as if Fay'dor were sitting next to me. "Soon," it said. "Soon."

twenty-seven

Kamela

Am I dead? I clutched a whimpering Jeryn to my breast. "Are you, little one?" I whispered to my daughter. She gurgled a drooling reply. I wiped her face with the back of my free hand and surveyed this strange, ethereal place, as well as my former neighbors, all of whom seemed to be sleeping. *Are all of us dead?*

It was Jeryn's crying that had awakened me, for I too had been asleep…if sleep it was. I had a vague memory of Na'an appearing to me. Was it here in this place? If it was, did that make all of this a dream? *Do the dead dream? Do the dead sleep?*

If we were dead and this was Kea Kana, the antechamber to the next life, the version I was experiencing was not at all the same as Ben's in The SunQuest. He described a tropical paradise of vibrant, perfumed flowers and brilliantly colored birds. This place had no color. It was not drab like the Mhor-Jenn. Nor did it appear as though its color had been washed away. It was as though color was not a quality that this place possessed. And although Jeryn had perceptible weight and mass, nothing else appeared to have any.

"Allaya," I whispered to the slumbering-seeming figure next to me. No response. Gently, I nudged her shoulder. It was reassuringly solid. She snorted softly and curled into a ball. She didn't open her eyes. I did the same to her cousin Flek, who lay on his back on the other side of me, his head tilted slightly upward and his mouth agape. His only response was to shut his mouth and turn his head away.

Still holding Jeryn, I attempted and failed to stand. It was as though my legs were no longer connected to my will because I could not get them to obey. Yet they were not paralyzed, for as weakened as they were, I could feel them.

I scanned the space, trying to gain a clearer sense of it, but I could not even tell whether it was indoors or outdoors. It lacked walls and a ceiling, and its floor, while supporting us, lacked substance. Because of the luminescent tendrils of cool mist that sinuated lazily around me, it occurred to me that we might be cocooned inside a cloud. I quickly dismissed the thought as being too fanciful…as if any explanation for this place and its occupants could be considered too fanciful.

Was anyone else stirring? I sensed subtle movement through the mist and tried to call out. The most I could manage was a throaty whisper that not even Jeryn acknowledged. With my next breath (*do the dead still breathe?*), my eyelids grew heavy. I thought I caught another glimpse of Na'an. Then, nothing.

From its perch atop the golden canopy crowning a lone jaq'òra, a verro surveys the devastated countryside. The jaq'òra is the only tree along the perimeter of this abandoned farm neither damaged nor felled by the tempest. Its former neighbors, uprooted by roiling floodwaters and stripped of their foliage, lie strewn across neglected fields now buried under a viscous layer of swampy sludge.

In the middle distance stand two barns, miraculously untouched by the storm. They are separated by a low hill and connected by a winding gravel path. The nearer barn is empty; outside the farther one, two men and a woman confer. Two black stallions stand packed and saddled behind them. Although the verro cannot hear what the humans say, their movements and postures make it clear that there is little agreement among them. Every few minutes one or another of them looks up, hopefully. The skies, however, are empty of anything but a distant cloud and the two suns, which beat down on the humans with all the harshness of a midsummer afternoon.

The verro tilts his head to the larger of the two suns, to Aygra. When Aygra passes behind the cloud, it will be time to act. That will be the sorcerer's signal, just as the cloud, on this otherwise cloudless day, is the sorcerer's creation.

The verro is impatient. He knows of more immediately gratifying ways to spend an afternoon. There are scores if not hundreds of destroyed homes, barns and shops to pillage, although not for the paltry value of their now-exposed contents. What would a verro do with gold? No, verros are fed by human emotion. Some verros flourish in the presence of love and joy, and those birds' proximity only enhances those emotions. These, this verro believes, are no better than bylta'a, those tiny, timid creatures whose sole purpose is to provide him with a quick snack. True verros, in this one's view, thrive on pain, anguish and loss. The more tragic the circumstances, the more fuel to be derived from it. And artifacts touched by such circumstances provide an uninterrupted source of that fuel, which is why this verro has a growing hoard of them in his cave deep in the Forest of Ardh.

Alas, instead of spending the day in joyful pillage, he is trapped here atop this tree, waiting for the sorcerer's signal. It will be worth it. The sorcerer's reward will be many times more valuable than a day's plunder...if the sorcerer keeps his bargain.

The cloud drifts closer to Aygra. It should not be long now.

If Hara'q's story had persuaded me to travel on with them, I was now having second thoughts. The horses were packed and ready, but Baq'shì had not returned to guide us, and my two new companions were engaged in an increasingly heated quarrel about where to go next.

Hara'q demanded that we travel north. "That," he declared, offering no evidence other than his self-described "native horse sense," "is where Bryn Doon *must* lie." What arrogance. The little sympathy his story had stirred in me immediately dissolved.

I was more inclined to trust Pyrà, even if I remained unconvinced that he was the Bard of Bryn Doon, should such a person actually exist outside Gran's story. In this instance, however, I could not trust him. He insisted, with little more explanation for his position than Hara'q had offered for his, that we first make our way to Castle Flor. "Something is there that we need, something that will help us get to Bryn Doon."

"You will find only cruelty and unhappiness there," I argued, reluctantly taking Hara'q's side. "Nothing more."

"You yourself said that we need to get the horses to Bryn Doon as quickly as possible," Hara'q reminded Pyrà. "Castle Flor is nothing but a distraction, and any distraction increases the danger to them, and to us."

"And if the key to speedily getting us back to Bryn Doon lies at Castle Flor?"

"You cannot know that it does."

"You can't know that it doesn't."

Where was Baq'shì? Tuning out both Hara'q and Pyrà, I scanned the sky. If they would not listen to each other, I was certain they would heed a messenger from Rev'Àn. Well, almost certain. Would I? What if she were to guide us to Castle Flor? Would I follow? I prayed to be spared that decision.

The sky was clear but for that same single cloud I had spotted earlier. Strangely, despite the light breeze, it hovered motionless halfway to the western horizon, as though it waited for Aygra. Moments later, sun and cloud met. As they did, a shrill screech sliced through my companions' bickering. Startled, they looked up. Was this, finally, Baq'shì, arrived to settle their dispute? If it was, where was she? Even as the screeching grew louder, the sky remained empty. Then, as though it had been thrust at us through an opening in the heavens, a verro dove earthward. It circled us once then shot straight up until it was barely a speck, before plummeting back toward us. When it was so close that I could see its eyes — one gold, the other silver — it careered eastward, its shrieks growing increasingly urgent.

All disagreements forgotten, Hara'q urged T'tammo and Sajàno in the same direction as the verro. The stallions, however, refused to budge. The bird we were certain was Baq'shì wheeled back toward us, issued an ear-piercing scream and again veered east, its wings beating frantically.

Hara'q whispered something in T'tammo's ear. The stallion shook his head but stood fast. Then Pyrà did likewise, stroking the horse's mane. T'tammo snorted and tossed his head in response, then nudged Sajàno forward.

We were on our way. And I was about to meet my destiny… whatever that was.

twenty-nine

Pyuà

At last we had our guide. Or had we? Some indefinable something about this verro felt off, although if it wasn't Baq'shì, it could have been her twin. Even T'tammo seemed reluctant to follow the bird at first, agreeing to do so only when I whispered a few words of reassurance in his ear. I trusted T'tammo on this, more than I did my own inner sensings, but I was reluctant to ignite another quarrel with Hara'q, who expressed not the slightest doubt that this was Rev'Àn's bird.

On one point, however, he and I were in absolute agreement: It was imperative that we move the horses to Bryn Doon, as swiftly as we could manage it. As for the bird, I was willing to go where it led us, at least initially. T'tammo and I would pay close heed to it in case it was an imposter. I had not abandoned my conviction that something of consequence awaited us at Castle Flor, but I would say nothing of it for the time being. Instead, with me at the lead, Mattilde astride Sajàno and Hara'q a few paces behind T'tammo, we launched our journey in earnest, following maybe-Baq'shì out of the oasis surrounding the barns and into the devastation wrought by the storm.

Fortunately, we were soon able to join a hard-packed dirt road, which despite being pocked with muddy potholes as large as small ponds, was preferable to slogging cross-country through fields awash with slop. This was farm country, or it had been. It was impossible to know whether the barns, farmhouses and outbuildings we passed, all stripped to skeletal remains, had been wrecked by the storm or whether the storm had completed what time and neglect had initiated.

From what Mattilde told us, Beneficia had rarely displayed more than a fleeting interest in the people she was meant to be governing, focusing instead on her personal comfort and a growing obsession with horses.

It had already been mid-afternoon by the time we set out, and it was now approaching dusk. We needed to find a rare patch of dry land where we could stop for the night. I called up to Baq'shì, if that's who it was, to guide us to someplace suitable, but the bird was intent on keeping us moving. If we halted, as briefly as to adjust a strap, it would swoop down behind us, beating its wings and screeching wildly. And if we didn't immediately get going again, it would land on my head, digging its claws into my scalp.

Aygra and B'na had already dropped below the western and eastern horizons and daylight was fading rapidly when we found ourselves climbing a series of switchbacks past jagged rocky outcroppings. Soon after, we happened on a broad rocky ledge slightly angled up from the road. It was not entirely flat, but it was the flattest land we had encountered since leaving the farmland behind, and from what we could discern in the failing light, the land beyond appeared to be even less suitable. Better still, a cave at the far end could serve as shelter if we needed it. But only if we needed it; its opening was tiny and none of us was eager to try to squeeze in.

Despite, the bird's angry cawing, Hara'q went in search of whatever dry wood he could find for a fire, while Mattilde and I clambered up the ledge, the horses behind us, and prepared to make camp.

Night fell quickly. One moment our craggy surroundings were veiled in the dusky blue of twilight; the next, the only light was the flickering of our fire and the occasional spark that danced up to join the stars. And the only sound was the crackle of the kindling. Because of the afternoon's set-tos, we had spoken little on the journey that brought us here, saying no more than was necessary to follow the verro. Even through dinner, we each kept our own counsel. I could not know what Hara'q and Mattilde were thinking, but I was increasingly convinced that it was not Baq'shì we had been following. Yet I did not trust myself enough to share it aloud. Instead, I lowered my lids, pretending to doze. Soon, I was no longer pretending.

When I opened my eyes again, the fire was little more than a pulsing glow. Mattilde and Hara'q were asleep, the day's tension erased from their faces. Hara'q snored softly and Mattilde's eyes twitched; perhaps

Rev'Àn had returned with some additional direction for us. I could but hope.

I rose quietly so as not to disturb them and made my way to where T'tammo and Sajàno stood, lightly dozing. T'tammo sensed my presence and opened one eye. He blinked, then opened the other, nuzzling his face against mine.

I don't know how long I stood there, my face buried in T'tammo's mane. But when I finally pulled free, M'nor had already risen in the north and hung at eye level, seeming to stare directly at me. Then, as she had done with Toshar in a MoonQuest that I could no longer dismiss as myth but had to embrace as history, she spoke.

"The story," she said, "it is time for the story. *Your* story." Her voice, which I felt in my chest more than heard with my ears, was so soft that I would have mistaken it for the breeze had not T'tammo and Sajàno raised their heads and turned them toward the moon.

It had to be M'nor speaking, yet bard though I apparently was, I did not know how to respond. Which story was she wanting me to tell? Which was *my* story? Was it The MoonQuest, with which she was so powerfully linked? Or was it, like the story the Bryn'qà had helped me scrive at the outset of our journey, one that would reveal itself only in the telling?

I pulled the Bryn'qà from my belt and held it up to the moon. Silver light poured through it, and I felt its warmth on my face. I felt the story.

"It's *your* story," I exclaimed to the horses. They whinnied and nodded their heads. Sparks flew off their manes. This time, for the first time, I knew what they were saying: that it was also my story, even if I didn't yet know what that meant.

"Once upon a time," I began, holding the Bryn'qà to my heart, "when time itself was new and the land that would one day be Q'ntana and neighboring dominions was so young that it was still rising from the deepest depths of the Mir, Prithi reached out to all the creatures of the sea — to the baleyas, delfians, rainbow ovals, tartarucas, seahorses and other floaters and swimmers, as well as to the thor'qyas, qymaq'as, horqyr'as and other sea-floor crawlers, scuttlers and scramblers. Which of them, Prithi asked, would consent to become the first inhabitants of this dry world?

"At first, none would. Why would they abandon the near-infinite freedom of open waters for the limitations of land? Why not, they suggested, approach the seabirds? Surely, flying creatures must yearn for resting perches more solid than the rocking waters of the Mir.

"Only Prithi knows Prithi's heart. Even Kumba, the Great Dragon of Creation, cannot know why Prithi acts as Prithi does. And Prithi's plan for these new lands did not include the seabirds. Not yet.

"Prithi neither forces nor imposes. Prithi allows. So Prithi, who knows no time but all time, waited. As Prithi waited, the land that would be Q'ntana and neighboring dominions continued to rise from the waters and take form — into mountains and plains, into deserts, valleys and jungles, into gentle meadows and jagged cliffs, into rolling hills and craggy precipices. Saplings grew into towering trees, tightly closed buds exploded into flowers and fruit, and troughs and channels filled with sparkling waters to become lakes, rivers and streams."

M'nor had continued her ascent as I spoke, and she now hovered overhead, casting a silvery glow over our tiny campsite. Mattilde and Hara'q still slept. Still pressing the Bryn'qà to my chest, I shut my eyes and continued.

"Only when the earth had taken on some semblance of its current form did two seahorses answer Prithi's call, volunteering to move onto the dry land that had risen around them. The dry land was Bokka Baka'à. The seahorses were Rykka and Ta'ar."

Rykka and Ta'ar? Those were the mystical horses of both Toshar's MoonQuest and Ben's SunQuest. My mind tried and failed to make sense of the story I was telling. All I could do was free it to carry me forward.

"Once Rykka and Ta'ar made their willingness known, Prithi directed them not to the island's crystalline shore but to the saltwater channel that flowed hundreds of v'reks underground from the Mir to Lago Bana'à, then under Bokka Baka'à to the base of Benq'a Baka'à, the sacred crater at the island's center. As they allowed the current to carry them to the crater's underwater opening, coarse hair replaced the scaly plates that had covered their bodies, hair that matched their seahorse coloring: Rykka's, the pale blue of morning sky; Ta'ar's, the smoky plum of twilight. And as the current propelled them forward, their bodies lengthened and swelled and their four fin-like limbs extended into muscular, hoof-tipped legs. When, finally, they climbed from the crater, they no longer resembled the seahorses they had always been. Instead, they were the new world's first horses."

A snorting whinny pulled me from my storytelling reverie and

I opened my eyes. At some point during my account, Hara'q and Mattilde had awoken. They now sat at my feet, entranced.

"I-I knew none of that," Hara'q whispered when he found his voice. "How do you—?" He stopped and shook his head.

Mattilde touched his arm. "The Bard of Bryn Doon."

He nodded. "The Bard of Bryn Doon."

The Bard of Bryn Doon. For the first time, I almost felt worthy of the name. I shut my eyes and continued.

thirty
Hara'q

One of the many things I have retained from my equine past is my inability to fall into a deep sleep. I do no more than doze through much of the night, and it takes little to wake me. I don't know what woke me this night, but when I opened my eyes and saw that Pyrà was missing, I flew to my feet. The moon had risen by then, which made it easy to locate him.

If I was not surprised to find him with T'tammo and Sajàno, I was surprised that not only was he telling them a story, they appeared to be paying rapt attention. Until then, it had vexed me that I was captivated by stories, assuming it to be one of the flaws of my human nature. Seeing how engrossed T'tammo and Sajàno were, I was relieved. My love of stories was not some distortion of my horse-self. It was unexpectedly integral to it.

I crept closer, yet not too close. I did not want to break the spell Pyrà's story was casting, not only on the horses but on himself.

"For their courage in volunteering to be the new world's first land creatures," Pyrà continued, "Prithi called them from the shores of Lago Bana'à, where they gazed wistfully into the waters they had left behind for all time, to the mouth of the Benq'a Baka'à crater. When they arrived, Kumba was waiting for them as Prithi's emissary, to gift them with three rewards."

"What's happening?" Mattilde whispered. So intent was I on Pyrà's tale that I had not heard her approach.

"Shh." I hissed. I did not want to miss a word. How had I not known this story?

"First, Kumba breathed a fiery thunderbolt onto their foreheads, which branded each of them with a distinctive white flash that gave them the gift of lightning speed.

"Second, Kumba breathed a dual column of fire into the air, which fractured into millions of sparks. As the sparks fell to the ground, they carved out the discrete province thenceforth known as Bryn Doon. This, Kumba granted to Rykka and Ta'ar as their eternal home and made them sovereign over all its territory and over the mares and stallions who would soon join them there.

"Prithi's third honor was the most singular: Rykka and Ta'ar could choose either unfettered freedom within Bryn Doon's borders or a life in service to Kumba and to M'ranna, the land that would one day be known as Q'ntana. The latter would also bestow a form of immortality upon them and upon all the mares and stallions of Bryn Doon.

"Without hesitation, Rykka and Ta'ar bowed their heads to Kumba and pledged their unconditional and eternal fealty. Kumba then exhaled the full force of its fiery breath into Benq'a Baka'à. When the flames cleared, Benq'a Baka'à had been fashioned into a creation portal for the horses of Bryn Doon, who would not be born of mare and stallion but would instead rise through the crater from the sea, as Rykka and Ta'ar had done."

Pyrà opened his eyes. Still half in whatever trance the story had carried him, he seemed unsure not only of where he was but who he was. He set down the Bryn'qà, though only long enough to drink from the water skin Mattilde handed him. As he passed it back, he stared at her, not as though he knew her from our brief travels but in that way Kamela would often describe, as though he could see into her soul and knew her from that place of inexplicable depth.

By now M'nor had disappeared under the southern horizon and the faint glow of a nascent dawn was painting the slender wisps of cloud in pink and orange pastels. Pyrà scanned the sky as though the rest of the story was written in those candy-colored tendrils.

If it was, it would have to wait to reveal itself, for as Pyrà opened his mouth to continue, the off-key, high-pitched voice of what I assumed to be a child wafted toward us, shattering the storytelling spell: "Oik and Ork pursue an Awk / The Awk will not be caught / The Awk turns 'round, scoops up a rock / Now Oik and Ork are not."

Mattilde clenched her fists until her knuckles turned white. All color drained from her face. "No," she gasped. "It can't be."

Aygra had barely slipped above the eastern horizon when Beneficia skipped into view, still singing her ridiculous ditty, a simpleton's grin plastered on her mud-splattered face and layers of smelly skins hanging awkwardly from a frame that, though still ample, seemed to have lost some heft. After I spotted her dancing past the barn where I had taken shelter after the storm, I had hoped never to set eyes on her again. At least then, she had not seen me. Now, she not only saw me, but despite the spell that now enchanted her, she recognized me.

"Mistress," she shrieked. She barreled toward me, her arms outstretched.

I shrank back, not quickly enough. She engulfed me in a suffocating hug, then fell to her knees.

"Mistress," she repeated, "I thought I would never, ever, ever see you again. But here you are!" She scrambled to her feet and embraced me again.

"Get off me." I tried to extricate myself from her vise-like grip, but she clung to me. "Get her off me," I shouted at Pyrà and Hara'q, who stared, wonder struck, at the spectacle.

Before they could pry me free, Beneficia dropped back to her knees. "Forgive me, mistress," she cried. "I had no right. But…but…I was afraid…you were dead." At that, she burst into tears, clutching my knees.

"Get. Off. Me."

Beneficia finally released me and slunk back. She settled by the mouth of the cave, still sobbing, her knees pressed to her chest. "I'm sorry, mistress," she whimpered. "I thought— I should never have— I didn't know— I didn't think… I just thank Prithi you're safe…that I can still serve you…if you'll have me. Will you?"

"It's Beneficia," I said to Pyrà and Hara'q.

"I thought she was *your* mistress," Hara'q said.

"She has gone mad. She must have. How else—?" I shook my head. Beneficia blubbered incoherently. I knew I should feel sorry for her, but I couldn't. Whatever had happened to her, whoever she had become, she deserved it. And more. It was impossible for me to forget all the ways she had belittled me…all the ways she had belittled Gran. I turned away from her and scanned the sky. "It must be time to move on. Where's that bird?"

"What about—?" Hara'q jerked his head toward Beneficia. Her sobs had subsided into sniffles, and she was back to singing her song.

Since first meeting him, I had suspected Pyrà of being too soft-hearted for his own good. Now I suspected that he was too soft-hearted for ours. He knelt next to Beneficia, trying to get some sense out of her. But all she would do when she wasn't singing was cry "my mistress," over and over.

"She will have to come with us," Pyrà said at last. "We can't leave her here."

"Come with us? You're as mad as she is. She has been wandering alone for days and has come to no harm. Let her continue."

"Mattilde…"

"No. Her or me. If you insist on lumbering yourself with—with that—" I pointed at Beneficia and I was so angry that my finger trembled, "—you go without me. Whatever my destiny is, it cannot be with her. I will find my own way."

Hara'q remained silent as Pyrà petitioned on Beneficia's behalf. I couldn't know whether it was because he agreed with Pyrà, didn't want to take my side against him or simply didn't care. In the end, all he said was, "Let us not make rash decisions on an empty stomach."

We ate in uneasy silence. I had said all I had to say, and Pyrà was wise enough to not argue. As for Beneficia, she had to be coaxed to eat — not by me. When, finally, she agreed, she carried a heel of bread and single slice of cheese back to her place by the cave. "I cannot eat at the same table as my mistress," she said.

Moments later, our verro charged at us from wherever it had spent the night. It flapped its wings first at Pyrà then at Hara'q, as though urging them to hurry.

Beneficia was not immediately aware of the bird. She was too busy singing to herself and ripping crumbs from the heel of bread. Most fell to the ground, which didn't stop her from eating them. Only when the verro squawked loudly did Beneficia look up. As soon as she saw the bird, she leapt up, screaming.

"No," she cried, waving her arms. "Bàq'sha. Bàq'sha Bàq'sha Bàq'sha." Then she dropped back to the ground and covered her head. "Bàq'sha," she whimpered. "Ardoxx. No. Ardoxx. Bad."

Ardoxx? I felt the blood drain from my face. If this verro had anything to do with Ardoxx, it was to be avoided. Reluctantly, I made my way to Beneficia.

"Mistress?" she whispered, stabbing her finger at me. "Danger."

It took all the grace I could muster to speak to her with anything but bitterness. "Tell me, Beneficia," I said. "That bird. It's Baq'shì, isn't it?"

She looked back at me with horror. "Oh, no, mistress. Verro is Bàq'sha. Bad bird. Evil bird." She squeezed her eyes shut and buried her face in her hands. "Sorcerer's bird." Her voice was muffled and shaking. Her whole body convulsed as she burst into tears. "You must go. *Go.*"

I wanted more than anything to slap her and walk away. Instead, I took her in my arms and rocked her until the shuddering stopped. At the same time, I tried to get Pyrà's attention without the bird noticing. In the end, it was Hara'q who came over.

"What's she on about?"

"Shh. Keep your voice down." I drew him nearer and shared what Beneficia had told me.

He pulled me a few steps away, out of earshot of both Beneficia and the bird. "Do you believe her?"

I tried to erase what Beneficia had been from my mind and focus instead on what she had become. "The Beneficia I know is cunning, but… Even if she were as cunning as this, she would die before she would knowingly act like anyone's servant."

"Are you certain?"

Was I? My Beneficia was selfish and haughty. If it could save her, was she capable of demeaning herself? To this extent?

"I want to believe she is acting. It makes it easier for me to continue hating her. But if I am honest, truly honest, I don't think she is. If she says this verro serves Ardoxx, she must be right. What do we do? Ardoxx is more powerful than you can imagine."

"Perhaps." Hara'q paused. "But he lacks one key power." He grinned. I had never seen him display even the hint of a smile. "Horse sense."

No one hears what the horse man says to the verro as he grips the back of the bird's neck with one hand and holds a dagger to its throat with the other. Nor does anyone see the horse man pluck a feather from its right wing before he lifts the bird and hurls it into the air.

With uncharacteristic silence, the bird flaps its wings, gains control of its trajectory, shoots into the sky and disappears.

Once he is satisfied that the bird will not circle back, the horse man tosses the feather onto the embers in the fire pit. Once it has sizzled into ash, he rejoins the bard and the girl, who have observed the incident with a combination of awe and alarm. Only then does the other woman, the one dressed in skins, cease her wailing.

The sorcerer sees none of this.

*　　*　　*

The sorcerer stares into his scrying stone, willing the fog that veils his view to clear. If the verro is doing what he is meant to be doing, the band of interlopers should soon be visible.

The verro has been commanded to ambush his sister and lure the interlopers on the three-day journey that will carry them deep into the Forest of Ardh, so deep that they will be unable to find their way through without assistance. They will have none. For if the verro obeys the sorcerer's orders, he will have abandoned them in the Gry'a Grove. One night among the Gry'a and they will agree to anything to be released from the nightstalkers' demonic grip. Only when the travelers are desperate will the sorcerer appear. He will offer them their lives in exchange for the two horses and the two bokka stones. They will surely agree, for they are weak, frightened humans. Even the horse man has been infected enough by his humanity that he will give in. Of that the sorcerer has no doubt.

The verro may not be trustworthy, but he is greedy. He will do what the sorcerer asks of him, most especially anything that allows him to exercise his loathing for his sister.

The stone has not yet cleared. The sorcerer does his best to be patient. His best, however, is not good enough. His fingers drum with increasing force and rapidity at the edge of the stone. When, finally, the fog dissipates from the scrying stone, the sorcerer cries out in a rage that causes the earth to tremble. He extends the fingers of both hands and pushes bolts of lightning through all ten fingernails. The deadly charge shoots through the forest and hundreds of v'reks beyond, igniting every tree and destroying every village in its path.

"She will die," he declares in a voice as quiet as it is icy. "They will all die."

ILLUMINATION

thirty-two
Beneficia

It would take some time before my senses were restored to something resembling adult understanding. Until then, I *was* the serving girl Beneficia, indentured to Mattilde, the *Lady* Mattilde. We had been separated — I had no memory of how — and were now reunited.

At first, I was overjoyed, for serving my mistress was all I lived for, and also alarmed, for my mistress seemed determined not only to avoid me but to leave me behind. Had I displeased her? Had I angered her? If only I knew what I had done so I could make amends.

Then, the verro showed up. Not any verro. Bàq'sha. The sorcerer's Bàq'sha. And everything changed.

"What now?" Hara'q asked once he had rid us of Bàq'sha. "What about her?" Beneficia still cowered by the cave. Her eyes shut, she rocked back and forth, breathing her Ork and Oik ditty like some sort of mantra. Although her face, arms and legs were still splattered with mud, her skin had, strangely, lost its blotchiness. Now, it almost glowed.

Mattilde stared at the spot in the sky where we had last seen Bàq'sha. A wisp of cloud masked first B'na then Aygra. When they cleared, the light seemed somehow brighter.

"She may have saved our lives," I said.

"I know." She knelt next to Beneficia and regarded her closely. "Whatever she is now, she is not the Lady of Flor. Even the Beneficia I knew, as scheming, manipulative and heartless as she was, could never sustain a charade like this. I don't know what happened to that Beneficia, who she has become or why she keeps calling me mistress, but—" She sighed. "I suppose she will have to come with us."

She stood and nudged me and Hara'q away from Beneficia. "One condition," she said too softly for Beneficia to hear.

"What is it?" I asked.

"If she is truly as helpless as she seems, I agree we can't leave her on her own. But—" Her face clouded as she recalled the indignities inflicted on her by her former mistress. "But the instant, the *instant*, this sickness or spell has passed and she acts like the old Beneficia, we leave her behind. I don't care where we are or what we're doing. In that instant, I withdraw all consent and all protection. Then, it *will* be her or me. Agreed?"

I stroked the Bryn'qà. Somewhere inside the quill was Beneficia's story, a story that was key to our journey. I was certain of it. I was equally certain that the old Beneficia was gone, never to reemerge. Once again, I didn't know how I knew these things. I simply did. Perhaps that was what my mysterious bardship was all about. Its story was likely also buried in the quill.

"Agreed," we replied in unison.

Mattilde helped Beneficia to her feet. "Come," she said with unexpected tenderness. "It is time to go."

Beneficia wiped the tears from her face with the back of a dirty hand. "You won't leave me again?"

Mattilde's face hardened for a moment. It had to be difficult to separate this Beneficia from the one she had always known. Yet when Beneficia looked up at her with the eyes of a helpless child, all she could do was shake her head.

It might have been time to go, but where? All any of us knew was that Bryn Doon was to be our final destination. But how to get there from here? Although I continued to feel a strong pull to Castle Flor, there was no way to know where it was from where we were, wherever that was. Even were Mattilde to agree to go, she could not direct us. Her knowledge of Flor was limited to the castle's immediate environs. Nor, in her present state, could Beneficia. That was assuming we were still in Flor. Who knew where Bàq'sha had been taking us? Into a trap, more than likely. In the end, we decided to remain where we were for one more night and hope for a clearer direction in the morning.

*　*　*

M'nor had set, and the only light twinkled down at us from the stars when T'tammo's whinnying woke me. The others still slept as I crept over to him.

Back home in the Mhor-Jenn, I had communed with him every day and some nights too, mostly because I'd had no one else to talk to. Village children avoided me, and adults always seemed frightened of me. All I'd had were my horses.

T'tammo whinnied again.

"Do you know something? Do you know where we are to go today? If you do, I wish you would tell me."

The stallion snorted and gently butted his head at my chest, something he had frequently done on Mòrq'an Mellà. Then, I had often sensed what he was trying to tell me. Now, I sensed nothing.

thirty-four
Hara'q

I let Pyrà think I was asleep while he stole over to visit with T'tammo. He often spent time with the horses before dawn, and I didn't want to get in the way. As I did most mornings, I watched their silhouetted forms and marveled at the connection they shared. Would I ever again experience that closeness with my brothers? Only if we made it to Bryn Doon and only if my natural form were to be restored. At this point on our journey, neither was guaranteed.

Mattilde and Beneficia still slept when Pyrà returned to the fire's dying embers. Mattilde was curled up across from us, her eyelids fluttering in dream. Beneficia was snuggled up behind her, snoring softly.

"A peculiar pair," I said to Pyrà.

"Like us." He chuckled and poked at the coals. A tiny flame ignited.

"We can't stay here another day," I said.

"No."

"Do you know where we are to go?"

He shrugged and poked at the fire again. The single flame swelled and undulated, rising taller against the velvet sky.

"Do you have a story that will guide us?"

"If there is, it has yet to show itself."

"Even to a bard?"

Pyrà laughed softly. "I am learning that bards do not direct stories. Stories direct bards. I cannot summon a story any more than you can. All I can do is be ready for when one chooses to be known." He pulled the Bryn'qà from his belt. "Even this has its own will."

"That makes no sense. Stories are not alive. Nor are feathers, whatever their source."

"You are wrong, my friend. Stories are as alive as you and I."

"I don't understand."

"I didn't either, at first. Then I began to see that stories are like dreams. They come to me not because I want them but because they have a message for me. I cannot command a story to appear and deliver its message any more than I can command a dream. So, yes, stories are alive. They are alive, but they have no voice of their own."

I felt a glimmer of understanding. "They need a bard to give them voice?"

"King Ben said that we are all bards in Q'ntana. That's how I first knew I must be one." Sparks flew off the flame. "If that is so, you must be one as well."

That was too ridiculous. Yes, horses loved stories. But horses did not tell stories. I studied Pyrà, who appeared to be hypnotized by the fire, which had now grown to almost man-size. Did we? "There is only one Bard of Bryn Doon," I said at last.

"Apparently," he said, his eyes still on the lone flame. It now towered over us, the size of a giant, and had taken on something resembling human form, with long, flickering arms that thrust toward us and a fiery head pierced by empty, black circles for eyes, a nose and a distended mouth.

I didn't know who or what it was, but it was no friend. Uncorking my water skin, I flung its contents at the flame. But what ought to have doused it only made it larger and more menacing.

Pyrà and I shrank back as it stretched toward us. When it failed to reach us, it turned its attention to Mattilde and Beneficia, still asleep.

What happened next was so quick that it was over in an instant, though it felt like an eternity.

"Mattilde," Pyrà cried.

Mattilde jerked awake, jostling Beneficia, whose eyes shot open as the fiery wraith leapt toward her.

"Ardoxx," she shrilled.

Mattilde screamed and threw herself on top of Beneficia. The figure froze, its gaping hole of a mouth gripped in a silent yowl. Mattilde hugged Beneficia as close to her as she could. "You have no power here," she hissed, spitting into the flame. The apparition writhed, wheezed and whistled, made one feeble attempt at a lunge, then extinguished, leaving a cold fire pit and the sharp, black chill of a moonless night.

"He'll be back," I declared.

Mattilde rolled away from me in shock, and I felt Pyrà's and Hara'q's eyes drill into me through the darkness. Even I was stunned by the tone of my voice. My words too. For an instant, the horrors of the previous moments were forgotten.

Only for an instant. Before any of us could speak, another specter rose from the fire pit. This one was a whorl of silvery luminescence that sinuated to the sound of a melodic tinkling — as though someone were strumming a stringed lythe in the gentle rapids of a rushing stream. When the dancing light stilled, Pyrà, Mattilde and I all spoke at once.

"Gran!"

We each called out the same name. We each saw something different. Someone different. And we were each right, even as we were all wrong. The figure now standing solidly before us in a glowing halo was not my grandmother, any more than it was Mattilde's or Pyrà's. Nor was it Rykka, the mystical forebear that Hara'q was convinced he saw.

"Beneficia is correct," she said. "He *will* be back. Sooner than you can know and in ways you may not easily recognize. So I must speak quickly, for he will renew his power and I must be gone before he does."

She didn't step from the fire pit so much as glide from it, as though she passed over the smoothest of surfaces on the smoothest of wheels. She moved to each of us in turn, tapping the fourth finger of her left hand to every brow. As she did, a glow from her finger passed into each forehead. At least, that is how it appeared and felt to me. How it seemed to Hara'q who saw her not as human-like but as a horse,

I cannot say. Nor can I know what the others experienced when she touched them. For all we would share of our journey in the time ahead, Pyrà, Hara'q, Mattilde and I never once spoke of this.

All I knew was that when she pressed her finger to my forehead, an awareness of every happiness I had ever experienced raced through my heart and mind, not erasing any of the harsh times I had known or instigated but flooding them all with a halo of compassion. Never had I felt so loved…or forgiven. And there was much in my life for which I needed forgiveness, not least the bulk of my interactions with Mattilde and her grandmother. For the briefest of breaths, I felt the pain of that and of so much else, including the loss of the grandmother that this being so resembled. Then it passed, to be replaced by what I could only describe as an abiding sense of the perfection in all things in Prithi's world. Then, that feeling, too, dissipated as the being lifted her finger and moved to my right, to Pyrà.

"I am Flora Mìna," she said once she had touched us all. As she spoke, the solidity of her appearance melted back into the silvery luminescence that had replaced Ardoxx in the fire pit. Only her face remained, a face that at the same time seemed as youthful as a young girl and as ancient as the land itself. Her voice, no longer the voice of my grandmother, was like no voice I had ever heard, somehow both high-pitched and rumbling, both clear and smoky.

"I am neither human nor animal," she continued, "although I can take on the form of either, and the form I take is the one best-suited to those to whom I appear. What am I? I am the spirit of Flor. I live in the rich loam of her earth. I live in the life-giving sap of her trees. I live in the sweet nectar of her flowers. I live in the crystal waters of her lakes, rivers and streams. I live in every cloud that scuds across her skies. I live in the molten core of every flame that flickers on her land. I have been that and more since the time before time when, at Prithi's direction, Kumba molded Flor from the clay of creation."

As stunned as I was by my transformation — my second transformation — the effect of Flora Mìna's presence was so hypnotic that it was hard to be aware of anything else.

"Once," she continued, "my presence was felt in every heart that beat in Flor. In every heart, in every moment. Once upon a time." Her face faded back into light. "That was then. Now…" Her voice dropped to a whisper. "Now, the greed of man and sorcerer alike has robbed me of my essence and, with it, has stripped Flor of its soul."

Her eyes burned through the light and into me, and I felt a pain in my chest so searing I thought I would die…so searing I wanted to die. It was the pain of shame.

I covered my face. "It is my fault," I cried, "all my fault. I betrayed my home." I turned to Mattilde. "I betrayed you." I turned back to Flora Mìna. "I betrayed Flor. Now," I gasped between sobs, "it is too late. For me. For Flor. For all of us."

I gaped from Beneficia to Flora Mìna and back. Which was more startling? Beneficia's transformation from barely coherent child to a mature adult unlike any I had ever experienced from her? Or the fire's transformation to, first Ardoxx then Flora Mìna? I could barely take in what was being said, so stunned was I…until Flora Mìna turned the fullness of her attention on me.

"Do you know the story of Flor?" she asked, her voice and presence more solid than they had been since her first appearance.

She no longer resembled Gran. Instead, she stood tall and slender in a lustrous gown that cascaded in glistering layers to her ankles. Her feet were bare and, like all her skin, smooth and white as the finest linen. If, earlier, her fingers had been bare, now she wore rings on five of them — on the thumb and middle and little fingers of her right hand and on the index and fourth fingers of her left. As with the choker at her throat, the stones in each ring were crystal-like and shimmered subtly in rainbow hues. It was from her neck up, however, that she was the most arresting. She had neither nose nor ears, and her multicolored hair was slick against her skull. Her mouth, full and red, appeared only when she was speaking and to the person to whom she was speaking. And her eyes, as crystalline as her rings and choker, only appeared to the person on whom she was focused. Her appearance ought to have been unsettling. It was anything but. It was mesmerizing.

Now, when she spoke, no one and nothing else existed. "Do you?" she asked again. Her eyes sparkled.

I shook my head. I felt as though I should be able to say yes, but I couldn't. All I knew was that I had been born to serve she who ruled

Flor, as had my Gran and all the Mattildes before us. That had been the truth of my world until something destroyed Beneficia's reason. Now I knew nothing, of either Flor's present or its future.

"That is not so," she said and waited. When I said nothing, she turned her attention to Pyrà. "Ben," she said, or I assumed she did because once her focus diverted from me, I saw no mouth. The name seemed to emanate from her.

Pyrà's eyes lit up. He had shared something with me of this ancient king of his homeland, who I knew to be his favorite figure in history.

"Tell her," Flora Mìna said.

Pyrà hesitated, unsure what it was he was to tell me. Then he nodded in sudden knowingness. "We are all bards," he said, taking my hand. "You too."

I shook my head once more. "I know nothing of storytelling."

"That is not so." Again, Flora Mìna directed her remarks to me. "But—"

"In the same way I embody the spirit of Flor," she said, "you embody its story. Its story and its history. Beneficia knows this, although she does not remember that she knows it. You know it as well, even if you, too, do not remember that you know it. You will rediscover it in the telling, and in the telling will you begin to know your destiny…to know it again for the first time."

My heart pounded so hard I feared it would explode out of me. I could barely breathe. I felt the others' eyes on me, yet I did not dare turn my head. Only by staring fixedly at Flora Mìna could I hope to hold the world steady. But the world refused to hold steady. It spun and somersaulted around me…faster, faster, faster…until I was certain I would throw up.

Then, without warning, it stopped. The spinning…the world… everything. Flora Mìna was gone. Pyrà and Hara'q were gone. T'tammo and Sajàno were gone. And Beneficia…?

All I could see was blackness, then…nothing.

Voices. Strange voices. Hovering over me. Too close. I want to tell them to be quiet. No, I want to tell them to go away. Yet although I feel my jaw moving and my mouth forming words, no sound emerges.

I clutch at my throat, trying to squeeze the words out. Nothing.

Nor do I see anything or anyone. Yet someone is here. I know it. And there is a somewhere here. I know that, too.

"Breathe." I hear the voice as though it echoes at me from some distant void; a husky voice…neither young nor old, neither male nor female. And I do. I breathe, suddenly realizing that I haven't been, that I have been holding my breath for so long that my chest is on fire.

As I do, as I breathe, the blackness dissipates, dissolving into swirling, fog-like tendrils that dance out of existence, revealing a scene so achingly familiar that it is all I can do to continue breathing: Gran and me, the day she died.

Gran lies pale and gaunt, her cheekbones jutting sharply from her face, her lips pressed together against the pain, her fist closed loosely over her bokka stone. Beneficia has refused us any of her innumerable physicians and healers. Nor has she permitted any from nearby villages to attend. It is she who would have to pay, and she will not. "She is dying," the un-beneficent Lady of the castle says. "Why waste gold on a woman will be dead by nightfall?" she asked coolly when I entreated her earlier this day.

In the end, Beneficia is correct. Gran's life light will extinguish with the last light of day. Mercifully, this vision spares me that horror. In its place, the misty threads return, this time accompanied by strobe-like flashes of white light.

When they clear, the scene is of a different chamber at a different time. It must be a different time. Or perhaps it is an imaginary one, for as I peer into the council chamber of Castle Flor, it is not Beneficia's face that gazes toward me from its throne-like High Seat, it is mine…an older version of mine. Or perhaps it is a younger version of Gran. Whoever it is stares directly at me, as though she not only sees me but is acknowledging me.

That instant of acknowledgment is fleeting, for in the next the chamber doors are flung open and a man who so resembles Ardoxx that he must be kin stalks past the sentries, not stopping until his face is nearly nose-to-nose with whoever it is that occupies the High Seat. Whoever it is, she does not flinch.

"And?" he snarls. "Have you changed your mind?"

Now I know the woman to be neither me nor Gran, because I know the man cannot be Ardoxx.

"You will not have Flor," she says. "Nor will I betray my cousins in Q'ntana."

Perhaps it is a trick of the light and shadow in the council chamber, or a trick of his sorcery, but he seems to grow taller, looming over her menacingly. "You will regret this, Mattilde. You and all who follow you." He grows taller still, and it is as though his darkness envelops not only the woman and not only the council chamber but all Flor.

Mattilde rises from the High Seat and her presence matches his. "Do your worst, but I repeat: You will not have Flor. However deep and however long your enchantment, it will not last. It cannot. Your sorcery cannot match the power of this land. The power of this land is eternal. Your sorcery is not. Should you not live to know this, your son will. Should he not live to know this, his son will."

With this last, it feels as though she speaks it as much to me as to the sorcerer, as though she stares through him in her time directly to me in mine. Even as I am barely conscious of my body, I feel a shiver run through me. I raise my eyes to hers and nod in affirmation.

"Very well, then," she says, tugging at the bell pull by her side.

Almost immediately, a Beneficia unlike any I have known enters the chamber. She is no different in countenance than the various iterations I have experienced in recent days. She could, in fact, be this Beneficia's twin, just as this Mattilde could be Gran's and this sorcerer, Ardoxx's. It is her demeanor that is different: modest, humble, courteous and obliging.

"Ma'am?" she asks, curtsying.

"The sorcerer has gifts for us," she replies, no trace of irony in her tone.

"For me, ma'am?"

"So it would seem."

The sorcerer ignores the serving girl. "I give you one final chance," he says to Mattilde. "The choice is yours."

"No," she says, "the choice is yours. I pray you make the right one." She speaks evenly and, again, seems to be directing her words as much toward me as toward him. I know what she is asking, and part of me longs to refuse, longs to force time back in on itself. I never imagined I would yearn for the daily drudgery of my former life. Yet in this moment I do. In this moment, the certainty of that simple slavery must be preferable to a destiny that presses itself so forcefully upon me. For in this moment, I know not only what is to happen next but what is mine to do about it.

"I pray you make the right choice," Mattilde repeats, her focus returning to the sorcerer, who, if he is aware of my 'presence,' is unconcerned by it. "Not for me, but for yourself."

"You are a fool," he growls.

"As are we all who walk the path Prithi has laid for us."

"Enough!" he roars. He levels one outstretched hand at Mattilde, the other at Beneficia. Sparks explode from his spear-like fingernails. Beneficia shrinks back until the sorcerer glares at her with a look so fierce she cannot move any farther. Mattilde, her face calm and composed, settles back into the High Seat,

her fist closed loosely over something I cannot see, even as I know, barely believing it to be true, what it is.

It is midday, yet light has fled not only the council chamber but the world beyond its windows, the sparks flying from the sorcerer's fingernails the only illumination, illumination that blinks rhythmically, revealing the scene in a series of jerkily static images.

First, the sparks flashing from his left hand wheel around Beneficia in an ever-tightening circle. Her mouth is frozen in a silent scream. Then, those from his right hand coil around Mattilde, who, if not unaware of the proceedings, appears unperturbed by them. Her eyelids flutter shut as her mouth turns up into the faintest of smiles.

Enraged, the sorcerer shrieks a guttural incantation. The sparks flash more intensely. The ground rumbles and heaves. An explosive thunderclap convulses the chamber as a blaze of brilliant green phosphorescence surges between the two women. Beneficia screams, then faints. Mattilde seems to have stopped breathing. My heart batters so boomingly against my chest that I fear it will burst from my body.

The sorcerer is screaming another incantation. Or is it the same one and he never stopped? How can I know when everything around me is spinning, spiraling so rapidly that my stomach heaves? To stop the reeling, I clench my fists to my side and squeeze my eyes shut. It doesn't help. It hardly seems possible, but it is more dizzying this way. Yet I daren't open my eyes or unclench my fists.

Someone is moaning, keening so piteously that I cannot bear to see what terrors have befallen him. Now, something grabs on to me, hugs me tightly. Too tightly. I gasp for breath. I can't breathe. I—

The mournful wail was mine. I had witnessed more than Mattilde's nightmare, I had experienced one of my own. As the sorcery had transformed Lady into serving girl and serving girl into Lady, it had also set in motion the slaughter of Bryn Doon's mares, the enslavement of its stallions and, ultimately, the subjugation of Q'ntana. I now knew the Great Enchantment to have been more venal than I could have imagined, for it had cursed not only my world but Mattilde's and Beneficia's. What other horrors might it have inflicted, and where? It did not bear thinking about.

For all my anguish, Mattilde's must have been deeper. I already knew much of my history; her revelation merely added to it. For Mattilde, though, *everything* she had assumed to be true about herself, her homeland and her heritage had been obliterated. I forced water down her throat though my hands were shaking.

"Here, let me." Beneficia gently prised my fingers from the water skin and tended to Mattilde, who seemed to be caught between our time and her vision of that other, long-ago one. Her eyes were open but a slit, and her fists were still tightly clenched.

I would have expected this to jolt Beneficia as dramatically as it had Mattilde, for her history and identity had been as radically recast. Strangely, it did not. Not immediately. Instead, it was as though the vision had freed her, and she fell easily into a role that was neither Lady nor serving girl but companion, an unexpected equal on an unanticipated journey.

However, once she had settled Mattilde by getting her to lie down with a wet cloth across her brow, her composure shattered. "I didn't know," she whispered. "Not any of it." She wrung her hands nervously and would meet neither my eyes nor Pyrà's.

Did I believe her? I did not disbelieve her, yet that was not the same as trusting her. She had undergone too many transformations in too short a time for me to feel sure of her. Apparently, she was no longer childlike and helpless. Had that been an act all along? Was this new persona an act as well? And what would Mattilde's attitude toward her former mistress now be?

I felt for the leather pouch that held my bokka, hoping the stone would answer some of these questions and tell me what to do — about Mattilde's revelations…about Beneficia's latest incarnation and whether she was still to accompany us…about how we were to find our way to Bryn Doon. Had it any guidance to offer, other than that it was not yet time to divulge its existence, it was not ready to share it.

I wondered if Pyrà was having more luck with his stone as he rolled it between his palms. The blank look on his face suggested not.

As the four of us silently pondered the night's discoveries and their implications for each of us, the faintest of glimmerings of light threaded up from the eastern and western horizons, heralding another day…another day with no clear direction.

After a second fogging-up episode that dragged on for too many days, the sorcerer's scrying stone has cleared and the travelers and their horses are again visible. Alas for the sorcerer, they are not visible to him. Frustrated by his inability to use his stone to track his prey, the sorcerer has journeyed to the neighboring kingdom of Grykk, ancestral home of the kings Fvorag and Gravel who, once upon a time with the assistance of his Great Enchantment and the support of Bo'Ra K'n, conquered and subjugated Q'ntana. Unfortunately, the last of the Fvorags was defeated, Gravel was humiliated, Bo'Ra K'n is no more and Q'ntana is now sovereign and free.

This makes Grykk the perfect ally, for Grykk is neither sovereign nor free. More accurately, the only Grykkan who is sovereign and free is its young ruler, Yali'Fà, who has inherited not only this tiny landlocked kingdom but generations of bitterness toward anyone and everything connected with Q'ntana, including its onetime nemesis, Bo'Ra K'n, the treacherous dream-walker who betrayed Grykk.

The sorcerer knows the evil forces that such bitterness can unleash. He knows, too, how to channel and manipulate those forces for his purposes. So he has come to Grykk to flatter and cajole Yali'Fà into proposing the very plan that he has already begun to implement unilaterally: the capture of the warrior stallions of Bryn Doon and the conquest of Q'ntana and Flor. If sorcery alone cannot achieve his aims, the sorcerer will follow Bo'Ra K'n's example and employ a foolish puppet to assist him. Once these kingdoms fall, the region's remaining lands will tumble one after the next until the sorcerer's suzerainty will surpass anything dreamt of by his rivals.

The sorcerer will erupt into a rage upon his return when, too late to intercept them, he learns that the travelers are making their way to Castle Flor. His fury will gain more force when he learns how and why.

By then, it will be too late.

BOKKA

thirty-eight

Pyrà

The late-afternoon suns blazed down on us, a pair of fiery spheres that offered no mercy on travelers weary from three days' climbing. When we had finally departed our campsite after Mattilde's vision, we'd had two choices, continue up the craggy road that had carried us there or retrace our steps. With no Baq'shì to guide us, we had opted to keep moving forward. Had that been the wrong choice? We now stood at a dead end: The ever-steepening road had petered out at the narrow apex of an escarpment that plunged heart-stoppingly to a forested valley dotted with the occasional plume of chimney smoke.

What I wouldn't have given for the shade of one of those trees and for the chill air suggested by the hearth fires. But even Hara'q, the most sure-footed of us, could see no way down the precipice. "We are going to have to return the way we came," he muttered after crouching on his hands and knees to scrutinize every sliver of rocky ledge, as if such close study could reveal some otherwise hidden route.

"I can't," Beneficia wheezed. As Flor's ruler, she had eaten well and rarely exerted herself. The result was a rotund frame perfectly adapted to sitting still and ordering people about, not to scaling near-perpendicular roads in scorching heat…nor to climbing back down them. Although she never uttered a word of complaint, her face had grown redder and redder until it now resembled nothing more than a giant bela nut, and her breath rasped out in staccato bursts.

"Unless…" Hara'q murmured.

"Unless what?" I asked. "If you have an idea, *any* idea, now is the time to share it." I tilted my head toward Beneficia. Eyes open barely a slit, she half-reclined against Mattilde, who was trying to get her to drink some of our depleting supply of water. "She needs a miracle. We all do."

If the air was oven-hot now, it would be numbingly raw once the suns set. We had barely managed to keep warm the previous three nights. A fourth might kill all of us, not only Beneficia.

Hara'q bent his head, eyes shut, as if in prayer. Then he pulled a pouch of smooth taupe hide from his pocket and removed from it a bokka stone. He set the stone on his palm where it glinted in the suns-light.

"You? You have one too?" Mattilde exclaimed. She retrieved hers, as did I.

Now, *three* of us carried bokka stones? What could it signify?

Beneficia pushed herself to sitting, her eyes now open wide. "Let me see," she croaked, motioning us to her, "all of them."

Reluctantly, Hara'q placed his stone on the ground in front of Beneficia. Mattilde and I laid ours next to it. Beneficia studied them then shuffled them into various configurations, inspecting each before again repositioning them. "There," she pronounced when she had arranged them so that Hara'q's and mine fit together. Strangely, Mattilde's no longer linked with mine. Instead, it sat apart. Yet even with a space on either side of hers, it was clear that, together, the stones formed three points of a five-pointed star.

"What does it mean?" Mattilde asked.

"That we have to find the two stones that complete the star," I said.

"I may have one of them," Beneficia whispered.

"Where?" the rest of us shouted in unison.

"Castle Flor," she replied, "if it is still there."

"The stone?" Mattilde asked.

"The castle."

Even should we somehow make it to Castle Flor, I knew the chances of finding my bokka in the rubbled remains of my former home were so slim as to be negligible. If we did find it and mine proved to be one of the bokka-star's missing points, and there was no guarantee that it was, I was fairly certain who had the other. The chances of getting it from him were slimmer still.

As for my bokka stone, it had intrigued me as a child, both for the unusual manner in which it had come into my possession and for the fact that it shimmered like no stone I had ever seen. Yet, I quickly grew bored with it; precious gems were considerably more captivating, especially when fashioned into jewelry so stunning as to make others of my sex sick with envy. Now it made me sick, and not with envy, to reflect on the cruel, selfish person I had so recently been.

The three stones still sat where I had arranged them, staring up at me accusingly, as though they were living, sentient beings, not merely chunks of rock…as though my carelessness with their kin had betrayed them. I shut my eyes against their indictment. Still, I felt shame.

"Beneficia." Mattilde's voice, gentle and caring. "Are you all right?" Then the touch of her hand, equally tender, on my arm. My eyes filled with tears. I deserved none of this. If only I could erase who I had been, especially to Mattilde. If only I could be sure to find my bokka stone…and the other one.

"Your story." This voice belonged to none of my companions. It was deep and gravelly, and it felt more like a rumble in my chest than a sound in my ears. "Your story," it repeated. "*It* is the key."

"The key to what?" I asked, opening my eyes.

"What key?" Hara'q barked.

I ignored him and touched the emptiness between Mattilde's stone and his. The stones' gaze seemed somehow to have softened. Or perhaps I imagined it as I had imagined the voice. I must have imagined it, all of it, unless I was losing my mind. Again.

Yet I knew I hadn't. The stones *were* speaking to me.

My story? Which story? The story of my bokka stone, of course. Have I the courage to revisit it? If I do, have I the courage to share it?

"Do you choose to keep silent?" The stones again. "Do you choose to remain in this spot and die? That will surely happen should you keep silent. Do you choose to let the others die with you? Are you still that selfish?"

Another voice, higher pitched than the first and seeming to come not from within me but from a distance away — and not merely a physical distance: "Do you choose to abandon me? Do you choose to abandon yourself?"

Now, the two voices in unison: "Do you choose to let Ardoxx win?"

I swallowed hard and reached for the stones. Hara'q tried to stop me, but Pyrà nudged his hand away. I cupped the three stones in my right hand and covered them with my left. A shudder shivered through me, so sharply that I could not breathe and I feared I would faint. Then it passed, and I no longer sat with Mattilde, Pyrà and Hara'q at the edge of a sheer cliff. I stood in the Flor market, a girl barely old enough to be out unsupervised.

It is market day, and the broad plain beyond the castle teems with people. Market day at Castle Flor happens only on the morning of every second new moon and it is the largest, most important market in the land. As such, sellers and buyers gather here from Flor and beyond, some more peculiar-looking or peculiarly dressed, or both, than any beings I have ever seen.

Some of the produce that fills the stalls is no less strange, with shapes, colors and sizes that leave me wondering what these fruits and vegetables, if that is what they are, might taste like. There are also more familiar offerings: bela, piila and tokku, kiribà, thomé and sascha. And my favorite: zzyzzyby cheese, which we rarely get at home. Mother calls it "peasant food," and she has Cook beaten every time he sneaks it up to my room. It isn't only fruit, vegetables and dairy products here. The air is redolent with the mouthwatering aromas of fresh-baked breads and tarts, something else I don't see unless Mother is away, which is not often.

If I had coins, I would buy a hunk of zzyzzyby. But I am not supposed to be here. That's because I am not allowed to leave the castle without Mother or Areya. Areya mostly, because Mother hardly ever takes me anywhere. I only got out this morning because Mother dismissed Areya, right at the breakfast table. The dismissal was not unusual; she dismisses all my tutors and governesses. In fact, Areya lasted longer than most. Some, like poor Monayka, don't make it through a single day. Areya managed to escape Mother's wrath through four full moons. At least Mother didn't have her put to death as she did with Homba.

I think Mother was a little intimidated by Areya, not that she would ever admit it. I know that Areya was the only one of my minders who ever stood up to her. When she did, it was a formidable sight. Areya stood two heads taller and a half a body wider than Mother and refused to be cowed by her. This morning, she refused to be fired. In the ensuing battle, insults weren't the only things hurled between them. I crept out when the first piece of crockery smashed against Mother's favorite tapestry and barely cooked egg yolks oozed down the no-longer flattering representation of her outfitted in her ceremonial regalia.

I hope the Great Flor doesn't strike me dead for thinking this, but I would not be unhappy if they killed each other. Then I would be the Lady of Flor and I could eat what I want and do what I want.

"What is it you would do?" a soft voice behind me asks. It is a young woman's voice, and when I turn my head, I see a stall I had not noticed before, which surprises me because I am certain I have passed every market stall here at least twice today.

There is no food at this stall, and the woman who stands between it and me is unlike any vendor. For one, she is young, too young to be a farmer's wife, and she is strikingly beautiful, neither weather-beaten from working the fields nor beaten down by the arduous life chiseled on so many faces. Buyers and vendors alike flock to the Flor market not because they want to but because there is nowhere else to trade what they produce for what they need. With few exceptions, their faces are hard and unsmiling.

This woman's face is neither. It is smooth and sensuous. And if she doesn't smile, nor does she frown. She stands nearly as tall as Areya but is slender, with snow-white skin and long raven hair that is braided into a crown and threaded with strands of scarlet silk. She is what I imagine a goddess would look like and maybe she is one, for when she speaks again her voice, soft though it is, not only rises above the market hubbub but carries a fearsome strength and power.

"What is it you would do?" she asks again, beckoning me to her stall.

"I-I—," I stammer, shaking my head. She scares me, though less than she fascinates me. I edge toward her.

"You know, my dear," she says in a soothing tone that I cannot help but trust, "even if you do not know you know."

I nod, not certain I understand.

Next I know, I am inside her stall with no memory of how I got there. It must be her stall. What else could it be? But I am so deeply inside something that oughtn't be this deep that the market commotion is little more than a distant hum, and the stall's opening is so far off that it is as though I view it through the wrong end of a spyglass.

Am I dreaming? I know from what happens next that I cannot be. Yet nothing about this woman and her stall seems real.

Now, I sit in a deep cushiony seat drinking a honeyed mead from a tall, pearlescent goblet. The goblet is stone and shimmers as I hold it up to the light, although it is not clear where the light is coming from, for neither lamp nor fire illuminate this place. At the same time, it is suffused in an incandescence brilliant as the suns' yet soft as the moon's.

When I have swallowed the final drop, the woman takes the goblet from my hands, holds it over her head to the mysterious source of the mysterious light, and in a voice sweeter than any I have ever heard, sings these words in a language I do not recognize but somehow understand.

Ah'hay eeyama mana'ya ki-hay

Ko'lama ma'nayo ee'ya

Ko-hay mana'ya ma-nay

On the final syllable, all light from this stall-chamber plunges into the goblet, which grows so blindingly bright that I can no longer make out the goblet's shape. Or maybe the goblet no longer has a shape. All I know is that when the light finally dissipates, the woman is holding an irregularly shaped stone.

"Do you know what 'bokka' means?" she asks as she presses it into my palm.

I shake my head.

"Destiny. Your destiny is bound up in this bokka stone, and its destiny is bound up in you. You sealed your destiny when you drank the Om Wamsa that was steeped in the bokka in its goblet form. Remember this moment, and when you are the Lady of Flor, you will know what this stone means and what to do with it. Until then—" she closes my fingers over it, "keep it safe and tell no one in the castle about it."

Next I know, I wake in my own bed, clutching the bokka stone and remembering every detail of what I know cannot have been a dream. I now know the woman's name, something I did not know when we were together: Ina Lei.

I hide the bokka behind a loose stone in the wall of my bedchamber. It is where I hide all my treasures.

Five moons later, Mother dies in a mishap as sudden as it is bizarre: She trips on the train of her favorite gown, pitches onto the floor and is dead the instant her head strikes the stone. In that same instant, I become the Lady of Flor and all memory of goddesses, stones, dreams and destinies dissolves.

Until now.

he low growl of distant thunder rumbles nearer, convulsing the earth as it sweeps through Flor with a single destination: an alpine escarpment that soars up from a densely forested valley. Near the rim of the smooth, upward-sloping shelf that crowns the escarpment, two men and two women cling to each other to prevent the trembling earth from pitching them over the edge. Two black stallions, more sure-footed than any humans, appear unconcerned by the tremors.

Even were there somewhere for them to flee, there is no way to flee, for there is nothing around or beneath them that does not groan and quake. And when the ground splits in an irregular-seeming pattern around the company, the rift widening until even the horses would refuse to leap over it, the two men and two women huddle together with alarm in their eyes.

The pattern seems irregular, but only at eye level. The verro circling high overhead, too high for the humans to see, even were they not focused on their perceived peril, discerns the rough outline of a five-pointed star and immediately recognizes its significance. Screeching loudly, but not loudly enough to be heard over the earth's rending, the verro returns whence it came.

The older of the two women clutches three pearlescent stones in her right hand, more concerned for their safety than for her own. Somehow, she is certain, the stones will save them. Though reluctant to trust her certainty, what choice does she have? She clenches her fist around them more tightly, so tightly that they seem to merge not only with her hand but with her whole body.

In that instant, she knows what is to be done.

She opens her fist to the three stones, which catch the light of both suns and flash brilliantly. With her left hand, she grabs onto the right hand of each of her companions and presses those hands onto hers, onto the stones, onto their stones.

First, the bard, then the horse man, then the serving-girl-turned-Lady.

The stones, warmed by her hands and warmed yet more by the suns, blaze searingly in the four-hands-as-one. Yet no one pulls free. Instead, they layer left hands upon right and breathe into the pain.

The rock beneath them shudders, rolls and teeters. Then in a single motion lurches free from the surrounding ground and plummets out of view.

The sorcerer, only now returned to his scrying stone, catches only the quickest flash of a glimpse as humans and horses disappear into the earth. Enraged, he slams his fist into the stone.

For any ordinary mortal, this act of fury would shatter hand and wrist.

The sorcerer is mortal, but no ordinary one. Neither hand nor wrist suffer any injury. Not so the scrying stone.

With a piercing, almost-human wail, the stone shatters into dust at the sorcerer's feet. His wrath further inflamed, the sorcerer storms out into the forest. Behind him, the tower implodes into a heap of rubble. Ahead of him, every tree in his path bursts into flame.

Overhead and unseen, the verro watches and follows.

Was I dreaming? If I was, it was like no dream I had ever dreamed. For one, my eyes were open and I was fully aware of all that had conveyed me to this moment: the lightning storms, the earth tremors that had destroyed our village, the descent down that endless stairway under the Dôma, my vision of Pyrà, my sighting of Na'an and this gauzy, colorless space that was more no-place than place.

If it was not a dream, were we under an enchantment? If so, to what purpose? Were we meant to be as weighted with inertia as we appeared? Every one of the villagers who had descended that staircase with me was here, each looking as dazed and bewildered as I felt. That was not entirely true. None seemed fully awake or capable of speaking, yet I felt more in possession of my faculties than I had since my first awareness of being here. And I could speak, couldn't I? Hadn't I spoken to Na'an? Hadn't I previously tried to engage my neighbors in conversation? Or had that been the dream?

I shook my head. This was too confusing.

I opened my mouth. "Falla," I croaked to my nearest neighbor, who had also been my closest neighbor in our village. She didn't react. My voice felt strained, as though I had not spoken in days and was struggling to make a sound. Maybe she hadn't heard me. "Falla?" I did my best to raise my voice, but it still sounded low and raspy. Falla blinked but stared straight ahead, as if in a trance.

"Na'an," I called out, or tried to. "Please, Na'an. If you are here, show yourself. Tell me why we are here, wherever that is. Tell me what you want of us, what you want of me." What there was of my voice caught in my throat. "Tell me about my son. Tell me he is safe."

Jeryn, curled in sleep on my lap, whimpered. Her eyelids fluttered.

I touched my fingers to my lips and rested them on her cheek. "What do you see, little one?" I whispered. "What do you hear? Has Na'an come to you?" She jerked her head, tilting and pointing it past me, as though she saw something through her closed eyes. I peered over my shoulder but saw nothing.

"Ask her," I pleaded. "Ask her for us."

I was certain we were going to die. How could we not? The mountain had opened up and swallowed us, and we now hurtled to our doom. Was one of my nightmares about to come true? Was *this* my destiny? What else could be happening?

Someone screamed. Was it me? Or was it one of the others? Or maybe it was the high-pitched whistle our rocky platform made as it plunged down and down and down and down to…to what?

I squeezed my eyes shut and held my breath, waiting for the inevitable crash that would slam us into the earth and smash us apart. The crash never came. Instead, the whistling stopped and so did we, not with bone-shattering abruptness but as gently as a feather settling onto a grassy verge.

I opened my eyes to find us exactly as we had been — was it only moments ago? — not in some cave deep inside the cliff and not in the verdant valley at its base, but in a suns-lit forest clearing next to a scattering of rocky rubble. Directly in front of us, a blackened path of scorched tree stumps pointed north in an arrow-straight line.

Perched atop the nearest stump was a verro. It flapped its wings, shot into the air, pitched back down, circled us and landed on T'tammo's back. Ignoring it, the horse stepped off the rocky slab and started nibbling on the wildflowers that carpeted the clearing. Sajàno followed.

"What took you so long?" the verro croaked in a guttural growl.

Hara'q leapt to his feet and swatted at the bird. "I told you what I would do to you if you returned."

"It isn't Bàq'sha," Pyrà whispered. "Or Baq'shì."

The verro ignored them both. "If you don't get a move on," he squawked, hopping from T'tammo's back to Sajàno's, "he'll get there before you and it'll all be over." He flapped his wings in Hara'q's face. "For all of you."

"Who are you?" Pyrà asked.

"Why should we trust you?" Hara'q added.

The verro slapped Hara'q with one of his wings, then dropped to the ground in front of Pyrà. "You either trust or you do not," he croaked. He raised himself until his ice-blue eyes were level with Pyrà's and stared unblinkingly into his. "I'm waiting."

"There is no halfway in between," Pyrà said, finally, in barely a whisper.

"*Braawk!*" The verro did a little dance as the rest of us gaped in confusion from Pyrà to the bird and back. Confusion shifted into astonishment when the verro's physical form melted into a wavery swirl of black that transformed first into a massive, single-eyed, tawny-haired creature, its wings broad enough to enfold us all, then into a fiery-plumed bird diminutive enough to perch on Hara'q's head. "*Braawk,*" he screeched again as he took on his previous verro form.

"Tashek?" Pyrà leaned into the bird.

Tashek winked and bobbed its head. "At your service, young bard."

"B-but," he stammered.

"All stories are real," he said in a voice that possessed neither gender nor timbre. It was a familiar voice, even as I was certain I had never heard it.

"H-he—" Pyrà turned to us, his finger stabbing at the bird. "The MoonQuest— Toshar— O'ric— M'nor? What—?"

"No time no time no time," Tashek shrieked, hopping from one foot to the other. "Trust. *Braawk!*" He spread his wings as if to take off, then must have had second thoughts, for he folded them back and stared so intensely that his body faded until all we saw were two ovals of icy blue that darted from me to Pyrà to Hara'q, finally settling on Beneficia.

"Bokka," he said to her, and his beak reappeared in time to peck lightly at her fist. She opened it to reveal the three stones. With his right claw, which now also rematerialized, he picked each up and dropped it in front of its owner.

"You have three," he continued, as the rest of his body re-formed in seemingly random sequence. "There are five."

"We know," Hara'q muttered.

"Indeed?"

"If we hadn't fallen through the mountain, we would already have been on our way to the fourth." Hara'q nodded at Beneficia. "At Castle Flor."

"Indeed?" Tashek tilted his head at Hara'q. "How?"

"I…uh— We…uh…"

"Indeed." He harrumphed. "*Now* you are on your way. Then, you were not. Then…" He straightened his head. "Then, you were stuck. Now…" He stared along the path created by the scorched tree stumps. "Now you are not."

"Can you take us to Castle Flor?" Pyrà asked.

Tashek shook his head.

"What use—" Hara'q began but stopped when Tashek glared at him.

"Can you help us find the fifth stone?" Pyrà asked.

"I could tell you who has it and why you need all five. But if I did, you would not need to trust. And trust you must."

"Trust?" I asked, speaking for the first time since we "landed" here. "In what?"

"Ah, Mattilde," Tashek crooned. "Trust the youngest to ask the wisest question."

I dropped my eyes. Was he mocking me?

"Why, in the story, of course."

Now I was certain he was mocking me.

"Here is what I can tell you of the story. The rest you must discover on your own, as you live it." He was speaking to all of us but seemed especially focused on Pyrà.

"First, only once the five bokka stones are reunited in the Star of Bryn Doon will it be possible for the story to complete…will it be possible for each of you to meet your destiny and find your rightful place." He extended a claw toward Pyrà's cloak and both T'tammo and Sajàno whickered, nodding their heads. "And for all the stallions to return safely home."

"We know where to find the fourth," Pyrà said.

"Maybe," Hara'q grumbled.

"Who has the fifth?"

Tashek poked Beneficia. "You know, don't you."

She nodded but could not meet his gaze.

"Well?"

"Ardoxx," she whispered.

forty-two

Pyrà

Although Beneficia was the only one among us who knew the way from the ruins of Ardoxx's tower to Castle Flor, we would not need her to guide us. The unbending line of burnt-out trees was more direct than any route she knew. Nor did we need Tashek to tell us that Ardoxx had carved out that path of destruction as the quickest way to the castle. Clearly, he was determined to find Beneficia's bokka stone before we did. Between his head start and his sorcery, he probably would. What chance did we have?

"Bokka," Tashek croaked in response to my silent despair. "Bokka bokka bokka. Bokka three."

"What does he mean?" Hara'q grumbled. "He is as bad as Fay'dor."

"Braawk!" Tashek screeched in his face. "Bokka three." He pecked at each stone in turn. "Bokka three brought you here. Bokka three will make bokka four and bokka five, if you let them…if you listen and *trust*. If you listen and trust, bokka five will unlock destinies four… and more."

With that, he bobbed his head and, piece by piece, faded from view. First his legs and body dissolved, then his wings, then his beak. The last to go were his eyes, which stared at me for what seemed forever, then blinked into nothingness.

*　　*　　*

Whatever shreds of reassurance Tashek's cryptic message had offered us dissolved as we followed Ardoxx's trail through the woods. The only evidence of the fire that had forged the trail were blackened tree stumps — all cold to the touch, which told us that Ardoxx was well ahead and might have already found Beneficia's bokka stone.

If he had, it could only have been through sorcery, we realized once we reached the edge of the woods and scanned the vast field of rocky rubble that had once been Castle Flor. Not a single wall stood, and nothing about the castle's layout was recognizable to either Beneficia or Mattilde, who gaped at the ruins in disbelief. Mattilde had fled in the dark before the stormwaters had caused serious damage, and Beneficia had wandered off without most of her senses, so she had never fully grasped the scale and scope of the destruction. Only a single chimney remained standing, but not for long. When a pair of twisted-necked vootahs lit on it, it teetered under their weight and collapsed in a cloud of dust, sending the giant birds off in caterwauling fury. Even the moat was now little more than a shallow, rock-filled trough.

"How will I ever find my bokka stone in…in *this*?" Beneficia fought back tears.

Mattilde squeezed Beneficia's hand. "Our bokka stones will find yours, if we let them," she said in a trembling voice that suggested she needed as much convincing as did Beneficia. "Isn't that what the Tashek bird, or whatever it was, said?"

"It's my fault." Beneficia pulled her hand free and covered her face. "I-I should have kept it safe, like she told me to."

"That's what you did," I said, "when you hid it with your other treasures. It's still safe," I added, forcing a smile.

"Too safe," Hara'q muttered.

The sorcerer's rage has not abated. If anything, it has multiplied manyfold. For all his powers, and they are fearsome, he has been unable to find that woman's bokka stone. No spell, chant or incantation has forced it out of its hiding place. Nor did his ultimatum succeed in getting it to reveal itself. For all his threats to pulverize the castle rubble into dust and the bokka stone with it, he knew he was powerless in that regard. The stone knew it as well.

When intimidation failed, he tried persuasion and, as unconvincing as it was, even to him, charm. He asserted that only he could reunite the stone with its companions, that only he possessed the wisdom to correctly employ them. He argued on behalf of the stone in his possession, the one he clutched in his fist.

It was to no avail. If a bokka stone refuses to be found, its magic will ensure that it remains hidden. Although the bokka's magic is no more powerful than his, it is a match for his. He will have to allow the bard, the horse man, the former Lady and the new Lady to collect it, if it allows itself to be collected by them, then seize it from them, along with their stones.

He knows it to be a risk. With four stones in their possession, the consolidated power of the travelers will be formidable...but only if they know it to be so. He will have to act swiftly.

The sorcerer uncurls his fist and curls his lip. That such a small stone can be the key to so much... It is unnatural. Yet he has lived long enough to know that what appears to have the least significance often proves to have the most.

That he fails in the moment to associate that knowingness with the four travelers does not bode well for him.

forty-three

Hara'q

As soon as I set eyes on what remained of Castle Flor, I feared our mission to be hopeless. Even if Beneficia could locate her childhood bedchamber, finding a small stone buried among its wreckage would surely prove impossible. Worse, the force of the explosion had not only flung ceilings, walls, floors and furnishings far from their original location, it had smashed them into unrecognizable shapes.

Still, we searched, shredding our clothes and scraping our skin as we scrabbled through the ruins. Because the risk of injury was so high, Pyrà had wanted us to stay together or at least work in pairs. In my view, however, the scale of the undertaking was too great for that. Ardoxx could return at any time. And who knew what other dangers awaited us? I argued that our only chance of success, as low as it already was, depended on us spreading out.

For once, Beneficia took my side, and that convinced Mattilde. Pyrà reluctantly agreed.

"You have the best chance of any of us," he said to me as we separated.

"You mean Beneficia does."

"No, you." He pulled his stone from his pocket. "These come from Bryn Doon and Benq'a Baka'à. All of them. None of us does. Only you. We lack that connection. If anyone can find a bokka stone in this mess, it is you."

As it turned out, his confidence in my homing skills was misplaced. Either I possessed no such abilities or they had been dulled not only by the years but by the curse of my humanness. I found nothing. Nor did the others.

Perhaps the stone was choosing not to be found. Or perhaps Ardoxx had already used his sorcery to retrieve it. All we knew, when the suns slipped below the horizon and daylight faded, was that we had failed.

"I have let you down," Beneficia moaned. She dropped to the ground, sobbing. We had reconvened by a giant tabletop-like slab beyond the farthest chunk of castle debris. We had left T'tammo and Sajàno there while we searched, and they were nibbling contentedly at the grasses that fringed it when we returned.

Mattilde tried to comfort her, but we were all disappointed. As futile as the endeavor had seemed at the outset, we needed that stone. Ardoxx's too. Somehow.

"What do we do now?" Mattilde asked.

"Find someplace more sheltered for the night," I replied. "Back in the woods could be good."

"No! Not back there." Beneficia shook her head.

"Why not?"

"Ardoxx. Those are his woods. He always traveled to the castle through there." She shuddered.

You didn't mind him when you were Her Ladyship, I wanted to retort. But I said nothing. I had grown to trust Mattilde. Perhaps I would grow to trust her former mistress. Perhaps, though I doubted it.

Pyrà scanned the land beyond the castle. Behind us to the east, lay the Forest of Ardh. Due west, where Aygra's corona was dimming, lay undulating hills that faded into the purple haze of dusk. To the north, a serpentine stream meandered through rolling meadowlands. South of us, the Forest of Ardh thinned into flat farmland, where a single farmhouse and barn stood sketched against the horizon.

"You know this country," he said to Beneficia and Mattilde. "What do you think?"

Mattilde shrugged. "I was never permitted much beyond the moat…"

Beneficia reddened. "I-I—"

"That wasn't an accusation," Mattilde said. "It was a fact."

Beneficia nodded. "If we are trying to leave Flor, the River Mala is the best way, although it will not take us to Bryn Doon. I know no way to get there. It could be possible to go to Q'ntana first and find our way to Bryn Doon from there. But there is no easy way. Flor and Q'ntana have never been friendly—"

"Not 'never,'" I muttered.

Beneficia stared at me. "Truly?"

"It was long ago. It cannot matter now."

"It does matter." She rose to her feet. Beneficia was the shortest among us, yet in that moment, she carried herself like the tallest, most regal of queens — head erect, shoulders back, spine straight — and spoke with an air of authority I had not previously heard from her. "If we were friends and allies once," she declared, "we can be again."

"You are not the Lady of Flor anymore," I said, more harshly than I ought to have.

Beneficia's face turned scarlet and her shoulders slumped. "I mean," she mumbled, "I mean…"

Mattilde turned on me, her eyes aflame. "Was that necessary? Flor's past was crueler to me than it was to you." She draped an arm over Beneficia's shoulder. "If I can accept it — and her — then the rest is none of your business."

I said nothing. Better to remain silent than admit she was right.

Pyrà touched my arm. "The past is passed, we let it go," he said softly. "If it was true in The MoonQuest, it must be true still." I could not meet his eyes. How could one as young as he be wiser than one as old as I? But, then, I wasn't the Bard of Bryn Doon. He may not have known in his own mind what it meant to be that legendary figure. It didn't stop him from acting like it.

"I'm sorry." I took Mattilde's hand in one of mine and Beneficia's in the other. Mattilde gave hers grudgingly; Beneficia, gratefully.

"I cannot know what Flor's future is," Pyrà said, joining his hands to ours, "but it seems we are already friends and allies."

Beneficia squeezed my hand. To my surprise, I squeezed back.

"As long as we stop Ardoxx," Mattilde added, injecting a note of dark reality.

"And get his bokka stone," Beneficia said.

"And yours," I said, doing my best to keep my voice free of any accusatory tone.

Suddenly, Pyrà pulled his hands free. "What is it, T'tammo? What have you got there?"

The horse had stopped nibbling and was trying to jam his nose into the narrow opening under the lip of the stone slab. When he couldn't, he pulled his nose free and pawed at the ground. Pyrà crouched and peered inside, but it was too dark to see anything.

"Don't," I warned, but he had already pushed his hand in and was feeling around. When he pulled it out, he was holding a pearlescent stone that, miraculously free of dirt, glinted in the final light of day.

The sorcerer opens one eye, then the other. Something has changed. He surveys his bedchamber. It is nearly dark, but nothing in the room appears to be out of place. Slowly, he rises from his bed. It is not a "thing" that has shifted. It is the air itself. It feels less heavy, less under his control.

"The bokka," he cries and strides to the window. M'nor has risen and although it still hangs low in the sky, its glow has lit upon the pearlescent stone resting on the window ledge. The sorcerer grabs it before the moon can, not that it could…not under normal circumstances. But these are not normal circumstances. This night…this night something is different. He dare not risk it.

Then he knows, and all previous fits of temper pale next to this one. He storms from his bedchamber and out into the darkening night, casting a spell as he goes that transforms his nightshirt into a heavy cloak that so matches the colorlessness of the night that he could well be invisible.

Strands of moonlight filter through the trees, but the sorcerer requires no external illumination. As he steps outside, his eyes, otherwise steely silver, glow blood-red, projecting twin beams of eeriness into the night.

M'nor's incandescence is an annoying distraction on this journey. And as he marches through the forest toward the scattered remains of Castle Flor, he curses the long ago bard whose exploits reignited the moon's light and the new bard whose meddling is interfering with his plans.

When the sorcerer reaches the edge of the forest and surveys the field of rubble, he is certain. Even if his powers cannot tell him where the bokka stone was, he knows it is gone.

So be it. He raises his right hand level with his eyes, spreads his fingers and points them at the castle site. The bolts of lightning that shoot from his fingernails do more than pulverize the ruins into a field of fine dust. They transform the dust into disappearing sands.

Nothing will ever stand upon this cursed land again. And any who step onto it will sink into a gruesome death.

With that, the sorcerer turns and disappears back into the forest.

forty-four
Pyrà

Now that T'tammo had found Beneficia's stone for us, we deter-mined to put as much distance as we could between us and the castle ruins before it grew too dark to travel. Unspoken by all of us was a similar eagerness to get as far as possible from both the Forest of Ardh and Ardoxx.

Unfortunately, there was no way to avoid him permanently, not if we wanted to get our hands on his bokka stone. To accomplish that, we would need to find it before he found us and to somehow outwit him and neutralize his sorcery. That time would come soon enough. For now, our water skins needed topping up, we needed to bathe and T'tammo and Sajàno had been without water for too long. Hara'q expressed concern that the riverbank — flat, open and treeless as it was — was too unprotected to be safe. By then, though, it was nearly dark and M'nor had yet to rise. With not enough daylight remaining for us to find somewhere safer, he agreed that we ought to spend the night by the River Mala.

While the horses lapped thirstily from the river, where Mattilde and Beneficia were bathing, Hara'q and I laid out the bedrolls and our rapidly depleting provisions. As generously as he and I had been outfitted through the early days of our journey, our food supply had not been replenished once we left the barn. Since then, we had not managed to supplement it with much other than the occasional fruits and greens and rarer wild game. We were now four travelers not two, four *hungry* travelers, and I was not sure how much farther we could manage on the little we had left. We would have to trust that we would not be abandoned on this journey. Something would show up. It had to.

*   *   *

We had just finished our meager, moonlit dinner when the earth shuddered so violently that the otherwise placid river frothed and our normally unflappable horses reared. The trembling lasted only a moment, but the moment felt interminable.

"Ardoxx," Beneficia whispered. "It has to be."

None of us doubted the sorcerer's responsibility for the tremor. Nor did we doubt that, despite our best efforts to distance ourselves from him, he was perilously near.

With no wood for a fire, we huddled together — not merely to conserve heat on this chilly night but to help allay our apprehension. Ardoxx was on all our minds.

"What do we do if manage to get all five stones?" Beneficia asked.

"*When*," I corrected her with as much confidence as I could muster. "When we have all five stones."

"Yes," she agreed with more certainty than I felt, "when we have all five stones."

Recovering the fourth bokka had been a fortuitous accident. Had we left the horses anywhere else while we searched the castle — even had we left them a short distance away — we would never have found it. And it was one thing to stumble on a bokka stone, unopposed. It was another to spirit one away from the most powerful *and* venomous sorcerer in all of Flor…or anywhere.

Could we do it? If so, how? If the Bard of Bryn Doon was supposed to know, I did not. I fingered my cloak with all its stallions. What if we did manage the impossible and secured Ardoxx's stone? How then were we to get the horses back to Bryn Doon? Again, if the Bard of Bryn Doon was meant to know, I did not. Puffy clouds scudded across the moon, dappling the moonlight. Was I this bard? How could I be?

Beneficia waited patiently for my answer. I watched her out of the corner of my eye, even as my gaze was directed straight ahead, into the dark. Without thinking, I reached for the Bryn'qà, tucked into the belt of my tunic, and fingered it. It felt much like any other feather, if slightly more bristly. It didn't sound like any other feather. As I stroked it, its barbs began to sing, as though I were plucking a stringed lythe, one only I could hear, for the others noticed nothing. Yet I did not play the Bryn'qà; the Bryn'qà played me. And the melody that thrummed through me was like no music I had ever heard.

There had not been much music in our village. Ganeyq had a lythe and his wife, Janeya, had a flute. Those were the only musical instruments I knew. Even then, they had played them only rarely, on special occasions. Yet as expertly as they played and as pleasing as were their songs, they were little more than gratings and gruntings next to the mellifluous tones now being produced by the Bryn'qà.

I knew Beneficia still waited for my answer. Hara'q and Mattilde, too, no doubt. But try as I might to keep them open, my eyelids drifted together. All I could do was feel the music move into me…through me…out of me. The voice was mine, yet I had no command of what it spoke. Spoke not sang, for the music formed itself into words, the Bryn'qà's words…

"Once upon a time," I began, opening my eyes a slit and speaking not only to my companions but to T'tammo, Sajàno and all the stallions impressed into my cloak, and not only to them but up to M'nor, over into the River Mala and out to all Flor, all Q'ntana and all surrounding lands. I spoke, too, into the heart of Ardoxx, if he had one. If he did not, I spoke into the place in his breast where a heart might one day beat.

Her question forgotten, Beneficia gazed at me, entranced by the four words that had launched every bardly tale since the first back at the beginning of time, and that had transported every listener — child and adult alike — with their promise of the magic that only stories can bring. The others were no less hypnotized. Even T'tammo and Sajàno turned their heads toward me. And as unlikely as it seemed, I felt the eyes of my cloak's one hundred eighty-five horses on me as well.

"Once upon a time," I repeated, shutting my eyes. And under my words of this night I heard others from other times…

"If we are all bards in Q'ntana, then I must be a bard. Is that not so?"

"It is, little one."

"You are certain?"

"If the story says it, then it must be so. Stories do not lie."

Then…

"You are the Bard of Bryn Doon. That is your destiny."

"Once upon a time—"

The sorcerer jerks awake. He is disoriented, remembering only that he returned to his bed after having destroyed what remained of Castle Flor. He then fell into a deep sleep, dreamless until—

"Once upon a time—"

He hears it again, and this time he knows it to be no nightmare, for he is wide awake. If the four despised words come from somewhere within him, they are not his. Nor is the voice his. It is—

"Prakk," he curses. "Prakk estafi." That bard. He is inside his head. No. Worse than that— He clutches his chest, gasping for breath. The sorcerer knows he will not die from this. He cannot die from this, even as the pain so rips at him that he wishes it would take him. Then, the desire for vengeance overtakes not the pain, which intensifies despite the dozen incantations he cries out, but the desire for oblivion.

He staggers to the window ledge and raises a fist at the moon. "You will not win this time," he cries out, his voice hoarse and strained. "You cannot stop me."

"Once upon a time, in the earliest days of Ben the King..."

"I will prevail," he wheezes. As he clutches at the window sill to keep from collapsing, his fist unclenches, releasing the bokka stone that has been in his hand since he fell asleep. It tumbles soundlessly to the floor. The shallowest of a raspy breath later, the sorcerer follows.

He will not know that he hears the story. Yet hear it he does.

forty-five

Kamela

*O*nce upon a time—

"Pyrà? Is that you?" I could not see him, yet I felt certain it was my son's voice…if not exactly the voice I remembered.

Was I dreaming? It was difficult to be certain in this cloud-like nowhere of a place where sound and sight were muted.

No, this had to be a dream. The intonation and timbre belonged to the Pyrà I remembered, but that "once upon a time" was deeper, more mature, more knowing. It belonged to a young man, not to a boy. It must have been a dream. Unless… No, Pyrà could not have grown up already. We could not have been wherever here was long enough for that, not when no one here had aged.

We hadn't, had we? I studied my daughter, who lay bundled in my arms, asleep. She was no older. Or was she? I sighed. If I could not be certain of that, I could not be certain of anything.

Once upon a time, in the time of Ben the King…

"Jeryn." I nudged her lightly. She didn't respond. "Do you hear it?" I whispered. "Do you hear your brother?" *Is it your brother?* I wanted to add. I didn't dare.

Unlike Pyrà, who as an infant drifted out of sleep as gently and quietly as he drifted into it, Jeryn dropped in and out of slumber with jarring abruptness. One moment she slept so deeply that nothing short of a world-ending cataclysm could stir her; the next, she wailed so piercingly you would think she had been victim to the cruelest torture.

She wailed now. It had been foolish to wake her, but who else could I consult? I had long ago tired of talking to myself, and although their eyes were open, my neighbors seemed unaware of everything — of me, of their surroundings, of each other, of themselves. So I did not attempt to hush Jeryn's wailing. Why bother? No one here would notice.

More than that, it would be pointless. Jeryn rarely responded as other infants did to rocking and crooning. She had known her mind about that since birth. About other things too. What would she be like when was able to speak, when she was able to quarrel? I didn't dare think about it. Then, the possibility of an infinitely worse fate struck me. Were we doomed to this suspended state indefinitely? I shuddered.

Once upon a time, in the earliest days of Ben the King, Kumba dispatched an emissary from far-distant Hana Mar Ò Q'inaya to the only village in the Mhor-Jenn…

Finally, Jeryn's caterwauling ceased. Her eyes opened the narrowest of slits, darted to the left, darted to the right, then lit on me. She frowned, shut them again and fell back to sleep, drool dribbling down her chin. Barely a breath later, though, they shot open again. She raised her head and stared straight ahead, moving her mouth as though she spoke to someone only she could see with words only that someone could hear. Then, she scratched the side of her head and fell back against my arm, her eyes half-shut and a contented smile on her lips — the same stance and expression she adopted when I told her a story. Now, however, I was not the one telling it. More wonder struck than she at the marvel of it, I was listening with her to her brother's telling.

Once upon a time, in the earliest days of Ben the King, Kumba dispatched an emissary to the only village in the Mhor-Jenn, that isolated, desolate province that was new home to the exiled families of the Black Riders and their black mounts. The emissary had but one purpose: to call on He Who Holds the Memory of His Race and impart to him a different kind of memory: a future memory.

This emissary could take many forms and had done so over the epochs of its service to the great dragon in its many forms. And although the emissary had particular forms it favored — what shapeshifter does not? — this occasion called for a new form altogether…an unprecedented form. For the first time in the timeless time of its existence, it would complete its mission for Kumba as a human, a female human, and call itself by a different name.

It was late on a moonless night when Ka'eyla arrived at the hut of He Who Holds the Memory of His Race. Had any in the village been awake and out-of-doors, they would first have discerned a shimmery swirl of gold appear suddenly in front of the windowless hut, as if out of nowhere. It hung in the air, then eddied in multiple directions at once until a human female took shape.

Tall, with wavy sable tresses that rippled past the waist of her silvery robe and framed a flawless, ebony face, Ka'eyla stood motionless at the entry to the hut. She tilted her head as though listening to something, then she nodded, smoothed her robe and stepped out of view.

Once inside the one-room hut, she scanned its rustic furnishings. A rough-hewn stool was pushed partway under a small, irregularly shaped table set with a single beaten-tin plate, a matching mug and the nub of a sooty candle angled into a candleholder so coated with wax drippings that its shape and composition were unidentifiable. A lone bookshelf was all that hung on otherwise-bare walls, empty but for a slender leather-bound volume. Next to the sleeping pallet stood a second table, taller and slimmer than the dining table, holding a pitcher and washbasin, also of tin. Sprawled across the sleeping pallet, his legs splayed, lay He Who Holds the Memory of His Race, deeper in sleep than was his custom.

Ka'eyla watched his chest rise and fall and his eyes race back and forth under his dark lids. She had never known sleep, being neither human nor animal, and found the notion of spending a full third, or more, of one's life with the dreamwalkers to be a peculiar one. After a few moments of this, she bobbed her head, mouthed an acerbic "at your service" at whatever had spoken to her and stepped closer to the sleeping figure. She reached into a pocket of her robe and pulled out a smooth, pearlescent stone. From another pocket, she produced a small pouch of taupe-colored hide. She then inserted the stone into the pouch.

A human female could not have slipped the pouch under the sleeping figure's pillow without waking him. However, she was human in form only and possessed sufficient magic to accomplish the task. That same magic would ensure that he would believe this encounter to have been a dream and that he would not notice the pouch until he awoke.

Once the pouch was tucked out of sight, Ka'eyla stepped back and began to sing. Her song was the reverse of a lullaby, for it was designed to wake the sleeping, not send the waking to sleep. It was a wordless song and, for one who normally slept as lightly as did He Who Holds the Memory of His Race, it worked almost immediately.

"I am Ka'eyla," she spoke before He Who Holds the Memory of His Race could question her presence in his hut. "I have been sent by Kumba."

Though never without resentment at his fate, he dared not be rude. For although it was Kumba, through Ben the King, who had exiled him, the great dragon could have snuffed out his existence as easily as wiggle a single feather of his giant wingspan. So He Who Holds the Memory of His Race swallowed his rage and instead bowed his head.

"Do you remember the story of the Bard of Bryn Doon?" she asked.

For all that he had been bound, unwillingly, to remember, he could touch no recall of such a figure. "I do not," he replied.

"Then I will tell it to you, and you who hold the memory of your race will carry it forward into the future until the moment comes to act on it."

"Once upon a future time," she began, "a bard will emerge in these lands who knows not that he is a bard. Like another bard of another time, he will be 'the oldest of the young and the youngest of the old.' Unlike that other bard of that other time, he will not know of his bardship. Rather, he will grow into an awareness of it. From that awareness, he will grow into his destiny, which is your destiny as well the destiny of all your exiled brothers.

"He will be known as the Bard of Bryn Doon and, when the time is right once upon this future time, his stories will lead you and your brothers home."

At these words, He Who Holds the Memory of His Race felt his eyes fill with tears. "When is this to be?" he asked.

"Once upon a future time," she replied. "As I said."

"The future," he said hopefully, "can begin with the rising of the suns… or with my next breath."

"Or not."

"Or not," he repeated sadly.

"Were you promised you would return home? By the king known as Ben?"

He nodded. "Once upon a future time. Those were his words as well."

"Then you shall. Once upon a future time. The king known as Ben is a man of his word."

"When? Please, can you say when? This place… This body… I can't." The tears pooling in his eyes rolled down his cheeks.

"Once upon a future time," she repeated, barely above a whisper. Then she touched a hand to his forehead and sang her earlier melody, this time in reverse. Within a single breath, he was asleep.

As the shapeshifter dissolved back into stardust, it may have wondered why a dreamwalker had not been dispatched in its stead. However, it was not the shapeshifter's place to question Kumba. Instead, with a loud "braawk" that woke everyone in the village — everyone but He Who Holds the Memory of His Race — the shapeshifter faded into the night.

Pyrà's voice faded with it. And as Jeryn again sat up, clapping her hands and gurgling with delight, I thought I caught the briefest glimpse of what she must have been seeing: the silhouette of my son and his companions against the velvet of a moonless night.

forty-six
Pyrà

I continued to stroke the Bryn'qà, but there was no more story to tell, not then. More stories would come, stories of the future as much as of the past, and it was those stories that *would* carry us home. All of us, not only Hara'q and his brothers. And not necessarily home to Bryn Doon, but to whichever home was each of ours to go. Would mine be Bryn Doon, with the stallions? Only the stories could know, and they would reveal that knowingness in their time, not mine.

But it would take more than stories to get us home. It would take the power of the bokka stones. All five.

I had yet to answer Beneficia's question…or perhaps I had. What would we do *when* we had all five? We would be ready to return home.

*　*　*

M'nor had set as I recounted the story I hadn't known I knew. Now, it was so dark that I could barely make out the forms of Hara'q, Beneficia and Mattilde, though they sat less than an arm's length from me. Stars twinkled above us, grouped in unfamiliar constellations and too far distant to cast any useful light.

No one slept, but it was not until the twin halos of Aygra and B'na crowned the eastern and western horizons that anyone spoke.

"Is it possible that Ka'eyla was not a dream?" Hara'q asked. He pulled his bokka from the pouch and balanced it on his open palm.

"All stories are true," was all I managed to say in reply. Despite the countless generations that had passed since Ka'eyla faded into the Mhor-Jenn night, I still felt myself back inside Hara'q's hut in a moment that had taken place long before my birth, my mother's or her mother's. And I remained as incredulous for my reasons as Hara'q must have been for his.

I was only barely aware that Mattilde and Beneficia had stripped, bathed and dressed again and now whispered together on the riverbank's narrow gravel beach. I was more aware that my stomach growled and that we had no food left. My stories might get us home. They might get us Ardoxx's bokka stone, although I could not be certain of that. I was fairly certain, though, that they could never conjure up the sustenance we would need if we were to make those feats achievable. T'tammo and Sajàno would be fine. There was plenty of grass to keep them going. That would not work for the rest of us, not even for Hara'q, despite his equine past.

My eyes drifted shut. Allowing the Bryn'qà to tell its story through me had energized me and had easily kept me awake through the night. Now that the story was done, though, an overpowering fatigue washed over me and, despite my hunger, I fell into a dreamless sleep.

*   *   *

"Pyrà." Haraq's voice sliced into my awareness. *Pyrà!"*

"Wha—?" Something jostled my shoulders lightly, then with more pressure. I forced my eyes open, but all I could see was Hara'q's face, so near to mine that our noses nearly touched. It was twisted with rage.

"Look!" He pulled away and pointed toward the river, his finger trembling.

"At what?" I asked, confused. "There's nothing there."

"That's right," he shouted. "Nothing. No one." His eyes bulged. "Mattilde and Beneficia," he said with cold fury. "They're gone. And they have taken the horses with them."

forty-seven
Mattilde

"**A**re you certain this is a good idea?" I asked.

"It will be the perfect surprise," Beneficia replied.

"Not if they wake before we get back," I said, still unsure about the wisdom of Beneficia's plan or how I had let her persuade me to go along with it. We had just crossed over the low hill that blocked our campsite from view. A hazy ground mist veiled the castle ruins ahead.

"I have to prove myself," she had argued when we sat on a rock by the river, drying ourselves after our bath, "especially to Hara'q. I know he doesn't trust me, and I can't blame him. Maybe if I can surprise him with food, enough to last us several days or more, he will accept me."

"He does accept you."

Beneficia shook her head. "It's my bokka stone he accepts. If we hadn't found it..." She pulled her tunic over her head. In fact, it was a spare tunic of mine, and although it fit too tightly, it was preferable to the smelly animal skins she had been wearing when she found us. "Maybe we'll also find something there that fits me better."

"It still doesn't feel right." It didn't, yet here I was, riding T'tammo alongside Beneficia on Sajàno, on our way to the abandoned farmhouse we had sighted from the castle grounds. It was in view now, and I was hoping it was the haze that made it appear farther away than I had thought. Would we get back before the others awoke? If we didn't, I could only imagine what Hara'q would say.

"I feel responsible for what I did," Beneficia said, gazing toward the farmhouse. "It was wrong of me to evict the farmers. I understand that now."

"You didn't merely evict them," I said. "You threw them out with no warning and no chance to collect more than a few belongings. It was horrible. It was cruel."

Beneficia angled Sajàno so that he blocked my way. I stopped. "It *was* horrible," she said. "It *was* cruel. That is who I was then. I can't change it. I wish I could, but I can't." She scanned the land, eerily empty of people. As Lady of Flor, she had evicted not only a few farm families. She had cleared the land for a twenty-v'rek radius from the castle. "I promise you this," she said, turning back to me. "When this is over, whatever 'this' is, I will make it right, not only for those families but for every Floriccan I harmed. Even if it takes the rest of my life."

I would never have believed the old Beneficia, who would not have hesitated to manipulate me by saying something like that. I believed this one.

"This — getting food and other supplies — makes it possible to take a small portion of the bad I did and turn it into something good. Maybe not for those farmers…at least not right away. But for Pyrà, Hara'q and all the horses. For Bryn Doon, Q'ntana and Flor." She reached over to touch my arm. "And for you."

I placed my hand over hers. "We take only what we need. Agreed?"

Instead of replying, Beneficia leaned into Sajàno, murmured something in his ear, and the horse took off toward the castle site. T'tammo needed no prompting to chase after him. We had ridden for only a few minutes more when we found ourselves in the midst of a fog so thick we could barely see the ground beneath us — or each other, even though we now rode side-by-side. More than thick, the fog felt soupy, almost viscous. It coated my skin with a slimy film, soaked my clothes and reeked of rot and decay. A few steps into it, the horses stopped and refused to continue, despite our prompting.

"Do you hear that?" Beneficia asked after we had stood motionless for some moments.

"What?"

"Listen."

I heard nothing at first, only my breath, labored from whatever gases were swirling around us, and my heart, which raced in mounting panic. Then I did: a burbly, gurgly, boiling sound that made my stomach turn. I gagged.

"We have to turn around," she said, "*very* carefully." She urged

Sajàno into a tight circle. "And must retrace our steps." She clicked her tongue. Gingerly, the horse stepped free of the fog. T'tammo needed no encouragement to follow.

"What was that?" I asked, grateful to be able to breathe freely again, even if my hair and clothes still carried that nausea-making stench.

"Disappearing sands," she replied and shuddered. "I don't know what happened to the castle, but a few more steps and we would have been sucked in."

I slid off T'tammo, fell to my knees and vomited. "We'd better get back," I whispered when I stopped shaking and could speak again.

Beneficia nodded. I looked back at the fog. It seemed thicker now, more noxious. And it was oozing toward us.

Even after I explained about the farmhouse and the food and supplies, I don't know what Hara'q might have done to us had Pyrà not been there to intervene. It wasn't what he said. It was the icy chill in his words. It was the fury in his eyes. It was white-knuckled fists that took too long to unclench.

"You could have killed T'tammo and Sajàno," he spat. "At least they had the sense to stop." He glared at me. "Too bad they didn't have the sense to throw you into the sands first."

I said nothing. How could I defend myself? I couldn't look at him.

Mattilde could. Mattilde did. Not only did she refuse to let me take all the blame, she refused to apologize.

"We need food," she shot back. "We tried to get some. Maybe it was not the best plan—"

Hara'q rolled his eyes.

"I didn't see you suggesting a better one," she retorted. "We still need food, and I still say the farmhouse is the best place to find some."

"Fine. Go to your farmhouse, but leave the horses here. We can feast on whatever you bring back…if you make it back." He shrugged. "Maybe it will be better if you don't."

"You need us," she countered.

"We need your bokka stones." He tapped his left palm with his right index finger. "Leave them with me. I'll keep them safe for you, for when you return. If you return."

"Enough," Pyrà said. His voice was gentle but firm. He had kept silent since our return, and I didn't yet know how he felt about our misadventure. Did his tone demonstrate compassion or quiet rage? Or was it something else? Had we failed him?

Far worse than angering Hara'q, I feared disappointing Pyrà.

"We need more than their bokka stones," he said to Hara'q. "We need them. Both of them." He pulled his stone from his cloak pocket and turned it over in his hand. "We didn't happen on these stones by chance. Each of our bokka stones chose us. Mattilde's and Beneficia's as much as yours and mine."

He smiled at me, although he still addressed Hara'q. "Even were that not true, Mattilde and Beneficia are as much a part of this journey as you are, as I am. I don't know how that is so, but I do know that their stories and ours are intertwined. Not only ours." He stroked his cloak where a trio of horses covered his heart. "Only in nurturing that connection will we succeed, will each of us find our way home."

"It was foolish," Hara'q muttered.

"Each of us is certain to do more than one foolish thing before this is over." He winked at Hara'q. "Even you." He paused. "Perhaps it wasn't so foolish after all. Now we know about dangers of which we were previously ignorant. Now, when we travel to Beneficia's farmhouse, we can choose a safer way."

Hara'q raised an eyebrow.

"We still need food. We still need each other."

Scrying stones cannot be conjured up on a whim. One cannot merely snap one's fingers or speak a few lines of spell and have one take shape with its full depth and breadth of visionary capabilities. Even the most powerful of sorcerers, and this sorcerer numbers among them, must follow a prescribed practice that is as ancient as the land itself, one that calls for focus, time and patience.

This sorcerer has no lack of the first quality. His extraordinary powers of concentration have helped turned him into the unrivaled sorcerer he has become. Unfortunately, however, he has never possessed any more than a modicum of the latter. As for time, the giant gold-and-silver hourglass that floats unsupported next to the massive fireplace in his study continues to taunt him about its increasing insufficiency.

The sorcerer glares at the hourglass and curses himself for his temper. The hourglass, which measures epochs not hours, has nearly run its course, threatening to empty his designs of their effect as irrevocably as the time-piece's upper clear-crystal chamber is emptying the lower of its sparkling black sands. What he wouldn't give for a reserve scrying stone. Alas, a spare is not possible. The magic of the first would be disabled were he to attempt a second.

The sorcerer restrains himself from smashing the hourglass. Destroying it would change nothing other than a physical representation of the remaining time. Time would continue to run out, regardless. Instead, he exorcises his choler on the study's floor-to-ceiling window, which explodes in a shower of fine glass out into the courtyard. Unlike the hourglass, it can easily be replaced. The scrying stone can also be replaced, though not easily. Yet it must be, for without a scrying stone to track the four travelers' locations and movements, it might prove impossible to seize their bokka stones and capture the stallions of Bryn Doon.

He sighs, turns away from the odious hourglass, begins his preparations and curses himself once more.

forty-nine
Hara'q

I was not as angry as I had let the others believe. Yet how could I reveal to them how frightened I was? I could barely admit it to myself. Fear was not an emotion I was familiar with.

As a horse, I had been fearless, even in battle, one of the few situations where my life could have been at risk. And as a human in the Mhor-Jenn, there had been little about my life to inspire fear. After all, I was no less immortal on two legs than I had been on four, not that the thought of death had alarmed me before now. In fact, such had been my life that I might have welcomed it. What had there been to live for when I did little other than sit outside my dwelling and silently watch my neighbors be born, grow old and die, only to watch those neighbors be replaced by new ones, again and again and again? All I did in those days was observe, engaging with others only when it could not be avoided. All I did was ask Prithi for deliverance from that place and this body and wait…and do my best to avoid Fay'dor whenever he showed up.

Now that deliverance had arrived, it was unlike anything I could have anticipated. For one, it involved regular human interaction, something for which my too-long years in the Mhor-Jenn had not prepared me. For another, it was fraught with the sort of uncertainty I had rarely been required to deal with. And uncertainty, I was discovering, terrified me. Even through those loathsome times when I served as a mount first for the King's Men then for the Black Riders, no initiative had ever been required of me; I went and did where and how I was directed. That had been no less true amid the unpredictability of the battlefield.

Even if I was now handicapped by having only two feet on the ground instead the more solid four, I wanted always to know upon which road those two feet were planted and where that road would carry them. On this journey, I rarely knew either. How could anyone not be frightened by that?

Then, there were Mattilde and Beneficia. I did not understand them, not because they were women, but because they were human. Humans, I was discovering, rarely said what they meant, and their actions rarely revealed their true feelings. I did not know how to parse Mattilde's and Beneficia's words and actions for their deeper meaning and intent before reacting or responding. Yet were I to take their words and actions at face value, the results could prove disastrous.

It would be unfortunate were my confusion to lead to any action or inaction that might harm Mattilde or Beneficia. For all that they baffled and exasperated me, I would not want to see them hurt. It would be devastating, however, were we to lose Pyrà, for without the Bard of Bryn Doon, I might never make it home. Worse, it would be cataclysmic were my incompetence to doom my brothers. If that were to happen, I could never forgive myself. It was that outcome I feared most of all.

If the two women on this journey remained an enigma, Pyrà, fortunately, was less of one. He had been communing with T'tammo and the others almost since he was born, so in his own way he was nearly as equine as I was. Not that I would have wished it, but it might have been helpful on this journey could I have been as human as he was.

fifty

Pyrà

"T'tammo will decide," I announced when the dispute between Hara'q and Beneficia had grown so heated that the rift it was creating risked jeopardizing our undertaking. Their relationship, never without strain, had been stretched to near breaking with the recent misadventure. With this new argument, an unbridgeable breach seemed inevitable.

Beneficia, her remorse over her furtive outing having faded, urged us to take a westerly arc to the farmhouse to avoid the possibility of running into Ardoxx in the Forest of Ardh. She acknowledged that it would take longer but insisted it would be safer, especially considering her near-fatal encounter with the disappearing sands, which we all acknowledged must have been Ardoxx's doing.

Hara'q pushed for the quicker route, one that would carry us southeast through the forest. He argued that the sooner we were restocked with provisions, the sooner we could resume our journey.

Through the twin tirades, Mattilde kept silent. I suspected she did so because she agreed with Hara'q but did not want to do it publicly.

I had no strong feelings either way. Whether we took the quick path or the slower one, we still had business with Ardoxx, so we would not be leaving the area any time soon. And as the most direct path was out of the question — it would lead us through the now-deadly castle site — I decided to leave the decision to T'tammo.

Beneficia paled when the stallion tossed his head toward the forest. But she did not object. Instead, she swallowed hard and clutched at Mattilde's hand so tightly that Mattilde winced.

We walked six abreast when we left the campsite, with T'tammo a few steps ahead bearing our remaining supplies. I was on foot next to him, with Beneficia alongside me, Mattilde alongside her, and Hara'q and Sajàno completing our formation. When we moved off the suns-lit river plain and into the forest gloom, the dense woods forced us into single file behind T'tammo. We had no choice but to trust him to guide us, for we were able to catch only an occasional glimpse of the suns through the forest canopy and quickly lost all sense of direction.

The deeper into the forest T'tammo led us, the more menacingly the trees pressed in on us. Little daylight pierced the heavy weave of upper boughs, allowing for only the barest evidence of life at ground level. We crunched on a forest floor of dead leaves, tripped over putrefying roots and were lacerated by the knife-like twigs that poked at us from coarse trunks. There was no cool freshness here, nor the woodsy fragrance of fresh growth. Everything here smelt of rot. Even the air tasted rancid.

When we had traveled a different part of this same forest on our way to Castle Flor, it had not struck us as malignant, even at the ruins of Ardoxx's tower. Here, every step felt as though we slogged through a sticky swamp of malevolence.

"I-I can't," I heard Beneficia cry from behind Mattilde. "I can't take another step."

I tapped T'tammo's backside. He stopped, his head raised in alertness to what might lie ahead but his ears turned back to gauge what was happening behind him. When I turned around, Beneficia was on all fours, her face white and sweaty. Mattilde squatted in front of her, wiping her brow. Hara'q knelt behind her.

"I don't know what happened," Hara'q said. "She was walking normally, then staggered and fell, as though she had been struck." He reached around her to press his water skin to her lips. She took a long pull and gagged. "Slowly," he whispered. She nodded and drank again.

"It's this place," she rasped. "I have never experienced anything so…so…"

"Evil," Mattilde and Hara'q said together.

She nodded.

"Can you go on now?" I asked, dreading her answer. I could think of no worse place to be stuck, especially after nightfall. I prayed she was strong enough to continue. I prayed, too, that even if she were, we would be free of this place well before dark.

"I think so." With Mattilde's and Hara'q's help, she rose unsteadily.

"I'm sorry," Hara'q said, the first time I had ever heard him utter those words.

"What for?" I asked.

"For being so stubborn about this being the best way." Still supporting Beneficia with one hand, he apologized to her as well. "You were right," he said.

From her expression, I could see that she was ready to snap back at him. Then her face softened. "You could not have known," she said. "If this is the way T'tammo is taking us," she added, her voice nearly normal, "then it must be the right way, whatever happens." She took another sip of water and stood taller. "I'm ready now."

Hara'q patted her shoulder. "If you need to stop again…" he began.

"I won't."

Beneficia was right. She would not be the cause of our next stop. But stop we would, and not by choice.

*A*s the sorcerer steps more deeply into the forest, clutching his bokka stone in one hand and his staff in the other, he mentally ticks off the ingredients he will need.

Seven equal lengths of a caiio branch from a single tree.

The white feather of a yanna. Yanna are bright yellow, with only three white crown feathers.

A thimbleful of fresh k'nrah blood.

A sea-smoothed pebble gathered near freshwater and a river-smoothed pebble gathered near the sea.

Four drops of his own blood from his left thumb.

Four locks of his hair.

The beating heart of a live ma'laqeya.

Surprisingly, what he does not need is a slab of stone. Properly combined and with the correct incantations, these ingredients will, themselves, manufacture a scrying stone. Not any scrying stone, but one perfectly attuned to his needs and to his vision.

The sorcerer's staff and bokka are integral to the ritual. Not as ingredients, but as catalysts. When the moment arrives, the sorcerer will lay them next to the beating heart of the ma'laqeya and chant the series of incantations that will effect the transformation.

It is a peculiar recipe, and he is convinced that there must be a simpler way. Until he discovers one, however, the sorcerer has no choice but to rely on this method, revealed to him by Fa'lé Q'a in one of their final lessons together.

The procedure would be quicker and less elaborate were he permitted to employ sorcery to conjure up a finished stone right in his study. Unfortunately, that is not possible. When the sorcerer attempted it, defying his teacher who had warned against it, the incantation not only created nothing, it destroyed Fa'lé Q'a's home and nearly killed them both.

Fortunately, however, sorcery can be used to conjure up some of the ingredients. He is required to pluck the yanna feather, collect the k'nrah blood, prick *his thumb and cut his own hair. He must also capture the ma'laqeya, cut it open while it still lives and extract its beating heart. All other components may be collected through sorcery, although the sorcery must be carried out on the spot where the stone will have its home. The sorcerer does not get to choose the location; the stone does, and each stone has its preference. Once the stone takes shape, he will raise a tower around it.*

If he is not permitted to use sorcery to produce a k'nrah and a yanna, the arcanely irritating rules of scrying-stone creation permit him to capture several of each and keep them caged in his compound against future need. As for the ma'laqeya, that only the hearts of the wildest are potent enough for effective scrying stones is inconvenient. It is yet more inconvenient that wild ma'laqeya are notoriously wily and difficult to ensnare.

Once the sorcerer has gathered the remaining ingredients in this new stone's chosen location — a remote clearing in the densest part of the Forest of Ardh — he will set himself the task of capturing a ma'laqeya. He will use the heart for its assigned purpose and boil the rest as a stew. Consuming the complete beast — meat, bone and muscle — will bind him more closely to the stone.

That is for later. For now, the sorcerer stops and checks the sky for the position of the suns, barely visible through the trees. He cocks his head in the direction of his compound. He can hear the sand in the hourglass warning him that soon there will be no time.

As he has done more than once this day, the sorcerer curses this most complex of spells and vows to simplify it. That too is for later.

If only his sorcery were potent enough to stop the suns. Because it is not, the sorcerer affixes his bokka stone to the head of the staff and hurries deeper into the forest. The scrying stone must be ready this day. There is no time to lose.

The Sorcerer's Staff

As narrow and barely navigable as the path through the forest had been before Beneficia's collapse, it was now barely discernible. I could not even be certain that it was a path at all. Were it a human guiding us or anything other than a horse, I would have considered us irretrievably lost. Still, it was hard not to question T'tammo's wisdom in carrying us along this route, if it could accurately be called such. Yet T'tammo showed not the slightest hesitation, moving as quickly and confidently as the terrain and dense vegetation allowed.

I knew Beneficia must be tired. The others too. Even I was starting to flag. T'tammo, however, pushed on, deaf to any suggestion that we take a break. Every dozen steps or so, I would rest my hand on Beneficia's shoulder in a feeble attempt to encourage her. There was nothing else to be done and nothing to be said. All we could do was follow the horse.

Before long, the flimsy excuse for a path that we had been traveling petered out, and we found ourselves stumbling blindly through an increasingly tight weave of trees. This went on until the forest grew so thick that I could not see how we would ever find our way out.

Then, without warning, T'tammo stopped.

I would learn later that Pyrà had been communicating with T'tammo in some manner and that the horse had continued to reassure him that he knew where he was going. Then, I was convinced that T'tammo had finally lost his way.

"We're almost there," Pyrà said, barely audibly.

"Where?" Mattilde asked.

Not to the farmhouse.

"I think I know where we are," Beneficia said, "and it is not good."

Pyrà hushed her. "Keep still," he said as loudly as he dared. "Our lives may depend on it."

Moments later, I heard a faint rustling. I held my breath. It drew nearer. A small animal, perhaps? Behind it, something larger and louder was slicing through the underbrush. Suddenly, a furry ball of bristly orange sprang into the air. Mattilde stifled a scream. Only when it landed on T'tammo's back did I realize what it was: a ma'laqeya. If T'tammo didn't flinch, Pyrà did, when the ma'laqeya leapt into his arms.

Before any of us could react, a figure charged toward us waving a spiral-wood staff topped with a pearlescent stone and marked with a familiar rune: a circle scored with a vertical line. It was the same symbol Fay'dor had made with his fingers in my vision in his tea bowl.

The figure was tall with stony gray eyes, a thick mane of snowy hair that tumbled to his shoulders and a braided white beard that fell halfway down his chest. He wore a blue robe so dark it could almost have been black, which was fastened at his throat by a coppery clasp shaped like a giant eye. I had never seen the man before, nor had Mattilde or Beneficia described him. Yet, I knew immediately who he was.

Ardoxx.

What occurred next was over in an instant...although it was an instant that played out in seemingly endless slow motion.

Ardoxx roared, a primal growl that shook the earth. He raised his left hand to eye level, spread his fingers and pointed them at us. I could see flashes of blinding white forming at the tips of his fingernails. But before thunderbolts could shoot at us, three things happened in lightning succession.

First, the ma'laqeya shrilled an ear-splitting shriek, flew from Pyrà's arms and vanished into the forest. Then, T'tammo reared and punched Ardoxx with his front legs, deflecting the thunderbolts, which shot upward, igniting the tree cover.

As startling as those were, what happened next left me astonished and envious. As one, all one hundred eighty-five of my brothers flew from Pyrà's cloak, baying bloodcurdlingly. Then, with T'tammo at the forefront, they lunged at Ardoxx. For a split second, I thought they had trampled him. When, in the next breath, they disappeared back into the cloak, I realized he had vanished. His sorcery had saved him.

That was all it saved. On the ground in front of T'tammo lay a spiral-wood staff, a bokka stone affixed to its head.

fifty -two

Mattilde

No one moved. No one spoke. No one breathed.

If a large area around us had not been flattened by the stallions, it would have been easier to believe that none of what I witnessed had occurred. It would have been easier to believe I had imagined all of it. It would have been easier to continue to doubt that the horses embroidered into Pyrà's cloak were real.

Then there was Ardoxx's staff. I knew it to be his; I had seen him with it often enough in Castle Flor, though without the bokka stone. Now it lay on the ground in front of us, more proof that I had imagined none of it.

My next awareness was of the four of us gathered around the staff, with T'tammo and Sajàno on either side of Pyrà. I had no memory of us rearranging ourselves, yet we must have…unless that was more magic.

Still, no one spoke. After a few moments, Pyrà knelt as if to pick up the staff, but before he could reach for it, it leapt into his arms. Someone gasped. I think it was Hara'q, but I was too startled to be certain.

Pyrà stood, cradling the staff in his arms and being careful not to touch the bokka stone. He ran his hand along the ancient spiral of twined light and dark woods, smoothed into a warm patina by all the other hands that must have stroked it through the ages. Then he held it to his ear and shut his eyes. A soft humming vibrated from it… or from Pyrà…or from both. He nodded, opened his eyes and raised his arm, lifting the staff over his head. At that, T'tammo and Sajàno, bowed their heads and bent a knee. Hara'q turned his head away, but not before I noticed tears streaming down his face.

"This was crafted in the earliest days of these lands by Kumba," he said, repeating for us what the staff had told him. "Kumba fashioned it from branches of the first sha'maya trees."

I knew from Gran Mattilde that the sha'mayas were the oldest of trees, older than the pyynch'ns, and that some few now living were saplings when Kumba planted them at the beginning time.

"White from the white sha'maya that still thrives in these lands and red from the red sha'maya that was lost to us during the time of the first Fvorag." He paused. "H-how?" he stammered. "Are you certain?" He stared at the staff, speechless. "Those trees," he began, "were once found only in Bryn Doon." He trembled. "It can't be…" He touched the bokka stone for the first time.

"What is it?" I asked, taking his arm to steady him.

"It is the staff of the Bard of Bryn Doon," Hara'q whispered. He buried his head in T'tammo's neck. His next words, though muffled by T'tammo's mane, were clear. "It has come home to the Bard. It has come home to the Bard that he might take us home."

It is only when his body, stooped and haggard from the herculean effort, re-forms inside the wrought-iron gated entry to his compound that the sorcerer realizes that he no longer holds his staff. Too depleted to rage at the fact that he has not only failed to forge a new scrying stone and seize the travelers' bokka stones, he has lost his bokka and, with it, the staff that, being as old as the oldest of ancient sha'maya trees, was harvested and fashioned for the most ancient of his forebears.

He staggers up the carriage road, weakened by his practice of the ultimate sorcery: instantaneous disappearance and relocation without aid of either potion or incantation. Yet what other choice had there been? The horses would have ground him into the earth had he not invoked it when he did.

When the sorcerer reaches the broad wood-plank door to his compound's principal dwelling, he keels over against it. The door falls open and he collapses, unconscious, onto the gray slate of the entryway floor, into the center of the shadow cast by the barred clerestory window two stories up.

fifty-three

Pyrà

For the longest time I could neither speak nor move. All I could do was stare into the bokka stone. As I did, I sensed not only all its history but all Q'ntana's, Flor's and Bryn Doon's. I could not have articulated that history, yet I knew it. More than that, I knew that I had always known it. It had taken the staff to awaken it, and much more, within me.

It was not until T'tammo nudged me, indicating that it was time for us to walk on, that I realized that I had been oblivious to everything but the staff. The sky had turned golden with dusk, and we needed to make our way out of the forest — to the farmhouse, if we could find it. This was still Ardoxx's realm. Who knew when he might return? What I did know was that should he return for the staff, I would die before relinquishing it. I could tell that Hara'q felt similarly.

Still, despite T'tammo's nudging, I found it difficult to budge from the spot where the staff had found me. For all it had put us through, it somehow felt sacred.

"T'tammo is right," Hara'q said as gently as his character permitted. "It is best we go."

I knew he was right, but… "One minute more?" I asked.

He nodded.

I reached for my bokka stone and held it next to the one atop the staff. Had we had found the missing point of the five-pointed bokka star? Like two contiguous puzzle pieces, they would easily fit together. Yet try as I might to join them, a stronger force kept them apart.

"Not yet," I heard from the staff. "Soon, but not yet."

*   *   *

All this time we had been nearer to the edge of the forest than we had realized…than T'tammo had allowed us to believe. For once we had gathered ourselves and got moving again, we soon left the forest behind.

The staff felt at once natural and alien in my grasp. On the one hand, I must always have carried it, and any part of my life that took place before it landed in my grasp could only have been a barely credible fable. The Mhor-Jenn? If it existed at all, it was someone else's reality, not possibly my own. On the other hand, I now felt more like the callow, untested youth I had been before stepping into Fay'dor's tent than I did any kind of bard, let alone a legendary one upon whom so many destinies apparently relied. This frightened part of me longed to fling the staff back into the deepest, most impenetrable part of the forest so as to be free of its pull. My mind rebelled at the contradiction.

As the final threads of the day's light vanished, the farmhouse appeared on the horizon, a faint smudge of charcoal against the deepening sky. Until then, we had been spread out, grateful to be free of the single-file confines of the forest. Hara'q and Mattilde strolled ahead, chattering amiably as though they were friends of longstanding rather than recent antagonists. Beneficia walked with Sajàno; a bond had developed between them after the incident at Castle Flor. And I walked alongside T'tammo, as grateful for his silent comfort here as I had been for it on the slopes of Mòrq'an Mellà. With nightfall, however, we once again lined up behind T'tammo, the only one of our company knowing enough to guide us through the dark.

When we arrived at the farmhouse as M'nor was rising in the north, the horses retired to the barn, its broad doors opened wide as though they had been expected. The house, however, did not feel as welcoming. Its front door was shut and all the windows were shuttered. In the low-angled moonlight, the two-story structure loomed menacingly above us.

We stood out front for the longest time, none of us eager to try the door. I edged nearer to Mattilde and took her hand. Beneficia grabbed her other hand and pulled Hara'q toward her. Then, with Hara'q at the lead, we shuffled as one around the house. I wasn't sure what we were searching for — an open kitchen door, perhaps? — but it felt more productive than standing mutely by the front door and safer somehow

242

than unlatching it. The back door, however, was pulled shut as well.

"Maybe this is not the best idea after all," Mattilde said when we had completed our circuit. "Maybe we should join T'tammo and Sajàno in the barn."

"There's no food in the barn," Beneficia said, pulling free, "unless you're hungry for hay." She stepped up to the door. "I don't know why we are so hesitant," she added, resting her hand on the latch, "unless…" She shook her head. "No. Why would he be here?"

Swallowing hard, she pushed the door open. A blaze of flickering light flared out, casting Beneficia in silhouette and illuminating the rest of our group.

"Is someone there, Grenja?" a sonorous voice called from deep within the house.

Beneficia leapt back.

"I think they be here, Q'aff." A higher-pitched voice. "Better late than not at all, for surely."

"Well, don't be making them stand there in the dark, Grenja. It cannot be hospitittible. Not at all." A thumping sound followed. It sounded like a cane thudding on steps. "I'm coming down."

"No, no. Of course. Of course not. For surely."

A moment later a figure appeared in the doorway. Backlit by the glow from within the front room, its features were impossible to discern, as was its gender. All I could tell was that it stood on two legs and was tall and thin.

"It's about timely. You be late, you know. For surely."

We were too stunned to say anything, Beneficia most of all.

"Don't be standing there like grawkins." The figure motioned for us to follow, turned and disappeared inside. "Come. Come. Your supper will be getting cold, for surely."

We stood in mute astonishment until we heard the other voice, now nearer.

"Where be they, Grenja? I cannot see them. Not at all."

"B-but, it's supposed to be empty," Beneficia finally sputtered. "I ordered it emptied. It should be empty."

"Well, it isn't, is it," Hara'q said. "Do we go in or get the vray out of here?"

Suddenly, the staff felt warm in my hand, as though signaling something. I hoped it was something reassuring. I stepped forward. "In," I said. "We go in."

I was the last in, reluctant to face the farm couple I had evicted and uncertain how embarrassed I ought to be, given that they had defied my order. When I stepped inside, Grenja and Q'aff were kneeling in front of Mattilde.

"It be an honor to have you in our home, your Ladyship" Q'aff said, his head bowed.

"An honor, your Ladyship," Grenja repeated. "For surely."

"It has been a long time coming, your Ladyship," Q'aff continued. "Too long."

"Too long, your Ladyship. For surely."

"Thank Prithi you be safe and well, your Ladyship." Q'aff looked up, noticed me and scowled.

"I— I'm not. You— I mean we…" Mattilde's voice trailed off. "Please," she said finally, "stand up."

Q'aff leaned into his cane of tightly twisted pyynch'n wood and, with great effort, pulled himself up. He then helped Grenja to standing.

So lean as to be nearly twig-like, Q'aff stood a head taller than Mattilde and two heads taller than Grenja. His suns-bronzed face was long and lined, with a prominent nose and pale blue eyes that seemed too large for his face and thick lips that were chapped and cracked. His claw-like fingers gripped his cane so tightly that his bony knuckles were white with the strain. Without her severe stoop, Grenja might have been nearly as tall as Mattilde. As it was, with her arched back and ample torso, she was like a soft, plump ball to Q'aff's brittle stick. Her face was equally round, with pink puffed-out cheeks, a tiny button nose and jungle-green eyes as dark as Q'aff's were light.

Before I'd had my nearest tenants evicted, I had met most of them. Maroona had always insisted that we host them yearly once harvest was completed, a practice the Beneficia I had been had abhorred. Had I ever seen these memorable two before now, I knew I would have recalled them. But they were strangers to me. Who were they and why were they here, in a house that ought to have been empty?

"This is—" Mattilde turned to me to complete her introductions.

"The usurper," Q'aff snapped.

"For surely," Grenja agreed. She stepped toward me — more a rolling motion than steps — and I steeled myself against the harsh words I expected. "But not her fault." She beamed at me, a smile so broad it filled her face and so warm I knew it to be genuine. "For surely." She nodded knowingly. "Pay no heed to Q'aff's words," she continued, "or to his demeanors," she added when he glared at both of us. "His heart be bigger than both."

"For surely," he said, and his stern lips broke into a grin. He then led us out of the front room, with its scores of flickering tapers covering every surface, and into the dining room, where a large farm table had been pushed against the wall and was laden with food-stuffs of every variety imaginable — cooked meats, fresh fruit, giant wheels of cheese, and breads that smelled as though they had barely left the oven. Here, the fires were confined to a fieldstone fireplace, yet they illuminated this room as generously as candles had lit the other.

"This be for you, the all of it," Grenja announced, prodding Pyrà toward the table. "For surely."

"How—"

"Did we know you be coming?" Q'aff asked.

Pyrà nodded.

"We knew," was all he would say. "Grenja has been preparing for—" He counted on the fingers of both hands, then shrugged. "A lengthy time."

Grenja pushed a plate into each of our hands. "Eat as much as you want. Whatever you cannot fit in your stomachs will fit in your travel bags. We also be having clean, fresh clothes for you and enough other supplies to see you through the next leg of your journey."

Pyrà tried to thank her, but she shook her head. "For the Bard of Bryn Doon and his companions, no feast be rich enough and no amount of care anywhere near sufficient. For surely."

I hung back as the others filled their plates. "Thank you," I said to Grenja and Q'aff. "The others are more than deserving, but I—"

"You were living out Prithi's will," Q'aff said, his voice warmer than it had previously been, "as were we all."

I shook my head. "It cannot have been Prithi's will that I sought to have you evicted. I am so sorry for that. So very sorry."

"It was Prithi's will that you not succeed." Q'aff roared with laughter. "For here we still be, as we have since the days of the first Mattilde."

"That cannot be possible," I said. "That would make you—"

"Old enough that it serves no purpose to argue with him." Grenja grinned and patted my hand. "Now, go eat. You be as deserving as the others. We will talk more later."

Q'aff winked at me. "For surely."

fifty-five

Pyrà

We sat outside under the moon and stars, our bellies so full that we could barely move. Before settling onto the star-patterned blanket Grenja had set out for us, we attempted to relieve her of the massive task of clearing up. She had refused, brooking no argument.

"For surely *not*. It will keep until after you are on your way in the morning, or whenever you choose to be off."

Then, we had insisted on making certain that T'tammo and Sajàno were comfortable. We'd had no cause for concern. The barn was more well-appointed than any barn we could have imagined. The floor was laid wall-to-wall with a thick carpet of soft grasses, and small stacks of fresh hay were scattered throughout, as were troughs of clean, cool water. A series of open stalls lined up against the far wall, each with its own trough and window, "in case they be having enough of each other's company," as Q'aff put it.

"We be expecting more horses," he continued. "Many more." He eyed my cloak.

I said nothing. As grateful as I was for his hospitality and for Grenja's, the cloak was too precious for me to risk revealing its true purpose, although I suspected from his glance that Q'aff not only knew what it was but tested my discretion. Not for the first time, I wondered who Q'aff and Grenja were. However, they were a match for my discretion and, like me, they revealed no more than was necessary.

*　*　*

"I see you have been dealing with Ardoxx," Q'aff said. He cupped a mug of tea in his hands. It had grown chilly out, but the rest of us had refused Grenja's offer of warming tea. It was impossible to consider even a sip of water after such a massive meal.

"What do you mean?" I asked. How could he know?

He held his hand over the staff. "Ardoxx would not be parting with this willingly."

"No."

"It be not his to hold on to."

"No?"

"It be the belonging of the Bard of Bryn Doon. It has always been the belonging of the Bard of Bryn Doon."

I said nothing.

"It be good to see it in rightful hands again after so lengthy."

"For surely," Grenja added. "It has been too lengthy."

I longed to ask him how he knew all he knew. It seemed impossible for him to know it first-hand. How old would he have to be for that? Unimaginably old. As old as Fay'dor, perhaps.

"Be you having your bokka stones?" he asked before I could formulate a question of my own, one that wouldn't sound rude. He knew about those too? "Be you having your Bryn'qà?"

"How can you know about that?" Beneficia asked.

"What I be kenning—"

"Hush," Grenja interjected. "This not be a time for your telling. It be a time for the bard's, for surely."

"You be right, as always you have been, my dear." He turned to me. "If you be having them, and I be more than suspecting that you do, it be *their* time. It be time to finish what you have been beginning… and to be beginning what you be near to finishing." He stared directly into my eyes, and despite the dim glow of moonlight, his gaze was discomfitingly piercing.

Again, I wondered who he could be. Would I ever know? One thing I did know, "for surely." He was no farmer.

fifty-six
Hara'q

There were moments during our time with Grenja and Q'aff when I was certain that Q'aff must be Fay'dor in disguise. How else could he know what he knew? How else to explain his age? In other moments, I feared that we had walked into an insidious trap…that either Q'aff was Ardoxx in a different form or that the sorcerer had conjured up Q'aff and Grenja to trick us into relinquishing our bokka stones and the staff.

This latter seemed all too conceivable when Q'aff urged Mattilde, Beneficia and me to pass our bokka stones to Pyrà so that he could fit them together with the one on the staff.

"Is that wise?" I asked Pyrà. "Are you certain this is the right time and place? Remember what happened in the forest when you attempted it with only yours."

To my amazement, Q'aff agreed with me. "Hara'q be right," he said. "You must not be doing it simply because I be thinking it a good idea. Be doing it only if you know it to be the right idea, the right idea for right now."

Perhaps Q'aff *was* genuine. Or perhaps this was part of the ruse.

"Ask the staff," Mattilde suggested.

Q'aff bowed his head. "Your Ladyship be wise, for surely."

"That be the best course, for surely," Grenja agreed. "You be sometimes too impetuous by far, Q'aff." She wagged a pudgy finger at him.

"Were I not so impetuous, my love, we would not be together." Q'aff leaned into Grenja and kissed her on the mouth.

Her pink cheeks darkened to scarlet and she dropped her eyes. "Oh, you. Still such a romantic, and after lengthy seasons upon seasons."

"For surely," he said and kissed her again.

While Q'aff and Grenja bantered, Pyrà held the staff to his ear, fingering the wood as though he were playing a flute. By the time our hosts had finished, so had he.

"What does it say?" Beneficia asked.

Pyrà studied each of us in turn, as though seeing us for the first time and weighing our measure for what was to come. His scrutiny was disconcerting. It was also heartening, for it seemed to mark a milestone on our journey — as much for him as for the rest of us. Gone was the youth he had in so many ways still been, despite the change in his outward appearance. What stood before us now was a young man who fully embodied his bardship. He *was* the Bard of Bryn Doon. The staff no longer counseled him; he and the staff were one.

When he spoke next, all timidity, uncertainty and hesitation were gone. There was an authority in his voice I had never heard before. I knew then that I could never again doubt him.

"We cannot step into the future until we acknowledge the past. We cannot live the next chapter of our story until we know our history. For it is only in knowing where we came from and how we got here that our destinies can reveal themselves to us.

"In order to free that history that it might free us, that it might complete us, this sacred staff of Bryn Doon must also be freed and completed." He touched his bokka to the right side of the stone that sat atop the staff. With a loud click, the two locked together as one, radiating a soft glow.

I knew what was next. I removed the bokka from my pouch and touched it to Pyrà's. It, too, clicked into place and the glow brightened. Beneficia and Mattilde followed suit, and the five-pointed star that then crowned the staff glowed brighter and brighter until its light swallowed the night.

In the light of this new day, Q'aff and Grenja had vanished, along with their farmhouse and barn. Only the patterned blanket beneath us remained as proof that we had not dreamt the episodes with Ardoxx, Q'aff and Grenja…that and the packs overflowing with provisions secured to T'tammo and Sajàno. And the staff, with its still-glowing Star of Bryn Doon.

The sound of a single click awakens the sorcerer, still collapsed on the tile floor of his front hall. It shudders through him as though it has risen from the earth beneath his compound. As clouded as his senses still are, he knows what the source is, and it bears no relation to his compound or its environs. He strains to summon sufficient sorcery to neutralize the source. Alas for him, he remains too weak. How can he cast a spell when he cannot summon the strength to whisper a single word or move a single finger? That he cannot do either stokes his fury, a fury he is powerless to express, which only adds more fuel to the fury.

A second click, so violent that he longs for the strength to clap his hands to his ears…not that it would dull the deafening thunder, for the hammer pounds inside his head, not outside it.

A third click, more explosive still, accompanied by a searing light that scorches his eyes. If he could scream, he would. If he could shut his eyes against the light, he would. He can do neither.

A final click, more intense than the first three combined. He feels it as a thousand thousand simultaneous knife thrusts. No part of his body is immune.

In the instant before daylight is extinguished and he loses all awareness, the sorcerer vows that this setback, however consequential, is not the end. He will rise, more powerful and determined than ever. He will. He will. He—

fifty-seven

Pyrà

"Once upon a time, at the beginning of time," I began, "twin sons were born to Aah'mos, third Bard of Bryn Doon, and his wife, Ray'a." The staff lay across my lap, its bokka crown lightly pulsing as I spoke. The Bryn'qà stood at an angle on the ground before me, scriving my story into the earth as I recounted it. For once, I was dictating a story to the quill, not the other way around. For once, too, I knew a story's words before I spoke them. Yet, as with all stories, I could not know this one's ending until I reached it.

We sat by the River Mala, a bit upstream from where we had camped earlier, having taken the long way around to avoid the forest this time, for fear of encountering Ardoxx. We were exhausted, the staff having stolen the night from us. Still, I knew there was a story that needed telling. At least one. Sleep would have to wait.

"The boys were called Malaqa'i and Ardoxx and were identical but for their eye color—"

"Ardoxx?" Beneficia exclaimed. "Impossible. That would make him—"

I ignored the outburst and continued. What was possible and what was impossible were not for any of us to judge. "The boys were called Malaqa'i and Ardoxx," I repeated, "and were identical but for their eye color. Malaqa'i's were as soft and green as the mosses that grew on the rocks on the eastern slopes of Brae N'ah; Ardoxx's were as hard and gray as the rocks themselves.

"Though it was by barely a few breaths, Malaqa'i emerged into the world first. By virtue of that happenstance, the laws of Bryn Doon and Q'ntana decreed that, upon his father's death, he would inherit not only the bardship but stewardship of all the land's mares and stallions.

"No law decreed that a first-born must wail without cease for a period of three moons, yet Malaqa'i did not know that, for that is what he did. Nor did any law decree that a second-born must never cry during that same period, or afterward. Yet Ardoxx did not know that, for he never did. Nor did he laugh. Not once.

"By contrast, his older brother, who ceased his wailing on the third new moon after his birth, replaced his tears of distress with tears of mirth. From that night forward, he personified exuberance, and the tales he wove as he grew into his birthright were always joyful. His brother's, on the other hand (for all Aah'mos's offspring were trained in the bardly arts), were at best grim. At worst, they were grisly…gratuitously grisly, for they offered no teaching other than that greed and malice were virtues to be celebrated, rather than vices to be avoided."

Mattilde sat across from me, her chin resting on the knees she hugged tightly with both arms. Her eyes opened barely a slit and her face as dreamy as if she were asleep, she listened raptly, seemingly aware only of the story and not of its teller or of the others who listened along with her.

Those others, Hara'q and Beneficia, sat to my left, unexpectedly pressed in as close together as they could be without touching. For the first time in all the seasons I had known him, Hara'q did not appear to be apprehensive. He looked almost relaxed. Could he be happy? Beneficia certainly was. Her face glowed with joy.

Across from them, T'tammo and Sajàno watched me expectantly, as though they knew this story but wanted to make certain I told it correctly. Even the horses on my cloak seemed to be paying close attention.

So this was what it was like to be aware of those to whom a story was being told. I had never noticed my "audience" before, so inwardly focused had I been. Observing them as I did now and seeing their expressions shift as the story unfolded was as engrossing to me as my story was to them, and it fueled me in a way nothing before had. Was this what it was like to be a bard? To be the Bard of Bryn Doon? If so, I had no doubt that I had found my destiny or, more accurately, that it had found me. So I continued…

"When Ardoxx attained his twenty-second year, knowing he would inherit nothing at his father's death, he fled to the wild jungles of Avìndrii to apprentice with the renegade sorcerer Fa'lé Q'a. His plan was to acquire the skills and powers in the dark arts that would enable him to seize Bryn Doon from his brother upon his father's passing. And should Aah'mos delay his demise for too long, Ardoxx was prepared to employ those same skills and powers to hasten him along.

"It took many, many seasons of intense and intensive study, for Fa'lé Q'a was a demanding master. Yet Ardoxx never once wavered. The morning at last arrived when his diligence was rewarded, when Fa'lé Q'a declared Ardoxx to be his equal in every way that mattered. There were those who whispered that Ardoxx was more than Fa'lé Q'a's equal, that student had surpassed master. Was this true? None could say for certain, apart from Ardoxx, who ardently believed it to be so, having cast a longevity spell upon himself that was beyond even Fa'lé Q'a's powers.

"On the day of his graduation, Ardoxx transported himself back to Bryn Doon, not as himself but as a nayla. The most deadly and stealthy of any creatures in the region, nayla were black as pitch and swift as hawks, effortlessly shredding their prey with teeth sharper than any blade, as much for the euphoria of the kill as for food.

"For seven nights, Ardoxx prowled the mountains, plains and forests of Bryn Doon with the bloodthirsty ferocity of a nayla, each slaughter inflaming his rage at his father and brother. On the eighth night, he slipped into his father's bedchamber and ripped out his throat out while he slept."

Beneficia gasped. Her hand flew to her mouth. Hara'q edged closer and took her other hand in his. I waited until she had regained her composure — from both my story and Hara'q's action — and continued.

"On the tenth night, Aah'mos having been buried and Malaqa'i having been installed that day as the fourth Bard of Bryn Doon, Ardoxx slipped into his brother's bedchamber. Tempted as he was to mete out the same manner of vengeance, he controlled himself. Fa'lé Q'a had taught him that discipline could be a sorcerer's most powerful weapon, and in that instant he understood that teaching as never before.

"Instead of executing him as he slept, Ardoxx licked his brother's face to awaken him. He knew that the bravest of men would panic were he to open his eyes to the greedy, yellow-eyed stare of a nayla. He knew, too, that his brother was not the bravest of men.

"When Malaqa'i opened his mouth to scream, Ardoxx pushed a

coarse-furred paw into it to silence him, boosting his brother's terror until what might have been his final breath. With that breath, Ardoxx leapt back and returned to his true form, sparing his brother.

"'Wh-what is it you want?' Malaqa'i could barely get the words out. His face was awash with a blend of tears and sweat, and his night-dress was soaked.

"Ardoxx's mouth twisted into a cruel smile. 'This,' he replied. He threw his right arm over his head then dropped it to direct all five pointy-nailed fingers at his brother. 'And this,' he cried as five bolts of lightning stuck Malaqa'i in the forehead.

"Before Malaqa'i could shriek with pain, he disappeared — from his bedchamber and from Bryn Doon. When next seen, he was wandering the streets of a remote Q'ntana village, stripped of all memory."

When I sensed what was to come next, it sucked the breath from my lungs. It explained everything, and it changed everything.

I could not speak the words of it. I didn't dare. Once it was expressed, it could not be unexpressed. Once I spoke it, it would bind that revelation to me and me to it, for all time. It was safer to say nothing, even as I knew that neither the staff nor the Bryn'qà would allow me to keep silent. The bokka crown throbbed, as though trying to communicate the urgency of the situation, and the Bryn'qà quivered in anticipation of the next words it would scrape into the ground.

"What is it? You have gone white." Mattilde pushed a water skin to my lips.

I gulped the cool liquid, but it could not relieve my terror. Like Malaqa'i, I felt powerless before my fate. Of course, I was like him.

"Malaqa'i," I managed to spit out. "He was— I am—"

Beneficia disentangled herself from Hara'q and rubbed my hands. "Your hands. They are like ice."

"He was what?" Mattilde asked.

Hara'q positioned himself behind me and rubbed my shoulders. "I know," he whispered. "I must have seen it as you saw it."

"You speak it, then," I said.

"You know I cannot."

"No," I sighed. "You cannot."

I took another sip and straightened my back, doing my best to display a strength I could not feel.

"My ancestor," I whispered. "Malaqa'i was my ancestor."

* * *

I wept for what felt like a lifetime but could as easily have been an instant.

"There is more," I said when I could speak again. "My parents."

"What about them?" Mattilde asked. She had refilled the water skin and again sat close to me.

"They are both descended from Malaqa'i." I paused. "I knew they were cousins, but…but I couldn't know how."

"Then it is settled," Beneficia declared. "You *are* the Bard of Bryn Doon. There is no other. There can be no other."

She was right. There could be no other. Fay'dor had known. He must have. But—

The blood fled from my face. If I was descended from Malaqa'i…

"Ardoxx," Mattilde whispered. "He's—"

"Yes. He is my uncle."

fifty-eight

Pyrà

I felt sick. That I shared even a droplet of blood with Ardoxx turned my stomach. I left the others and walked to the river.

While Mattilde, Beneficia and Hara'q laid out a meal from the provisions Grenja and Q'aff had packed for us, I stared at the River Mala's breeze-rippled waters. A pair of verros soared high overhead, black specks that vanished into the distant haze. Was one of them Baq'shì, flying up into Tikkana? Or was it her brother, racing off to report our whereabouts to Ardoxx…to my uncle?

Another pair of birds, gannu fluffy as tufts of cotton, floated down onto the water and skimmed toward me before taking off, cooing loudly.

On the opposite shore, a family of sleek, silver-black k'nrahs — two adults and six pups — gamboled through the weeds and rushes that poked out of the water, squealing and barking as they played a sort of hide-and-seek. After a while, they stopped and curled up in the sun to dry, the pups nestled sleepily between their parents.

Suddenly, I missed my family more than I could bear. It felt like lifetimes since I had hugged Kamela and held Jeryn. Fay'dor had assured me that they were safe. But now that I knew our history, I feared that Ardoxx might have taken them…or killed them. Was it Ardoxx who had destroyed our village? Had my mother, my sister and I been his true targets? Was Ardoxx somehow the reason my father had been trying to find a way out of the Mhor-Jenn? Had Lucca been seeking a way back to Bryn Doon? Would I ever see him again? Would I ever see any of them again?

Had Lucca known the truth about us? The whole, ugly truth?

It is not entirely ugly, my son.

"Father?" It was his voice. It had been so long since I'd seen him that I had almost forgotten his face. His face, but not his voice, that low, lightly gravely tone that sounded almost like the purr of a k'nrah.

"That must be it," I muttered. "Those k'nrah must be purring, and it is making me think of Papa."

Or it truly is me, my boy…only I can no long call you "my boy," can I, for you are no longer a boy.

I spun around. No one was there, only Hara'q, Mattilde and Beneficia, watching me silently as they ate.

"This is a waking dream. It must be."

A vision more than a dream, for what is the Bard of Bryn Doon if not a visionary?

"Then you're alive? Or…"

I am as alive as you are, no less flesh-and-blood than you.

"Then why I cannot see you? Where are you?"

Waiting for you.

"You talk in riddles. You're as bad as Fay'dor."

Just as I recognized his voice, I recognized his laugh — a single, explosive *ha*.

I am here and not here, Pyrà. I am in your heart, which means I am everywhere you are. Always.

"What about Maminka and Jeryn?"

We will all be together again, sooner than you can imagine, but…

"But what?"

But not in any way we have been before.

My stomach churned. Bile thrust its way up into my throat. Did he mean they were dead? I was afraid to ask.

How could we be as we were? You are no longer a boy. You are the Bard of Bryn Doon. That alone renders everything different from what it was.

"Why?"

No answer.

"Why am I the Bard of Bryn Doon? Why aren't you? Or Mother? Or Jeryn?"

Because it is your destiny, not ours. It is what you were born for. Now, go live it.

"What about Ardoxx?"

He has his destiny as well.

"Does he know? About me…about him…about our history?"

The breeze that had been lightly rippling the water, roared into a powerful gust. The k'nrah dove into the river and raced away through the whitecaps. Overhead, clouds that had been drifting lazily now scudded across the sky. A few fat raindrops splashed onto my head, and I could hear my companions struggling to pack everything away before it all flew off with the wind. Then, as quickly as the squall had begun, it ended. It was as though I had only imagined the threat of a storm. For everything swiftly returned to the way it had been, except for the k'nrah, who never resurfaced, and my father, whose voice and presence had scattered on the wind.

fifty-nine

Hara'q

If Pyrà slept that night, it was a restless slumber punctuated by frequent moonlight walks to the river. Whenever I opened my eyes, he was either wandering down to the water or back from it. And when I rose at dawn, he was staring into it, at the fiery reflection of the rising suns. When he noticed me, he motioned for me to join him.

I sat next to him, saying nothing. By now, I had journeyed with him long enough to curb my impatience. He would speak when he was ready.

He remained silent even when Mattilde and Beneficia carried bread and cheese to us. Then, he waited until the rest of us had eaten — he didn't touch his portion — before speaking. "There is more to the story of my ancestor," he said sadly, his chin resting on his staff, "and it must be spoken before we can continue." He gazed into the water. "I would like to do it here."

"Won't you eat something first?" Beneficia asked.

Pyrà shook his head.

"Some water, then?"

Pyrà took a single sip from the water skin she passed him. He sighed and began, his eyes never leaving the river.

"As malicious as we now know Ardoxx to have been," he said, "his evil did not end with his brother's exile. It took a new form.

"Ardoxx may have learned more sorcery than most and acquired more power than most, but Bryn Doon offered him little opportunity to employ the former in order to abuse the latter. The province was sparsely peopled, and its fabled horses held little attraction for him, at least initially.

"Why, then, had he seized the bardship of Bryn Doon? For no

reason other than that he could, as well as to punish his father and spite his brother. As for stories, he thought them dull and pointless. Why repeat some rambling fable when a few words of incantation could immediately bind others to his will. Stories bored him. Bryn Doon bored him.

"Had Ardoxx been perceptive enough to see beneath story's surface simplicity to its transfigurative power, a force more potent than his sorcery, he might have thought and acted differently. He did not, so he could not.

"Instead, he absented himself more and more frequently for longer and longer periods, traveling to lands far and near so that he could put his magic to better and more malignant use than was possible in Bryn Doon.

"It was on one of these forays that he encountered Fvorag I, King of Grykk, who had long coveted Q'ntana. And it reawakened within him not only his lust for greater power but his hunger for revenge, most particularly on Mattilde, Lady of Flor."

At this point in his telling, Pyrà propped his staff against his leg and pulled the Bryn'qà from his waistband. He stroked its vanes, then set it in front of Beneficia.

"You know how the story continues," he said to her. "Mattilde has already recounted part of it. It is now for you to complete it."

Beneficia blanched. "No," was all she said.

Pyrà pointed to the Bryn'qà. "It will help you."

"It speaks to bards," she said. "I'm no bard."

Pyrà picked up the Bryn'qà and set it on Beneficia's lap. "It whispers its stories to all who listen." He took her right hand and laid it atop the feather. "All can listen."

"No," she reiterated, but she didn't move her hand, though it shook violently. "Must I?"

"I cannot force you, but it is for each of us to speak our story. This continuing is more your story than mine. It is more your healing than mine."

I knew what was coming, and my heart broke for her. Yet I knew Pyrà was right. I knew, too, that my time to say yes to what I feared most would come before this journey was over.

Beneficia, her face still drained of color, shut her eyes and inhaled deeply. She held her breath, then released it with a loud sigh.

"The Lady Mattilde," she began, her voice wavering, "had had the misfortune of meeting Ardoxx during his apprenticeship, the jungles of Avìndrii being but a few days' journey from Flor and Flor possessing, should one have the sorcery to find them, diversions of the flesh and vine lacking in both Avìndrii and Bryn Doon.

"Once installed, increasingly unhappily, in Bryn Doon, Ardoxx returned to Flor often. Each time, he sought and received an audience with the Lady Mattilde, for she was a gracious host and rarely refused such requests from visitors.

"If Ardoxx was neither handsome nor agreeable by nature, he could be by sorcery. So that was how he presented himself. The Lady Mattilde was canny enough to see through his charade, but saw no harm in seeming to accept him as he appeared to be."

She stopped and pulled her hand from the Bryn'qà. "I-I can't go on."

"What if I told you that you can?" Pyrà asked gently.

"I doubt I would believe you."

"What if I were to tell you that this story could be the gateway to your destiny? What if I were to tell you that it was?"

Before that moment, I had never longed for anything other than to return to my natural form and to be home in Bryn Doon. Yet those longstanding yearnings paled next to a sudden desire to hold Beneficia and reassure her, to tell the story for her if that would help.

I was confused. And angry — at Beneficia for stirring up those feelings and at Pyrà for pressing Beneficia in such a way that such feelings could be aroused in me. Most of all, I was angry at myself. How had I let this happen? How had the independent, insular self I had cultivated through multiple generations been so easily shattered?

If only I could flee. But there was nowhere to go. For reasons I could not imagine, I too needed to hear this next piece of the story. I also needed to support Beneficia in the telling of it.

"The serving girl Beneficia," she continued haltingly, her hand again atop the Bryn'qà, "was unschooled in the ways of the world and was naive enough to be flattered by the sorcerer's outward charms. Every time he spoke to her, she blushed. And as unschooled as she was in the ways of the world, she was highly skilled in the ways of the castle. She took every opportunity to be present when Ardoxx had his audiences with the Lady Mattilde. When she could not be, she hovered in the castle's public hallways and hid in its secret passageways that she might eavesdrop and spy."

She paused, waiting for the Bryn'qà to give her more. "The day came when Ardoxx revealed himself to the Lady Mattilde. If he expected her to be shocked, she disappointed him. And if he expected her to agree to his proposition, he was more than disappointed when she did not. He was enraged.

"'You must have little regard for yourself, for me and for others if all you seek is power,' she said as kindly as she could, which only enraged him more. 'Were I to agree to bear your child and join forces with you, as you ask, I am certain that in short order you would seek dominion over me as you seek it over others.'

"With that, she retreated from the audience chamber, abandoning Ardoxx to his red-faced fury."

Beneficia picked up the Bryn'qà. "I don't want to say more," she sighed, "but I must."

My heart swelled with pride at her courage.

She massaged the feather and shut her eyes. When she opened them, she looked at Pyrà. He nodded, and she began.

"Once the Lady Mattilde had left the chamber, the serving girl Beneficia emerged from her hiding place behind a giant tapestry.

"'Is there anything I can fetch for you, sire?' she asked.

"Speechless with rage, the sorcerer shook his head.

"'May I show you the way out?'

"He nodded, and as he followed behind her along the maze of corridors, a journey intentionally lengthened by the serving girl, the spark of a plan — a plan for revenge — kindled within him.

"When at last they reached the great outer gate, he stopped and stared at her so intensely that she dropped her eyes and blushed a deep crimson.

"'How would you like to be chatelaine of this castle instead of its drudge?' he asked, still staring.

"So astounded was she that no words came.

"'Think about it,' he said.

"Only when he was nearly across the drawbridge did she find her tongue. 'Yes,' she cried. 'Yes, yes, yes, yes. *Yes!*'

"Ardoxx's lips curled in a sneering sort of smile as he turned to face her. 'I will be back for you,' he called to her, 'and it shall be so.'

"And it was."

Beneficia released the feather. Her eyes followed it as it fluttered to the ground. "I-I'm sorry," she whispered.

"You are not your ancestor," Mattilde said.

"I was."

I handed the Bryn'qà to Pyrà, who tucked it into his waistband, reached for his staff and half-stood, then dropped back to sitting. Again, he gazed out over the river.

"The Great Enchantment," he said after a long silence. "It was Ardoxx's revenge."

No one spoke after that, not until Aygra and B'na joined overhead at midday.

"You are not your ancestor either," I said.

Pyrà waited until the suns had separated, then he leaned into his staff and rose."Come," he said, starting back toward our campsite. "It is time we were on our way."

"Where?" I asked.

"To find Ardoxx."

"Please, no," Beneficia cried out to Pyrà. He stopped and turned around. None of us had followed him from the riverbank. "He will kill me, or worse. Whatever else any of you has done, none of you has betrayed him. I have. He will want me to pay." She shuddered. "He will make me pay."

"She's right," Hara'q said. "It is too risky. For all of us. We have the staff and his bokka stone. What more do we need from him?"

Pyrà rejoined us by the water. "It is a risk," he admitted. He paused and I hoped he was reconsidering. He wasn't. "I wish there were another way, but I cannot see how to avoid it…not if we are going to get the horses safely to Bryn Doon." He patted the sleeve of his cloak. "All of them."

"What do you mean?" Hara'q asked.

"One more story must unfold if we are to unravel the Great Enchantment's final strands. That is the only path to Bryn Doon. I wish I knew of another."

"Which story?" I asked.

Pyrà shrugged. "I wish I knew that too. All I know is that Ardoxx is the key to it. So it is to Ardoxx we must travel."

Although we could not be certain where to find him, Beneficia remarked that with both Castle Flor and his tower destroyed, he was likely at his compound in the Forest of Ardh. So, with her as our grudging guide, we followed the River Mala a short distance west, then turned south, toward the castle. For the only path she knew to Ardoxx's compound began there.

Our plan had been to skirt the disappearing sands by staying well clear of the mist that shrouded them but to get near enough to the castle for Beneficia to locate the path. Yet when we rounded the bend, no deadly gases greeted us. Instead, to our astonishment, nearly half the fog had dissipated, revealing a Castle Flor that was rebuilding itself in front of us. One corner tower stood nearly complete. Elsewhere, partial walls zigzagged through the site. And the moat, while not filled with water, was mostly clear of debris.

"The Enchantment," Pyrà exclaimed. "I knew it was reversing. I never expected this."

Beneficia's eyes lit up. "Can we...?"

I was relieved when Pyrà shook his head. My memories of the castle were radically different from hers. I was not keen to revisit it, even if it were no longer as a servant.

"It is too dangerous," he said. "There could still be pockets of disappearing sands, and we cannot know how solid any of it is."

"Or how real," Hara'q added.

"Oh, it is real," Pyrà said, "or at least in the process of becoming so. But until we know that it has been fully restored, it is best not to get too close."

We circled to the front of the site. While Beneficia scanned the forest for the path, I reflected on what there was of my old home, at once repulsed and fascinated by it. There was no drawbridge or front facade yet, only the partly open outer gate, unsupported by any wall. Beyond the gate, where the courtyard would have been, swirls of thick mist still eddied angrily, and from as near as a few hundred paces away, I could hear the sands' hungry gurgle. I turned back to face the forest with the others. Whether or not the castle rebuilt itself, I would be happy never to see it again. If I was to rule Flor someday as its Lady, I hoped it could be from a new Castle Flor, not this one.

Beneficia pointed to a barely discernible opening in the wall of tightly interlaced trees directly ahead of us. "That's it, I think," she said. "I will know better when we get closer, but if the castle gates are where they are supposed to be, that's about right."

It was. The opening was barely wide enough for us to slip through, though once we did it broadened enough to allow us to walk in pairs: Beneficia and Hara'q in front, the horses in the middle and Pyrà and me at the rear.

The path wound through the woods like a demented corkscrew, turning in on itself so often that I was certain we were backtracking to the castle rather than progressing toward Ardoxx's compound. Yet

Beneficia assured us more than once that this was the only path, each time her voice echoing in the eerily silent forest. No one else spoke until, after a dozen more twists and turns, she stopped.

"We're here," she announced.

Here? Where was here? Was Beneficia playing a cruel joke on us? Had she been fooling us all along? Was she still the unreformed mistress of Castle Flor? What else could explain what lay in front of us...or did not?

There was no compound here. Only trees, trees and more trees, in every direction and as far as the eye could see.

The sorcerer will not be surprised when the travelers arrive. He may not yet have access to a scrying stone, but even without the return of his full strength, he is not without resources.

For a start, he has directed his servant, Karùn, to prepare a potion for him that will hasten the restoration of some of his powers. Although possessed of no mystical gifts herself, Karùn knows his store of plants, herbs and preserved animal parts as well as he does. Better, perhaps, for it is she who alerts him when any supplies grow precariously low. It is she, too, who arranges for their replenishment, at least those requiring no sorcery for their collection.

Karùn has served the sorcerer for many decades, having succeeded her older sister, Kaya. Unquestioningly devoted to the sorcerer, Kaya would be serving still if she could. However, her bones had grown so brittle and dry with age that one day they crumbled into fine dust, leaving nothing behind but her indestructible leathery hide. It now hangs in the damp, mossy crypt beneath the compound, along with the remains of all her forebears.

Karùn is so stooped that she must push her neck as far back as it will go to see in front of her, and she is so wrinkled that her pale violet eyes are tucked deep into the folds of her skin. As hidden from view as her eyes are, they miss nothing. Nor do her ears, for her hearing is as acute as ever it was. And despite her lack of magical skills, she has a talent for so blending into her surroundings that she might as well be invisible.

Because of those gifts and skills, she is privy to more than she ought and, because of the sorcerer's vanity, more than he knows. She knows, for example, that he has summoned Bàq'sha and ordered him to monitor the travelers' movements. She also knows that the verro, emboldened by the sorcerer's weakened state, at first refused, consenting only when the sorcerer reminded him of the temporary nature of his condition and, should the verro not obey, the permanent nature of his disgruntlement.

And because she has befriended the verro, she knows something the sorcerer has not yet discovered: The travelers have nearly arrived.

BRYN DOON

sixty-one

Pyrà

"We're here," Beneficia announced. She stepped back a few paces and tilted her head. "I wish it were not so, but we are."

"What do you mean?" I asked. "There is nothing there." The path had ended and nothing but forest lay ahead.

"Don't look straight on," she said. "Turn your head like I'm doing and look from the corners of your eyes."

When I did as she suggested, I saw it. It was as though someone had laid a faint sketch of a walled compound on top of an equally faint sketch of the forest. From this angle, neither appeared solid. Each flickered, mirage-like, with first one then the other seeming to have more substance. Yet as soon as I straightened my gaze, I saw only forest. The compound had disappeared.

It took several tries before Hara'q and Mattilde could see it too, but none of us was able to hold the vision for more than a few seconds at a time.

"How do we get in?" Hara'q asked after several unsuccessful attempts to reach the gate. Each time, all he ended up doing was walking deeper into the forest.

Beneficia shrugged. "I came only at Ardoxx's invitation. When I reached this spot, it was the way you see it. At first. Then, it was as if the forest melted and the compound solidified. I didn't do anything to make it happen. I simply waited. Ardoxx must have performed some sort of magic to let me in."

If he had, he was unlikely to be as welcoming this time. And should he prove to be as welcoming, it would surely mean that he had some plan in mind to thwart us. He was a sorcerer, after all. Could he have used his sorcery to get us here? To make me think we needed to be here when, in truth, he needed us here to reclaim the staff and seize the cloak? Had I led us into a trap? I could see in Beneficia's and Mattilde's eyes that they asked the same questions. I knew Hara'q trusted me, but he also had to be having doubts.

No. We *were* in the right place. The key to the success of our journey lay inside that compound. Without that key, I would never return the horses to Bryn Doon, and Beneficia and Mattilde would not fulfill their destinies. I was as certain of it as I had been of anything on this journey…as certain as I had been of the truth of each of the stories that I had allowed to flow through me.

Stories… Hadn't I stated that another story was needed to unravel the last of the Great Enchantment? Perhaps the time to begin that story was now, not once we were inside.

Listening harder than I ever had, I ran my fingers up and down the Star of Bryn Doon's five points. Nothing. I reached for the Bryn'qà and stroked its fronds. Still nothing. Where was the story that would propel *our* story forward?

"There is nothing to listen for," I heard. "The story lives within you already. There is only to begin as all stories begin…"

"Once upon a time—"

"Is this truly the time and place for a story?" Hara'q interrupted. "We should search for some sort of shelter. We're too vulnerable here." He tilted his head in an attempt to see the compound then swore when he was unsuccessful.

"We are vulnerable everywhere," I replied, "and not only in this forest. I don't know what this story is or how it will protect us. What I do know is that it is our only protection."

I sat and began again. "Once upon a time…"

As I spoke those four words, the forest vanished. Not the forest in front of me that had blocked our way into the compound, but the forest around me, and with it Hara'q, Mattilde, Beneficia, T'tammo and Sajàno.

Instead, I stood at the head of a hallway so long and blindingly lit that I could not make out its ending, only a brighter light far in the distance. It was as though I looked into one of the suns. Shielding my eyes against the glare, I stepped forward. Although I could not hear my feet move along the polished marble floor, I did hear the tapping of my staff as it drew me nearer to that brilliance, each step causing the deep purple of its bokka crown to glow more radiantly.

As lengthy as that corridor was, it took no more than a few breaths for me to reach the end, where a pair of ornately carved wooden doors trimmed with runes outlined in gold leaf prevented further passage. I stood there, waiting for what seemed forever, unsure what to do next. Then, when I was about to give up and turn back, the staff rose, taking my hand with it, and touched one of the symbols.

From somewhere far distant, I heard a chorus of voices. "It's gone," they shouted. And it was. The doors had vanished.

In their place, a stranger old enough to be my father wavered into view. Tall with sea-blue eyes that crinkled at the corners as he smiled and wavy golden hair crowned with a simple coronet, he wore a cream linen robe, its only adornment a flaring sun embroidered over his heart. I knew I had never seen him before. Where in the Mhor-Jenn would I have encountered royalty? Yet there was something oddly familiar about him, as though maybe I had seen him once in a dream. Behind him, as though viewed through a gauzy curtain and unaware of both him and me, an elderly woman hunched over a long wooden table, preparing a decoction of some sort from the array of jars, tubes and phials spread out before her. She hummed a minor-key melody that, like the man, was strangely familiar. Although she did not sing them, I was certain there were words to it. Perhaps I had heard them in that same dream?

When I had first viewed the doors, I assumed them to be part of the entrance to Ardoxx's compound and that this story I was living as much as telling would take me inside to meet him. Now, I was no longer sure. Where was I and who was this stranger? And where were Hara'q, Mattilde, Beneficia and the horses?

"Pyrà." The stranger nodded his head in greeting. I knew the voice, gentle and silken, and suddenly I knew who this had to be but couldn't.

"Your majesty?" I dropped to one knee and bowed my head. If this was the legendary King Ben, how could he be standing here? Q'ntana's greatest monarch had been dead for hundreds of years.

"Rise, young bard," he said.

I rose, uncertainly, but kept my eyes lowered.

"Look at me, young bard."

Reluctantly, I raised my eyes to meet his. "Yes, I am Ben," he said. "However, I am not your king. For if you recall your SunQuest, you will know that Q'ntana has no need of kings, not anymore." He moved toward me.

I wanted to step back but didn't dare.

"Yet Q'ntana will always have need of bards. And Bryn Doon has been missing hers for too long. That she has been without one all this time…" A thoughtful expression crossed his face. "I take responsibility for that, young bard, although O'ric — you know O'ric, of course — would insist that the story has played out precisely as it needed to…as it always does." He shook his head to clear that thought. "Now, to the matter at hand."

I was confused and not a little scared. I had told many stories since setting out on this journey. I had told those stories as I heard them, although with the story of Aah'mos, Malaqa'i and Ardoxx, I had known much of the tale before starting. That was what bards did. That was how storytelling worked. But this was different. With the words "once upon a time," I was no longer merely recounting a story, I had tumbled inside it. Was part of me of still sitting with Hara'q, Mattilde and Beneficia speaking the words? Regardless, part or all of me had left the forest and was living this story from the inside out. The mere thought of it, the impossibility of it, made my stomach churn. I leaned heavily into my staff. Without it, I am certain I would have fainted.

"Wh-where am I, sir?"

"No 'sir,' young bard. For now, for the purposes of this story, 'Ben' is best. Simply Ben. As for where you are, it is difficult to describe. The best I can do is to say that you hover in the space between breaths, within the story you are experiencing at the same time as you are recounting it to your companions."

"That makes no sense."

Ben chuckled. "Why would you expect it to?"

"I-I don't think I understand."

His chuckle exploded into a guffaw. "No, I do not imagine you do. Nor would I, were I in your place." He touched my shoulder, and for the first time I noticed the fiery sunburst ring on his right index finger. It flared so dazzlingly as he spoke that it was hard for me to take my eyes off it. "Time is short," he continued in a more serious tone, "for the space between breaths cannot last indefinitely, and the story must continue." He pointed to the old woman still fussing with ingredients behind him. "That veil will dissolve in its own time, whether or not we are ready, and I must be gone before it does. I pray you to swallow your bewilderment and your questions so that I might explain myself, at least somewhat." He pointed his ring at my free hand, which now held a mirror-polished obsidian chalice filled nearly to the brim with warm mead.

"The Nayr," I gasped. This was the sacred chalice that on more than one occasion had played a powerful role in Q'ntana's history.

Ben waved his hand at it, dismissing my awe. "It will not be missed for now." He pushed it to my lips. "Drink. It will settle you."

I sipped the warm sweetness and immediately felt firmer on my feet and in my body.

"First," he said, "I must thank you."

"Why?"

"No time for questions. Remember?"

I took another sip and nodded, feeling for the first time as though I belonged in this time and place, whatever it was.

"When I restored peace to Q'ntana and exiled the Black Riders, along with their horses and families, I could not have foreseen how Ardoxx would react." He paused. "O'ric would maintain that my blindness was part of the story. Do you know O'ric? You didn't say." He continued, not waiting for my response. "Regardless, you are in the midst of completing what I set in motion, and for that you will always have my gratitude." He removed the ring from his index finger and slipped it onto mine. "And you will have this, which will assist you with the task ahead."

As Ben's ring touched my skin, a nearly unbearable throbbing pounded through my body, so startling that the Nayr slipped from my hand. It vanished before it hit the ground.

"As for the task ahead, it will reveal itself through this story. Trust it, trust the story and trust yourself, and all be well as, surely, it already is. That's what O'ric would say."

With that, he faded away, as did the gauzy film separating me from the old woman.

"You're here," she said, not looking up from her labors and in a voice that sounded like two rocks scraping against each other. "You're late."

sixty -two

Karùn

"Some hundreds of years late." I looked up from my fussing with Ardoxx's potion, having delayed the process as long as I could manage. Were he not so debilitated, he would have stomped in long ago, demanding that I finish. Were he not so debilitated, he would not have needed me to prepare it for him. Were he not so debilitated, he would not have needed it at all.

The old fool. I was a fool, too, for assuming that my service would get me home again, back to Bryn Doon.

Now, the Bard of Bryn Doon had finally arrived, but too late. I was too old to make the journey, or so I thought when he stepped out of nowhere into my kitchen. I knew him right away. How could I not? He so resembled the Ardoxx of all those seasons ago that he had to be kin. If he was kin, who else could he be?

He was more startled to see me than I to see him, this Bard of Bryn Doon. No one had told him about me. Yet, I knew all about him.

Had Ardoxx been less of a fool, he would have killed his brother. He thought it a greater punishment to let him live. What he could not imagine was that Malaqa'i would initiate a bloodline of his own. Unless Ardoxx was to prove cannier than his history suggested possible, this bloodline would destroy what he had set out to create.

There was no time to communicate all this to the young bard, who stared at me gape-mouthed. Not in words. Yet if he was the bard I prayed he was, true heir to Aah'mos and Malaqa'i, he would know. The story would tell him. It would tell him, too, that I would help him. Even were I too old and frail to make the trip home, I would help him.

"Karùn," he said at last, the story having conveyed in a few breaths what it would have taken me too long to speak. He strode to me and took me in his arms. "I have come to take you home," he said. He said it and I wept.

I was still weeping when he took the potion from the table and left.

The sorcerer pushes himself to sitting and reaches for the bell pull that hangs by his bed. He has been tugging on it all afternoon to summon the crone, to no avail. She has yet to deliver his potion. Fortunately for her, he is too weak to act on his impatience.

Had the crone not proven through their long years together to be loyal and devoted, he might suspect her of an intentional delay. But she is ancient, and possibly feeble — of mind, perhaps, as well as of body — so he has little choice but to wait. His household is small, and no one but she has his complete trust.

Once his strength is restored, he will see about replacing her. Simply because her sister worked for him until her bones could no longer support her does not mean that he must endure the crone's enfeeblement until she follows suit. A young Floriccan would do nicely, on multiple counts. And it is more than past time to sever the final link with Bryn Doon that she represents. To his mind, it is a most accursed place.

Perhaps this last tug on the bell pull has achieved its purpose. He hears shuffling steps in the corridor. They draw nearer, as, he is certain, does the return of his power and, with it, his destiny.

sixty -three

Mara'q

Something was wrong. I could feel it, even as everything appeared normal…as normal as anything could be described as having been since the Great Enchantment exiled me and cursed me with this body.

It was Pyrà. He had insisted that a story would get us inside Ardoxx's compound. Although it seemed unlikely to me that a story could possess such power, he was the Bard of Bryn Doon, and I had learned to give in to his pronouncements, despite any misgivings.

Now, I had to wonder whether he had overreached. The story he was recounting, about meeting King Ben and talking to that hunchback servant of Ardoxx's, could only be fiction. After all, he still sat in front of us as he spun the tale, the sorcerer's compound seemed no more solid than when Beneficia had shown us how to see it, and we seemed no nearer to being able to gain access to it, should that truly be key to a return to Bryn Doon for me and my brothers. As well, Bryn Doon's human numbers had always been few. Had this old woman's family been among them, how would I not know of it? Yes, fiction.

Doubtful though as I was of the accuracy of Pyrà's story, Mattilde and Beneficia were entranced. Perhaps humans were more susceptible to this manner of tale. However, the horse in me knew that we needed to either get inside the compound and do what needed doing to get us home or remove ourselves from this forest, the quicker the better.

As Pyrà continued, I found myself paying less and less attention to him and more to Beneficia. What little sunlight filtered through the trees dappled her auburn hair. Unusually short though it was, barely over her ears and slashed raggedly rather than fashioned into any style, it looked silky and smooth.

Had I a proper head at the end of my neck instead of this human abomination, I would nuzzle her hair with it and make soft snorting sounds into it. And were she a mare, well—

What am I thinking? Bryn Doon horses do not mate. And as we are all one with each other, brother to brother and sister to sister as much as brother to sister, coupling for any other reason is so rare as to be nearly nonexistent.

And yet...

Beneficia's eyes shone as she listened intently to Pyrà, as immersed in his story as I was not. Her lips, full and red, were slightly parted, and I caught a glimpse of teeth that were straight and remarkably white. If the rest of us grew more ragged and disheveled with each passing day, Beneficia seemed less rumpled and more refined. It was as though she was growing into herself, and it showed in her appearance.

Admittedly, I was not being honest with myself or fair to the others. We had all grown through this journey, so much so that we were probably unrecognizable to our former selves. I was certain that the others, were they to stop to acknowledge it, would celebrate that growth within themselves. Could I? Instead of answering the question, I averted my eyes from Beneficia and returned my attention to Pyrà and his story.

When Pyrà left, my first thought was to follow him to Ardoxx's bedchamber and spy on their interaction. My greatest desire in that moment would have been to witness the expression on Ardoxx's face when the fact of his failure dawned on him. For he would fail. For all Ardoxx's sorcery, the youth would best him…and not merely because the potion I had prepared resembled Ardoxx's recipe in taste alone. That, in part, was what had taken me so long. I had been experimenting with a concoction that would mimic his potion's taste while lacking its restorative power. There was another expression I longed to witness: When it dawned on Ardoxx that the potion had done nothing other than leave a sour taste in his mouth.

I would have preferred for him to know that I had betrayed him. Alas, he was more likely to blame it on my senility, and that would only buttress his determination to be rid of me.

Yes, I knew he had no intention of waiting until I met the same fate as Kaya. If he could, he would "deal with me" sooner than that and bring in a young Floriccan to replace me and bear him an heir. I would not give him that satisfaction. Even had Pyrà been further delayed, I would have done my best to prolong his weakened state, if only to prevent him from further weakening mine.

Leaving the kitchen in disarray, I made my way across the courtyard to the tiny one-room cottage that had been my home since Kaya's death. It contained little more than a cot, a wooden table and a single stool in front of a rough-stone fireplace and, next to the single uncurtained window overlooking the courtyard, a second, smaller table alongside a cushioned chair. There, if I returned before nightfall, I would sit with a mug of tea and watch whatever birds and wildlife found their way into the compound through the enchantment that kept most people out and me trapped within. Often, as I did that afternoon, my eyes would fall shut and I would slip into a light sleep. This day, however, something woke me long before it was time to return to the main house to prepare Ardoxx's dinner...not that he was likely to be in a mood to either eat or view my face once the Bard of Bryn Doon had finished with him.

Apart from Ardoxx's temper, which would occasionally explode into a tantrum of bellowing curses and breakage, there was little other than rare birdsong and rarer animal cries to shatter the absolute stillness of the compound. So when a cacophony of human voices jabbed at my awareness, it was easier to assume that I was dreaming than that the courtyard teemed with women, children and men, all appearing to be as startled to find themselves in this place as I was to see them.

At first, I wondered whether I had died. Could Kea Kana resemble Ardoxx's courtyard and be a maelstrom of confusion? I considered that explanation, but only briefly. It seemed less a possibility than that the scene outside my window was real, as unlikely as that was.

Could this be Ardoxx's work? Had he regained his powers in spite of me and conjured up this crowd? To what end?

I shook my head. Whoever had brought these people was a more powerful sorcerer than Ardoxx could ever hope to be. Just then, something high in the sky caught my eye.

It can't be. I squeezed my eyes shut and opened them again. It was gone, yet I was certain of what I had seen: a giant dragon, soaring high above the treetops.

sixty -five

Hara'q

One moment, Pyrà sat with us, recounting an unlikely story that seemed to be moving our story forward not a smidge. The next, he grew as wavery as Ardoxx's compound and vanished.

What happened after that took place in less than a breath. Beneficia screamed. The horses reared. Mattilde leapt to her feet, calling out Pyrà's name. Then, as though the entire world blinked, everything went black, darker than the darkest of moonless nights. When the light returned an instant later, we stood on the other side of the gate, the forest now as blurred as the compound had been, and we were not alone.

So unexpected and out of context were these people who now surrounded us that I did not immediately recognize them, not until they called out my name. It was the Mhor-Jenn villagers, those who had survived that final storm. There were Falla and Mayta, Flek, Janeya and Ganeyq, Kand'q and Valena'a. Even old Zeetah. And off at the edge of the crowd by the door to the main house stood Kamela, Jeryn in her arms. They were all here, Prithi knew how or why. I'd had little to do with these people when I lived in their midst. Now, I was overjoyed to see them.

That Pyrà was not among them at first alarmed me. Then I realized where he was: inside, with Ardoxx.

sixty-six

Pyrà

I stood at the foot of the broad staircase, holding the fluted vial I had taken from Karùn's kitchen. Steam swirled from the green viscous liquid that smelled more noxious than Auntie Mekla's stew, a dish she was so proud of that no one in our village had ever had the heart to tell her how vile it was. Had she survived the storms and what followed, she would be in the courtyard now, with all our neighbors. Mattilde, Beneficia and Hara'q would be there now as well, as would T'tammo and Sajàno. And Maminka and Jeryn. My heart stopped at the thought of seeing my mother and sister again, and what I wanted more than anything was to smash the potion against the wall and race out to them.

I could not, of course. Should I not see this next part of the story through, none of us would leave the compound alive. Could I do it?

King Ben thought I could. I would have to trust his wisdom, for I was not nearly as sanguine. All I knew was that I was to carry the potion to Ardoxx, and that my success or failure would depend on what transpired in his bedchamber. Given that I did not know what I was to say or do once I stood in front of him, failure seemed the more likely outcome. After all, however weakened he was, he was a sorcerer who possessed powers I could not imagine. I was but an inexperienced storyteller. How could possibly I outmaneuver him?

I trembled as I climbed those stairs. When I reached the top, I didn't dare stop for fear that what little courage I had mustered would abandon me. Nor did I hesitate when I reached his door. I opened it and stepped inside.

"Uncle." My voice sounded surprisingly strong, stronger than I felt.

"Who the vray are y—," he bellowed, then fell into a coughing fit. When he had recovered enough to speak, he leaned forward and squinted at me, then shrank back, all color draining from his face. "Malaqa'i," he gasped.

"*Uncle*," I repeated. How could I have feared this man? Lying there, pale, with red-rimmed, clouded eyes sunken into hollow cheeks, it was as though death were waiting to claim him. I almost felt sorry for him. Almost. I knew the potion in my hand could restore him, although not in the way he expected…or desired.

He sat up, leaned forward again and studied me. "Pfft," he said when he had completed his assessment. "You are not Malaqa'i. Whoever you are, boy, hand me that potion. It is mine." So focused was he on the vial that he had yet to notice the bigger prize, my staff.

I remained where I was, by the door. "All in good time, Uncle."

"Who are you?" His anger had returned. Now it was a cold rage, by far more dangerous than his previous outburst. Had he the power, I was certain that he would have shot a flame at me and burned me to ash.

I stepped closer. "You know who I am, Uncle."

Again, he scrutinized me. "You are that boy, that self-styled bard." This time, he pointed to the staff with a trembling finger. "That is mine. I will have it."

I took another step toward him. "It is mine now, Uncle. By rights."

"Uncle? Why do you call me uncle? I am no one's uncle, unless…" He shook his head. "No," he muttered, "it cannot be."

I now stood less than a staff-length from him. "It can and is, Uncle."

"My boy." His voice grew soft and coaxing, even as his eyes now blazed with a mix of fear, fury, loathing and greed. "My nephew. My kin. Son of many sons of my beloved Malaqa'i."

Beloved? It took all my self-possession to not respond with anger. If I was to succeed, I could not allow myself to be like him.

"You may not have this," I said, tapping the staff on the floor. "However, you may have this." I extended the potion toward him, but not close enough that he could reach it.

"Yes, yes, my boy. The potion. That is enough. More than enough. You see how sick I am? The potion will make your ailing uncle well again. Then we can have a proper reunion. There is so much I—"

"Stop!" I slammed the staff into the floor. "I know who you are. I know what you are. I know what you have done. I know what you would do if you could." I tightened my grip on the staff, continuing before he could interrupt.

"If this were my story, I know, too, what your fate would be. But this is not my story. It is Bryn Doon's, and as its bard I must tell it as it demands to be told, not as I would wish it to be." I paused. "More's the pity."

"You would take advantage of an old man's infirmity?" he whined.

I set the potion by my feet and raised the staff so that it was parallel with the floor. "I would do more. I would press this to your throat until you lifted the Great Enchantment, then I would press it more forcefully still, until you could no longer do any damage — to Bryn Doon or to any connected with it."

"*Ha*. You would not, not if you are truly my brother's descendant. You lack the stomach for it."

"You are right, and I am grateful for it. I would be no better than you if I did."

"You are weak," he spat, "like that brother of mine. You are weak, and I can crush you."

I picked up the vial. "Not without this."

He laid his head back on the pillow and smirked. "You will give it to me. You will give it to me because you are weak, because you haven't the spine to watch an old man die."

"I will give it to you because I am strong, strong enough to let the story unfold as it must."

"Pfft. Stories. They mean nothing."

"That is where you are wrong. And it will be your undoing. They mean everything."

Ardoxx waved his hand dismissively. "The potion, boy."

"Once upon a time," I began.

Ardoxx groaned, but there was little he could do to stop me.

"Once upon a time," I began again, "there was a once-powerful sorcerer who, through pride and arrogance, had crippled his powers. Not only was he impotent, he was no longer a sorcerer, for a sorcerer without sorcery is only a man, an empty shell of one at that."

Like a willful child, Ardoxx turned his head away. I half-expected him to cover it with his pillow or shut his eyes and block his ears.

"How the once-sorcerer came to find himself in this situation is too long a tale to tell here. Suffice it to say that like most prideful and arrogant men who discover that the pride and arrogance that have fueled their drive are ineffective in the face of a reverse, the once-sorcerer found himself facing an intolerable dilemma. He could accept assistance from someone he perceived as being weaker than he, or he could die. As the former would not only brand him a weakling, which was untenable, but create an obligation, which was more untenable still, he chose to die.

"And so he did."

Ardoxx jerked his head around to face me. "What kind of story is that?"

"Yours, Uncle."

"How can it be when I am not only happy but eager to accept your help? The help I seek is for you to pass the vial to me so that I may be cured." He spoke those words calmly, then exploded with rage. "Do it!"

"It will not help, Uncle."

"It will. This is my recipe, and Karùn has prepared it according to my instructions."

"She has not, Uncle."

Ardoxx roared. "She will die for this."

"You will die first, Uncle."

He said nothing.

"You see, Karùn is as eager to get to Bryn Doon as I am, as are these horses on my cloak. Uncle."

"You mean to say—" He jabbed at the air with his finger. "Your cloak. The horses. All of them? All along?"

I nodded. "All along, Uncle."

"Stop calling me uncle."

"You would deny your kin? You would deny your brother's descendant?"

"If that potion has no effect and I am to die, then leave me." He waved me off and again turned his head away.

"I never said the potion had no effect, Uncle."

"But—"

"It has an effect, simply not the one you seek. Not exactly. Although Karùn did not brew it to have this other effect, the story has ensured that it does."

"You and your stories. What do you want? Everyone wants something and everyone has a price, even a self-righteous so-called bard." Another coughing fit left him gasping for breath.

I waited until he was able to speak again.

"You want me to send you and that ungrateful hag to Bryn Doon? Restore my power and I will."

"Only when the once-sorcerer was nearer to death than he knew," I said, continuing the story, "did a life-saving and power-restoring possibility present itself."

Despite its story form, my telling attracted Ardoxx's notice. Even as he feigned a lack of interest, I could see that he now paid close attention.

"The architect of that possibility was the Prithi he had spurned. And Prithi's messenger was a bard, which displeased a once-sorcerer who had never had any use for bards or their tales."

"Get on with it."

"The once-sorcerer could be full-sorcerer once more, though only through a potion, one he had commissioned but that circumstance had altered."

"*Enough!*" Ardoxx pounded his fist on his nightstand, so violently that all its contents flew to the floor. The effort sapped him of his strength. "Make your offer or be gone from here," he wheezed.

"As you wish, Uncle." I raised the still-steaming vial to eye level. "Despite Karùn's tampering, this potion *will* restore your sorcery to you...with certain restrictions."

"No. I accept no restrictions from the likes of you."

"Very well, Uncle. I wish you a good death." I turned my back on him. Would he fall for my bluff? I needed him as much as he needed me, but I had no maneuvering room. I could not make the potion anything other than it was. I could not make the story anything other than it was. He would make his choice and we all would have to live with the consequences. I held my breath as I moved toward the doorway, silently praying that Ardoxx would surrender before I passed from the room. For once I crossed the threshold, it would be over. The potion would lose its enchantment, reverting to the worthless infusion Karùn had prepared.

"Wait." All fight had leached out of him. He sounded subdued, more exhausted and resigned than angry.

I stopped, inhaled deeply and turned around, saying nothing.

"What is it I must do?"

I moved back toward the bed, remaining just over an arm's reach away. "Once you remove what remains of the Great Enchantment," I explained, raising my staff to silence him. "No," I said, "I know you can do it. I know you still possess that power."

He grunted and waved his hand for me to continue.

"Once you remove what remains of the Great Enchantment, this potion will gain the capacity to restore your power within one turning of the sun of your having consumed it…with these stipulations: None of your sorcery or your descendants' sorcery will be able to reach into Bryn Doon or its inhabitants, human or animal, nor will it have any force on any of those now assembled in your courtyard."

"Who is in my courtyard?" He tried to push himself up to see out the window but lacked the strength. He collapsed back onto his pillow.

Ignoring him, I continued. "You and your descendants will be free to remain in Flor and to practice sorcery within its boundaries. However, any attempts at sorcery from you will have no effect on the governance of this land, on its governors or on its governed." I waited for him to take in the full effect of what I had spoken. "Do you understand, Uncle?"

Ardoxx muttered a curse.

"Do you understand, Uncle?"

"You tie my hands inexcusably," he replied.

"I tie nothing and no one, Uncle. I do my bardly duty and recount the story. Do you understand?"

He nodded his head and mumbled his assent.

"Know this, Uncle, any attempt to bypass or circumvent these restrictions will have the effect of diluting and diminishing those powers you still possess. Do you understand?"

"I understand, damn you," he shouted. "Get on with it."

"Good. Do you agree, Uncle? Do you agree to all the conditions and repercussions?"

I knew he would. What choice had he? I also knew that as soon as he swallowed the potion, he would begin plotting to bypass the conditions and avoid the repercussions. I didn't like it, but my job was to tell the story, not to like it.

"Well, Uncle?"

His fists clenched, and his face grew red from the strain of surrender and restraint. "Under one condition."

"I am not empowered to negotiate only to—"

"To tell the story blah blah blah. Yes, I know. However, this is a condition you ought to have no difficulty agreeing to, story or no story."

"What is that, Uncle?"

"That you *never* call me uncle again."

The sorcerer takes the potion from the bard. He wishes he had the luxury of tossing the steaming liquid into his priggish face. Alas, he cannot afford the gesture. He needs the liquid too much. He hates that he needs it. He despises himself for needing it. He loathes the bard who gives him no choice but to swallow it, and his pride with it.

First, however, he must lift what remains of the Great Enchantment, and this galls him more than anything. Perhaps it would be best were he to die.

He considers this possibility. He could leave the enchantment in place, pour out the potion and wait here to die…if Karùn does not kill him first. The enchantment would outlive him. At least he would have that.

"No," he roars to the empty chamber, for the bard has left him alone to complete his side of the contract. "No," he repeats, with a cold, quiet fury. Why end his life when his longevity spell remains intact. He will live to have his revenge, however long it takes.

Setting the vial on his nightstand, he rubs his hands together as vigorously as his strength will allow, then uses them to draw a series of complex runes into the air while speaking the undoing incantation.

Ma'kàlé ma'kànu ma'kaléy'aa

Ma'kaléy'aa ma'kàlé ma'kànu

Ma'kànu ma'kaléy'aa ma'kàlé

It is a simple spell, but it saps him of yet more power.

He picks up the vial and raises it to his lips. "It is not over," he whispers before swallowing the potion.

Then, as waves of cheering wash over him from the courtyard, he falls into a deep sleep.

"Kamela! Is that you?"

Was it? Had it not been for Jeryn cooing in my arms, I honestly could not have sworn to it. We — the whole village — were crowded into the low-walled courtyard of a compound of sorts. There was a main house — two whitewashed stories topped by a red-slate roof — three tiny cottages that mimicked it in style, and several windowless outbuildings. Beyond the wall, a dense forest fluttered in and out of view, as if I were dreaming it.

And what had happened to the previous dream? Whatever hazy reverie of a space into which we had been deposited when our village was destroyed had also fluttered in and out of view, until it vanished altogether, leaving us momentarily suspended in a black nothingness. When the light returned we stood here, in a new place no less alien than the old. At least my neighbors had been reanimated. They now chattered among themselves as though they were home in our village on market day.

"Kamela!" The voice was familiar.

"Hara'q?" I called back. "Where are you?"

In reply, a hand waved over the villagers' heads, drawing nearer as the body attached to it wove through the crowd. When that body reached me, it hugged me in a long, tight embrace. When it finally released me, it kissed first my forehead, then Jeryn's. And when it stepped back, it was smiling warmly.

It could not have been Hara'q. I had never known him to smile, other than grimly, or to show any affection. Yet I hoped it was, for only Hara'q could know where my son was.

"Pyrà?" I asked hesitantly.

Hara'q pointed at the main house. "It's complicated," he offered before I could ask. "What are you all doing here?"

I shrugged. "You tell me."

"Pyrà will know. It must be part of the story."

"Story?" What sense did that make? Along with his uncharacteristic grinning and kissing, he had to have gone mad. What other explanation could there have been? Yet if he was, we must all have been.

A wave of exhaustion washed over me. It didn't matter that all I had done for the past however-long was doze. All I wanted now was sleep.

Then, although it didn't seem possible, something stranger still occurred. The door to one of the tiny cottages opened and a woman who appeared to be older than time stepped out, scanned the crowd and, when she saw me and Hara'q, shuffled toward us.

"I do not know your name," she said to me, "but I know who you are. Your face— If you were a man, you could be Malaqa'i's twin. You must be kin to the Bard of— To Pyrà."

She turned to Hara'q before I could respond. "You are also familiar," she said, "yet I cannot place you. Who are you and why are you here?"

Hara'q — if it was truly he — kissed her hand. "I am Hara'q," he said, "and this is Kamela, Pyrà's mother."

I didn't hear what the old woman said next. All I heard was a buzz of voices that grew into a deafening roar. At the same time, daylight brightened blindingly around me and a throbbing pain ripped through my head.

"Kamela?" The voice was so distant that it seemed to come at me from another world.

I tried to reply, but I couldn't speak. I couldn't see. I couldn't feel.

"Jeryn…"

Then, nothing.

sixty-eight

Pyrà

I did not return to the courtyard right away. Instead, I returned to the kitchens, hoping to find Karùn there. The room was empty.

I should have felt joy, release, relief. After all, the Great Enchantment that had destroyed so many lives and been the cause of so much grief and suffering through so many generations would be lifted… was now being lifted.

Mattilde would gain her lawful place in a reconstituted Castle Flor. Beneficia would be free to live her destiny, not one imposed on her by a sorcerer. T'tammo, Sajàno and their brothers would return home to Bryn Doon. Hara'q would return as well, in his natural form.

And I? I supposed that a Bard of Bryn Doon's rightful place must be in Bryn Doon. Where else could it be? There was no return to the Mhor-Jenn, for there was less there now than when I had known it. Yet I had known no other home.

This journey had given me much. It had gifted me with the confidence, strength and courage that the boy I had been had neither known nor imagined possible. It had blessed me with companions who developed into dearer friends than I had ever known back in the Mhor-Jenn.

The journey had taken from me as well. It had cut short my childhood. It had destroyed every vestige of certainty, comfort and familiarity. I choked back a tear. It had stolen my family.

I knew it was time to return to the courtyard. If the Great Enchantment was falling away, it would be time for this story's next chapter. I stroked the sleeve of my cloak. It was time to free these horses for their journey home. What would Bryn Doon be like with only horses as companions? Without Maminka and Jeryn? Without my father?

It was time, but I was not ready. Not yet. I lowered myself onto a stool at the table, still cluttered with the makings of the potion, and dropped my head into my arms.

I was grateful that we had succeeded, but would it be a lasting success? Could it be as long as Ardoxx lived? If only I could race upstairs and snatch the potion from his lips before he drank it. If only… But that was not how the story went.

It made no sense, this story. Why would Prithi allow Ardoxx to not only live but regain even a fragment of his power? He was clever, that sorcerer. Somehow, he would find a way around the potion's limitations. Somehow, his scheming would cause more grief…more death. Where would it end? Or would it never end, replaying over and over and over until the end of time? Could I trust such a story?

"You either trust or you do not. *Braawk!*"

I lifted my head as a verro that must have flown in through an open window flung itself headfirst at a low cellar door half-hidden in a shadowy corner of the kitchen. The door had been shut; now it opened. As the verro disappeared into the cellar, a man staggered up the two steps from it into the kitchen, shielding his eyes against the light.

"There is no halfway in between," he said, his voice hoarse with disuse. His face was drawn, his hair and beard were long and stringy and his clothes hung loosely on a skeletal frame. "My son," he cried when he saw me, his eyes glistening with tears.

sixty-nine

Mattilde

renzied pandemonium could not begin to describe the scene in the courtyard. Pyrà's storytelling had ceased the instant we found ourselves inside Ardoxx's compound, not that it would have mattered had it not. We could never have heard him over the chaos created by the simultaneous arrival of the entire population of Hara'q's and Pyrà's village, as startled to find themselves in this strange place as we were.

Beneficia and I, the only strangers in the assembly, stood to one side with T'tammo and Sajàno as some four score men, women and children, acting as though they had not seen one another for the longest of intervals, greeted each other with much affection and even more commotion.

The strangest sight of all — for the villagers, it seemed, as much as for me and Beneficia — was our sober, serious Hara'q, who danced through the crowd, hugging and kissing anyone who would let him.

I would learn later that Pyrà's mother was among them, but that she had fainted in the excitement. At the time, though, all we could do was observe the confused reunion in stunned amazement.

A hush fell over the crowd as all eyes turned toward the main house, where Pyrà and a scarecrow of a man stood side-by-side on the front stoop.

"Pyrà!" a woman's voice cried out. Hara'q helped her through the crowd, and when they reached Pyrà, she pulled him into the tightest of embraces. It was only when Pyrà gently pulled himself free that the woman got a close look at the man at his side. "Lucca," she shrieked and fell into his arms as the crowd cheered.

"My friends," Pyrà called out when some of the hubbub had died down. "It warms my heart to see you all again when, for all my prayers, I never thought I would.

"The story of where you are and how you got here, of how we all got here—" He motioned for Beneficia and I to join him, and to bring the horses. "That story is too long to recount now, not when there is another story to tell, one that will at last see us all home."

As I stood on the steps of Ardoxx's house, it occurred to me that nearly everyone I had ever known was here with me in this courtyard. My parents and sister…all those I had grown up with…those I had journeyed with…even the stallions of Mòrq'an Mellà with whom I had passed so much of my childhood, although limited space demanded that they remain immobilized in my cloak, for now. And one more person, if he was a person: Hovering at the far edge of the crowd stood Fay'dor, a verro impatiently hopping from one claw to the next on the wall behind him.

I knew I had a story to tell, and I thought I knew what that story was. Yet having spoken my few words of introduction, I felt tongue-tied. I had recounted my stories to one, two or three people at a time. Never more than that. Never in front of everyone I knew in the world. And never was it a story that would radically alter so many lives with every word I spoke. They all watched me so expectantly, so hopefully. My knees shook. My stomach heaved. My mouth was as parched as the Mhor-Jenn. I was as terrified as I had been at any moment on this journey.

Then, a loud, obnoxious *braawk* issued from the verro's beak, and I knew I could wait no longer. I either trusted or I did not. There *was* no halfway in between.

"My name is Pyrà, son of Lucca and Kamela," I said, "and I am the Bard of Bryn Doon." I paused. "It is because of me that you have been forced from your home. That it was not your true home is no longer as important as it is to know that it is to your true home that this story will deliver you, if that is your true heart's wish. Is that your true heart's wish?"

The stunned silence that greeted my question lasted but an instant. The eruption of shouting that followed was so intense it was as though I had been struck.

"What have you done to our village?"

"Give us back our home!"

"I want my old life back!"

There were a few calls of "let him speak." Only a few. My first thought — my first desire — was to turn tail and escape back into the house. But I could not, if only because Ben's ring throbbed into my finger, reminding me of my duty and reigniting my courage.

This reaction had to be Ardoxx's work. Not only had he drunk the potion, he must have found a way to bypass its restrictions. I could not let him continue to manipulate the people I cared about. It stopped here. Now.

I slammed my staff onto the step. Not once. Not twice. But three times. Each time, the earth shook more forcefully and each time the sparks that flew from the bokka crown were bigger and brighter, until with the final crash of wood on stone, the crowd fell silent.

"Those who choose to return to the harsh, hardscrabble life in the Mhor-Jenn desert may." I pointed my staff to the left side of the courtyard. "Collect yourselves over there." First a few, then most villagers did. Only my parents and a half-dozen others remained where they stood.

I then pointed the staff to the other side of the courtyard. "Those of you ready to exchange the struggles you and your forebears have known in that bleak, unforgiving land for the gentle, embracing oasis that longs to lovingly welcome you home, gather on the right."

Lucca led Kamela, Karùn and their friends to the right side of the courtyard. When no one else moved, I had a flash of doubt. Was I being too presumptuous? Was I acting as arrogantly as Ardoxx? Or was this another sign of the sorcerer's cunning?

"Once upon a time," I began when I realized that only a story's power could rival his.

"No stories," Pora'q cried from deep within the crowd. "Send us home."

"It is the story that will send you home," I replied with as much quiet certainty as I could muster, before the shouting and catcalls could start again.

"Once upon a time, a sorcerer as cruel as he was powerful set out to eliminate any and all threats to his plans to gain dominion over Flor, Q'ntana and neighboring lands. Unfortunately, as great as was his power, it was not great enough to determine the precise source or location of the threats. So he set out to destroy village after village after village, indiscriminately and without regard for who might live or die as a consequence. Thus was the sole village in the Mhor-Jenn razed.

"It was because of that same sorcerer, who has lived longer than any mortal man has a right to live, that the ancestors of the residents of that same village were originally exiled there. But that story is for another time."

As I spoke, villagers from the left side of the courtyard began to drift over to the right, first singly, then in couples, then in clusters. Each new addition was warmly welcomed by those who had already made the choice for Bryn Doon.

"When by random happenstance, the sorcerer targeted the right village, the great dragon Kumba orchestrated the village's evacuation to a safe haven in Tikkana, the land of the dreamwalkers. There they remained until, the sorcerer having been disabled by his grandiosity, they were moved to the staging ground for their return home. That staging ground was in an enchanted location deep in the Forest of Ardh in the Principality of Flor. That location was a courtyard in the sorcery-veiled compound that was the sorcerer's home. This sorcerer. This compound. This courtyard."

Those still on the left side, just shy of two score, again shouted their anger. Now, the panic was theirs not mine. I waited a few breaths to allow their fear its expression, then raised the staff over my head. The silence was immediate.

"The first to leave the staging ground were those who had chosen to return to their village. Each man and woman who made that choice for themselves and for their children made it of their free will, knowing that once back in the Mhor-Jenn, there would be no further opportunity to leave. The Mhor-Jenn would be their home, their children's home and their children's children's home until the end of time."

I waited to see if any villagers would move across the courtyard at this point, in either direction. Samb'ha and Vyn'da grabbed their three children's hands and pulled them over to the Bryn Doon side. Lara'qi, who was eager to join them, argued with her widowed mother, Brazya, who was determined to stay.

"I can't," Brazya cried. "I just can't."

Lara'qi tugged on her mother's arm, but she stood fast, shaking her head, tears flowing down her cheeks.

They both begged me with their eyes to compel the other to her will. There was nothing I could do but wait.

Finally, after each one's pleading failed to persuade the other, Lara'qi released her mother's hand and crossed the courtyard. Both were sobbing as I continued.

"Two things then happened at once. Far away in the Mhor-Jenn, the village that had been destroyed rose again. And in the courtyard of the sorcerer, those who had chosen a new life witnessed those who had chosen to return to the old one fade and flutter in and out of sight until they were gone."

A gasp rose from those who remained as those on the left side of the courtyard vanished. Before there could be another outburst, I went on.

"Immediately afterward, those who had chosen to begin afresh in a new land that was the oldest domain in Prithi's world also faded and fluttered from the view of those few who now remained."

My voice caught on those last words. My mother, father and sister were gone. This time, I knew I would see them again, soon. Yet part of me still feared I might not. I had lost them once. How could I let them go again without embracing them or telling them I loved them?

I shook my head to clear the purposeless sentimentality. The story called, and I had no choice but to let it take me where it would, without delay.

It was time now to send my companions on their way and my heart broke, for I knew, even if they did not, that long years would pass until I might see them again. Before continuing, I did what there had not been the occasion to do with my family. I embraced first Mattilde then Beneficia and thanked them. When it came to Hara'q, he held on to me for a long time, and I felt his tears mingling with mine.

"I could not have done this without you," I whispered. "I could not have become this without you."

Hara'q pulled away, wiping the tears from his eyes. "Nor I without you."

"I must continue," I said.

"Yes, you must." He stepped back to rejoin Mattilde and Beneficia.

"For all her sorrow at leaving her companions, the Lady Mattilde knew her duty. She would return to Castle Flor to a life of service, not to a capricious mistress but to the people of her realm. In the moments previous to this one, she had offered her former mistress cosovereignty with her over Flor. In the most gracious of refusals, her former mistress had knelt before her and pledged her allegiance to the rightful Lady."

All this had occurred while I was thanking Hara'q.

"Now, the Lady Mattilde made her way down the carriage road, stepped through the gate as though it was not there and vanished into the woods, only to reappear barely a breath later at the open draw-bridge of the reconstructed Castle Flor."

Next, I beckoned to T'tammo, Sajàno and Hara'q. But before I could remove my cloak and lay it on the stonework in front of me, Hara'q stepped away from his brothers and nodded for me to continue.

"When it came time, at last, to free the horses to return to their fabled home, the one who had been cursed with human form embraced T'tammo and Sajàno, then stepped away from them to stand before the former Lady Beneficia of Flor.

"Taking her hand, he gazed into her eyes and spoke."

It was Hara'q's voice now that continued. "Wherever it is you choose to go, be it Bryn Doon, elsewhere in Q'ntana or somewhere in Flor, I will go with you if you will have me. Not as who I was, a stallion of Bryn Doon, and not as who I am, neither horse nor human. If you will have me, I will go with you as a fully human man, as mortal as you."

"The Lady Beneficia's hand flew to her mouth," I said, describing neither what had been nor what was to be, but what was occurring as I spoke.

"Are you certain?" Beneficia asked in her own voice.

Hara'q took her hands in his and kissed them. "More certain about this than about anything else in a long life I now know to have been lived only for this day and for the days to come."

Beneficia's eyes filled with tears. All she could do was lean into him and weep with joy. "I will gladly follow you to Bryn Doon," she said, "for that is your home."

"No," Hara'q countered, "Flor is your home. If this is where your heart calls you to be, it is my heart's choice as well."

When neither felt able to decide for the other, they agreed to let the story's wisdom determine their fate.

"Holding hands and with eyes only for each other," I continued, "and as others before them had done, the figures of Hara'q and Beneficia faded, fluttered and disappeared. Where to? To a new home that was neither Bryn Doon nor Flor, though inextricably linked to both: Alanda, the ancient and eternal capital of Q'ntana. There, Beneficia's cousin, Maroona, who had survived the destruction of Castle Flor, was waiting for them.

"Only the embodied horses, T'tammo and Sajàno, remained in the courtyard, along with their brethren in the mystical cloak. With a single tap of staff on cloak, all one hundred eighty-five horses leapt free and, with T'tammo and Sajàno, flung themselves over the courtyard wall, to Bryn Doon.

"The memory of their history now fully restored, the stallions of Bryn Doon had finally returned home to Bokka Baka'à. There, they were welcomed by Rykka and Ta'ar, the only of Bryn Doon's mares to have survived the Great Enchantment. As the horses arrived, T'tammo's true coloring was restored to the deep teal of the sea; Sajàno's, to the bright yellow-green of spring growth, and all their brethren to their original hues. That miracle was accompanied by another, one of which only Prithi was capable: All the mares who had been slaughtered through the Great Enchantment rose again as one from the restored Benq'a Baka'à crater.

"The last to leave the sorcerer's courtyard were two creatures who, until the instant of their departure, had not been present in those forms: a giant, green-scaled dragon with silver-feathered wings, four claws on its right foot and six on its left, and a fiery-plumed bird, its head crowned with upright feathers of orange, yellow and crimson. Together, they shot up through the trees and circled back around the compound before disappearing into the distant sky."

seventy-one

Pyrà

I stepped away from the front door and made my way across the empty courtyard and down the carriage road, my staff tap-tap-tapping on the stone cobbles. When I reached the gate, I turned to look back at the house, which, in a way I could not understand, represented not only all I had experienced since leaving the Mhor-Jenn with Hara'q but all I was leaving behind.

I knew I would miss the unlikely companions without whom I could never have lived this piece of my story. Yet I was grateful that they had found their rightful places, as I was about to. I knew, as well, that if the story had provided me with those companions for these chapters, it would provide me with new ones for the next.

The story that opened this telling with a bedtime fable in a faraway village was about to complete another installment. This completion would not be a final one, for stories have no fixed endings any more than they have fixed beginnings.

All that remained for me now was to let the story carry me to its next chapter.

As I gazed up, I saw Ardoxx, dressed once more in his sorcerer's robe, watching me from an open upstairs window. A verro I took to be Bàq'sha was perched on his shoulder.

"'Stories,' the bard said, as much to himself as to the sorcerer, 'are mightier than any other kind of wizardry. Nothing in Prithi's creation can rival them.' As if to demonstrate the immutability of that statement, the bard turned his back on the sorcerer, struck the gate three times with his staff and stepped through it, not into the Forest of Ardh but onto the mossy slopes of Brae N'ah in the storied land of Bryn Doon."

The sorcerer surveys the courtyard from the window of his study. With the bard and his rabble gone, it is empty, and mercifully quiet.

The potion has done its work, and the bard and his cohorts now lie beyond his reach, as does the traitor Karùn. The horses cannot be his, nor can Bryn Doon, Q'ntana or Flor. He has failed.

Yet the story is not over.

After a moment's reflection, the sorcerer thrusts his right hand upward through the open window, spreads his fingers and releases a series of blazing thunderbolts into the sky. They hang suspended for some moments, jagged slashes of fire as hot and bright as the suns and visible from one end of Flor to the other, and beyond.

Then, with his other hand, he draws a complex rune in the air in front of him. In an instant, the thunderbolts resume their journey into the heavens and, with an earth-trembling roar, the compound rockets after them.

No, the story is not over. The story is never over.

The Worlds of Bryn Doon

Aah'mos (*AH*-mohss) — Ardoxx's father

Abray (ah-*BRAY*) — Another name for Hara'q

Ah'hay eeyama mana'ya ki-hay / Ko'lama ma'nayo ee'ya / Ko-hay mana'ya ma-nay (ah-*HAY* ee-*YA*-ma ma-*NAH*-ya ki-*HAY* / Ko-*LAH*-ma ma-*NAH*-yo ee-*YA* / Ko-*HAY* ma-*NAH*-ya ma-*NAY*) — Ina Lei's invocation

Alanda (a-*LAWN*-dah) — Q'ntana's ancient capital; river in Q'ntana

Allaya (ah-*LAY*-ah) — Resident of the Mhor-Jenn

Àna (*AW*-nah) — Celestial being in *The StarQuest*

Ankiàna ka'eyna tookà jooq (un-kee-*AH*-na kah-*AY*-nah *TOOH*-kah *JHOOQ*) — One of Ardoxx's incantations

Ardh (*ARTH*) — A forest in Flor

Ardoxx (*AR*-doxx) — Evil sorcerer

Areya (ah-*RAY*-ah) — One of the young Beneficia's governesses

Avìndrii (a-*VIN*-dree) — Home of the renegade sorcerer Fa'lé Q'a

Aygra (*AY*-grah) — The larger of the two suns

Azùl (ah-*ZOOL*) — A Black Rider

Baleya (bah-*LAY*-ah) — Type of sea mammal

Bàq'sha (*BAHK*-sha) — Verro bird, twin brother to Baq'shì

Baq'shì (bahk-*SHI*) — Verro bird, twin sister to Bàq'sha

Baranna (bah-rah-*NAH*) — A forest in Flor

Bela (*BAY*-lah) — Type of red-fleshed nut

Ben (*BEN*) — Ancient king of Q'ntana and protagonist of *The SunQuest*

Beneficia (ben-eh-*FISS*-ee-yah) — Ruler of Flor; *Bryn Doon* journeyer

Benq'a Baka'à (*BENK*-ah bah-*KAH*) — Creation portal on Bokka Baka'à

Black Riders — Rogue soldiers in *The SunQuest*

B'na (bih-*NAH*) — The smaller of the two suns

Bokka (*BOW*-kah) — Sacred stone found only in Bryn Doon

Bokka Baka'à (*BOW*-kah bah-*KAH*) — Remote island in Bryn Doon

Bo'Rà K'n (bo-*RAH*-kin) — Dark force in *The MoonQuest, StarQuest* and *SunQuest*, now known as Rev'Àn

Brae N'ah (bray *NAH*) — Region in Bryn Doon

Brazya (*BRAH*-szia) — Lara'qi's mother; resident of the Mhor-Jenn

Bryn Doon (brin *DOON*) — Mystical province of Q'ntana

Bryn'qà (brin-*KAH*) — Scriving quill of Bryn Doon

Bylta'a (bill-*TAH*) — Tiny furry mammal, the size of a small mouse

Caiio (*KYE*-oh) — Type of tree

Castle Rose — Legendary castle in *The MoonQuest* and *SunQuest*

Delfian (*DELL*-fee-yun) — Type of sea creature

Do'ana Qi (doh-ahna *KEY*) — Area of quicksand in the Mhor-Jenn

Dôma (*DOH*-mah) — Rotunda at the center of the Mhor-Jenn village

Ee-ya-EE (ee-yah-*EE*) — Cry of the ganda bird

Eulisha (you-*LEE*-sha) — Elderbard in *The MoonQuest*

Fa'lé Q'a (fah-lay *KAH*) — Renegade sorcerer

Falla (*FAH*-lah) — Mayta's mother; resident of the Mhor-Jenn

Fay'dor (*FAY*-dohr) — An oracle

Flek (*FLECK*) — Resident of the Mhor-Jenn

Flor, Florrican (*FLOHR* / *FLOHR*-ih-kun) — Land where much of *The Bard of Bryn Doon* takes place; citizen of Flor

Flora Mìna (*FLOW*-rah *MEE*-nah) — The spirit of Flor

Fvorag (*FOR*-ag) — Former king of Q'ntana

Fyràm'i (fir-*AH*-mee) — A stallion of Bryn Doon

Ganeyq (gah-*NAYK*) — Janeya's husband; resident of the Mhor-Jenn

Ganda (*GAN*-duh) — Type of seabird

Gannu (ga-*NOO*) — Type of bird

G'goma (gih-*GO*-mah) — Type of slimy insect

Gravel (gruh-*VELL*) — Fvorag's grandson and a king of Q'ntana

Grawkin (*GRAW*-kin) — Easily frightened, rabbit-sized mammal

Grenja (*GREN*-yah) — Q'aff's wife

Gry'a Grove (*GREE*-yah) — Grove in the Forest of Ardh possessed by the Gry'a, demonic nightstalkers

Grykk, Grykkan (*GRICK* / *GRICK*'n) — Land adjacent to Q'ntana; citizen of Grykk

Hana Mar Ò Q'inaya (*HAH*-na mar oh-kee-*NYE*-ah) — Island home to Kumba's shapeshifter emissary

Hara'q (ha-*RAHK*) — Journeyer in *The Bard of Bryn Doon*

Homba (*HOHM*-bah) — One of the young Beneficia's governesses

Horqyr'a (hor-*KEE*-rah) — Type of sea creature

Ina Lei (ee-nah *LAY*) — Mysterious woman in the Flor market

Janeya (jah-*NAY*-ah) — Ganeyk's wife; resident of the Mhor-Jenn

Jaq'òra (jhah-*KOH*-rah) — Type of tree

Jeeka (*GEE*-kah) — Game animal native to Q'ntana and Flor

Jeryn (jerr-*INN*) — Pyrà's sister

Ka'eyla (kah-*AY*-lah) — A shapeshifter

Kamela (ka-*MEH*-lah) — Pyrà's mother

Kand'q (*KAN*-dick) — Valena'a's husband; resident of the Mhor-Jenn

Karùn (kah-*ROON*) — Ardoxx's servant

Kaya (*KYE*-ah) — Karùn's older sister

Kea Kana (kay-ah *KAH*-nah) — Destination for souls of the newly dead

Ken, Kenning (*KEN*-ning) — An intuitive knowingness

King's Men — Fvorag's brutal army in *The MoonQuest*

Kiribà (kee-ree-*BAH*) — Type of fruit with red skin and flesh

K'nrah (kin-*RAH*) — Small animal indigenous to the region

Krysh (*KRISH*) — Type of dense shrubbery

Kumba (*KOOM*-buh) — The Great Dragon of Creation

Kyri (*KEE*-ree) — A king of Q'ntana (also, my dog's name)

Lago Bana'à (lah-go b'*NAH*) — A lake in Bryn Doon

Lara'qi (lah-rah-*KEE*) — Brazya's daughter; resident of the Mhor-Jenn

Lucca (*LOO*-kah) — Pyrà's father

Lythe (rhymes with "writhe") — Stringed musical instrument

Ma'kàlé ma'kànu ma'kaléy'aa (mah-*KAH*-lay mah-*KAH*-noo ma-kah-*LAY*-ah) — Ardoxx's "undoing" incantation

Mala (*MAH*-lah) — Flor's major river

Malaqa'i (mah-lah-*KYE*) — Ardoxx's twin brother

Ma'laqeya (mah-lah-*KAY*-ah) — Large rodent native to Flor

Maminka (mah-*MIN*-kah) — Pyrà's pet name for his mother

Mandopleth (*MAN*-do-pleth) — Large, lumbering mammal

Maq'rah (mah-*KRAH*) — Vulture-like bird native to the Mhor-Jenn

Marella (mah-*RELL*-ah) — Insect indigenous to Flor

Maroona (mah-*ROO*-nah) — Beneficia's cousin

Matté (mah-*TAY*) — A stallion of Bryn Doon

Mattilde (mah-*TILD*) — Castle Flor's majordoma; *Bryn Doon* journeyer

Matushka (mah-*TOOSH*-kah) — Mattilde's Gran's pet name for her

Mayta / Maytasch (*MAY*-tuh / *MAY*-tush) — Falla's daughter; resident of the Mhor-Jenn

Mekla (*MEHK*-lah) — Pyrà's aunt

Mhor-Jenn (mohr-*JHENN*) — Remote desert region of Q'ntana

Mir (*MEER*) — The sea

M'nor (mih-*NOR*) — The moon

Monayka (mo-*NAY*-kah) — One of the young Beneficia's governesses

Mòrq'an Mellà (*MOHR*-kin mih-*LAH*) — Knoll by the Mhor-Jenn village

M'ranna (mih-*RAH*-nah) — Earlier name for Q'ntana

Na'an (rhymes with fawn) — Tikkan dreamwalker

Nayla (*NAY*-lah) — Vicious animal indigenous to the region

Nayr (*NAIR*) — Ancient chalice

Om Wamsa (ohm *WUM*-sah) — A mystical drink

O'ric (*OH*-rick) — Timeless oracle in *The MoonQuest* and *The SunQuest*

Orrican (*OH*-rih-kun) — Legendary dagger

Ooura (*OOH*-rah) — Type of ale

Piila (*PEE*-lah) — Type of fruit

Pora'q (*POH*-rack) — Resident of the Mhor-Jenn

Prakk estafi (*PRAHK* es-*TAH*-fee) — An expletive

Prithi (*PRIH*-thee) — The supreme deity

Pyrà (pirr-*AH*) — Journeyer in *The Bard of Bryn Doon*

Pyynch'n (*PINCH*-in) —Giant tree indigenous to the region

Q'aff (*CUFF*) — Grenja's husband

Q'ambra (*KAHM*-brah) — A village in Flor

Qanaria (kah-*NAH*-ree-yah) — Type of tree

Q'nta (kin-*TAH* — Protagonist of *The StarQuest*

Q'ntana (kin-*TAH*-nah) — Where the Mhor-Jenn, Bryn Doon are located

Qymaq'a (key-*MAH*-kah) — Type of sea creature

Ray'a (*RAY*-ah) — Ardoxx's mother

Rev'Àn (rih-*VAWN*) — Tikkan dreamwalker; see also Bo'Rà K'n

Rykka (*REE*-kah) — One of the surviving mares of Bryn Doon

Sajàno (sah-*JHA*-no) — A stallion of Bryn Doon
Samb'ha (*SAHM*-bah) — Vyn'da's husband; resident of the Mhor-Jenn
Sascha (*SAH*-shah) — Type of edible weed
Sha'maya (shah-*MY*-yah) — Type of tree

Ta'ar (*TAR*) — One of the surviving mares of Bryn Doon
Tartaruca (tar-*TAR*-u-kah) — Large, tortoise-like sea creature
Tashek (*TAH*-shek) — Shapeshifter
Thomé (toh-*MAY*) — Type of nut
Thor'qya (thor-*KEE*-yah) — Massive fish-like creature
Tikkan / Tikkana (tee-*KAWN*) — Ancient race of dreamwalkers; home of the Tikkan
Tokku (*TOH*-koo) — Type of fruit
Toshar (*TOH*-shar) — Protagonist of *The MoonQuest*
T'tammo (tuh-*TAHM*-mo) — A stallion of Bryn Doon

Valena'a (vah-*LAY*-nah) — Kand'q's wife; resident of the Mhor-Jenn
Vee'qo (*VEE*-koh) — A stallion of Bryn Doon
Verro (*VER*-roh) — A raven-sized bird native to Flor
Vootah (*VOO*-tah) — A giant bird of prey
Vray (*VRAY*) — An expletive
V'rek (*VRECK*) — Approximately one-quarter of a mile
Vyn'da (*VIN*-dah) — Sambh'a's wife; resident of the Mhor-Jenn village

Yali'Fà (yah-lee-*FAH*) — A king of Grykk
Yanna (*YAWN*-nah) — Type of bird
Yùq'a (*YOO*-kah) — A stallion of Bryn Doon

Zeetah (*ZEE*-tah) — Resident of the Mhor-Jenn village
Zzyzzyby (*ZIH*-zih-bee) — A type of pink cheese

Appreciation

Most authors devote a section like this to thanking the friends and colleagues who supported them along the way and helped make the book possible. Before I go there, however, my first expression of gratitude must go to the story itself, which thrust itself into my awareness one gray February morning in 2019 at a time when I believed that what I was then calling "The Q'ntana Trilogy" had completed itself six years earlier with *The SunQuest*. Given that story's ending, how could there possibly be more? Suddenly, to my astonishment, I knew there was. And when I scratched out an opening scene and heard Pyrà remind Kamela that "there's more to every story," I knew it must be true and that I must persevere to discover what it was.

If you have read the acknowledgments pages in any of my other books, you will know that I am highly sensitive to the energy of place. More accurately put, perhaps, my stories are, and they not I choose where they are to be written. It is to those places that I now offer profound gratitude…

> • to the animated buzz of Portland, Oregon's Pearl District, where *The Bard of Bryn Doon* searched me out and dictated its first few scenes without me knowing anything much about the story other than its title;
>
> • to Anderson, California, where a sunset stroll with my dog, Kyri (named for a key character in *The MoonQuest*), revealed for the first time the plot's broad strokes; and
>
> • to the inspiring Red Rock Country of Sedona, Arizona, where *The Bard of Bryn Doon* found its voice and completed itself.

The journey that dropped me in Anderson several times over the summer of 2019 and that ultimately landed me in Sedona was not an easy one, financially or emotionally. I was nominally homeless over those three months and on a journey not unlike that of Pyrà and his companions, although the only evil sorcerer I encountered on that trek was my own fear. To all the friends, online and off, who believed in me, cheered me on and/or helped financially through that challenging time, I owe you an enormous debt of gratitude. I don't know that I would have made it without you. I doubt there would have been a *Bard of Bryn Doon* without you.

There certainly would not have been a *Bard of Bryn Doon* without the loyal readers of my other *Q'ntana* books. Thank *you* for being such great fans and for spurring me on to continue the series.

To Joan Cerio, Sander Freedman and Kathleen Messmer: The only way I can repay your belief in me and my work, especially on those too-frequent days when I was hard-pressed to believe in either, is by keeping the words flowing. So that's what I'm doing — with this book and whatever follows. A heartfelt extra thanks to Kathleen Messmer for this book's evocative cover photo, which so eloquently captures the essence of Bryn Doon's stallions.

Finally, to Eve Hunter, who, sadly for all who loved her, has left her physical body: Thank you for all the ways you supported me so enthusiastically and encouraged me so heartfully when I returned to Sedona and as I worked on *The Bard of Bryn Doon*. I hope that wherever you are, you know how grateful I am.

About the Author

Mark David Gerson is the bestselling author of more than twenty books. His nonfiction includes popular titles for writers, inspiring personal growth books and compelling memoirs. As a novelist and screenwriter, he is best known for *The Legend of Q'ntana* fantasy series. His other fiction includes the novels of *The Sara Stories*, set largely in Montreal, his hometown. When not writing, Mark David coaches an international roster of writers and non-writers to help them get their stories onto the page and out into the world with ease.

For more about Mark David Gerson,
to sign up for his newsletter and to learn about
upcoming *Q'ntana* books and other releases,
visit www.markdavidgerson.com